Wearing the Cape

"This is such a solid book that I have difficulty believing it is Mr. Harmon's first novel. The story is polished, well edited, tightly plotted, and stocked with interesting characters. Like Peter Clines' debut novel, Ex-Humans, this sets the bar so high for follow-up work that I'm sure Mr. Harmon is feeling the pressure."

Michael of Dover, Delaware

Villains Inc.

"A riveting follow-up to Wearing the Cape, Harmon's sophomore novel continues to satisfy those of us who need a fix of well-written superhero fiction. Fans of the first book will not find its sequel lacking, and while it might be more of an adjustment to readers who haven't picked up the first book, it stands well enough on its own."

Avander Promontory

On the *Wearing the Cape* series.

"The Wearing the Cape series is the gold standard that all other superhero novels should aspire to."

Hero Sandwich

Young Sentinels reviewer.

The world of Wearing the Cape just keeps getting more interesting with each passing book. The characters grow deeper and old plots resurface in new ways.

Kindle Customer

Small Town Heroes.

Mr. Harmon knocks the ball out of the park once again in Small Town Heroes. His realistic take on an absurd reality is, as always, an extremely interesting read and his characters continue to be deep and immersive.

Another Amazon Reviewer

Marion G. Harmon

Books by M.G.Harmon
Wearing the Cape
Villains Inc.
Bite Me: Big Easy Nights
Young Sentinels
Small Town Heroes
Ronin Games

Short Stories by M.G.Harmon
Omega Night

Ronin Games

A *Wearing the Cape* Story

by

Marion G. Harmon

Copyright © 2015 Marion G. Harmon

Cover art by Jamal Campbell and Jessica Chang

All rights reserved.

ISBN-13:978-1517503093
ISBN-10:1517503094

DEDICATION

To the readers who make Hope more real than I ever can.

ACKNOWLEDGMENTS

To all the usual victims—I mean beta-readers. There are a few who read draft after draft for me, and amazingly pretend enthusiasm for the next flawed gem. And then there are the new readers, one of whom keeps shipping two major characters and presenting her argument like a lawyer's brief. Good try, but no. And thank you.

Ronin: *Historically, a masterless samurai (lit., a wave-man). Outside the political power-structure, ronin lived as mercenaries and bodyguards, or as outlaws and robbers when work could not be found. In Post-Event Japan "ronin" is slang for Active Non-Government Powers (ANGPs), freelance superhumans, criminal or otherwise, who use their powers without government sanction.*

Barlow's Guide to Superheroes

Episode One

Chapter One

"Let your plans be dark and impenetrable as night, and when you move, fall like a thunderbolt."

Sun Tzu, The Art of War

"Don't let them see you coming, and don't let them get back up."

Atlas

Artemis dropped out of mist and onto the table, and that would have pretty much ended the poker game even if my bursting through the warehouse's high windows in a shower of glass above them hadn't ruined the players' night. Lit by the crackling halo of her electrostatic field, Lei Zi floated through the shattered windows behind me and fired off a carefully calibrated electromagnetic pulse, the sticky charge of free electrons washing past me to send an electronics-killing surge through any unshielded devices inside the zone. *"Go, go, go!"* she chanted in my earbug on the open channel.

I let myself fall with the glass. No sense rushing anywhere while I was still picking targets.

"Hard targets here and here!" Shell used our neural link to outline two of the players at the table in virtual green. Painting them directly through my visual cortex, she left all but one of the rest in yellow and painted the last target in red: *unidentified*. I angled right. The green icon on Big Blondie identified him as a straight up A Class Ajax-Type, but the green three-headed dragon icon on the black haired man beside him named him my target—Zmey Gorynich.

A thrill chased through me like a shot from Lei Zi, equal parts excitement and nerves; three weeks work and prep, and tonight we got to rid Chicago of its latest monster. "I'm on Zmey! Svyatogor—"

"Is incoming!" Even dropping into a desperate fight, I could hear the laughter in Shell's voice. *"He says 'Don't be greedy!'"*

Below me Artemis snapped multiple stun-shots into the red unknown target with her electrolasers before leaping up and back into mist to clear the way for me. I fell right through her to destroy the table, swinging Malleus without pausing to straighten up—straight into the open, shocked face of the man Shell identified as Zmey. My hit threw him across the wide-open warehouse space.

An all-in hit backed by one hundred pounds of titanium maul would do that to anybody, and I had one horrific moment to wonder if our intelligence had been bad and I'd just killed someone I'd never met—but there was no blood, no brains, no unspeakable mess; just a man flying backwards from the force of my unrestrained hit. *"Score!"* Shell cheered. *"Don't let him touch—"*

"I know!" I shot after him, ignoring Blondie and the others still at the table. Svyatogor's briefing had let us know just how small the window we had in which we could hurt Zmey without paying a price, and I was going to get in every hit that I could in before the window closed. Behind me Artemis' elasers snapped again as she dropped back into flesh to engage the rest of her targets. The crunching smash of brick and mortar outside my field of attention told me Svyatogor had entered the warehouse. On my right Riptide blew a loading door off its hinges in an explosion of water. I kept my eyes on Zmey.

The warehouse wall stopped the Russian boss's bouncing roll and the cadaverously skinny man made it back upright before I caught him again. My hardest hit from Malleus hadn't even shaken him—just taken him off his feet—and the eyes he turned to me *glowed*.

"NO!"

Whatever his roaring, spitting denial meant, it was all he got out before I hit him again, smashing him back into the wall—this time it felt a lot heavier, like I'd hit an elephant.

Crap! Crap crap crap crap! The man was changing already!

"*Down!*" Shell yelled in my earbug and I dropped to the floor and rolled away as an iron club as big as me spun through the space I'd occupied and smashed Zmey *again*. A retina-burning flash of lightning-strike from Lei Zi lit him up, shaking even him, and then I was back in the air and out of his reach with Malleus held ready as he continued to change into something *else*.

"Yeah, that's not good," Shell said.

"Really? Do you *think*?"

Four hits from us had barely shaken him and now, stepping away from the wall, Zmey thickened and *stretched*. His long fingers grew longer, turning spidery, his skin marbling and darkening to coal-black as heat poured off him in waves. A volley of snaps behind me marked Artemis' continued work on the street-villains at the table. I ignored them. The liquid hiss of rushing water told me Riptide was doing his job, pulling in and backing up a load of his own ammunition, waiting on me. Another loud crash told me someone else—probably Grendel—had arrived to deal with the remaining Ajax-Type, but I didn't look around. Shell would tell me if there was a problem.

Speaking of which... "Shell? How's the evacuation coming?"

"*The CPD Superpower Response units are clearing the street and adjacent buildings. So far Rush, Variforce, and Watchman haven't had to keep anything in here from getting out there.*"

"Zmey..."

"*I know—that might be about to change. They're ready if it does.*"

That was good to know; Svyatogor had told us the Russian Bratva preferred to make their meeting places in urban areas, where heavy fighting could easily bring on heavy civilian casualties—*this* base sat right in the middle of a half-gentrified Chicago warehouse district. The former warehouse across the street had been turned into lofts, a shopping arcade, and a club, and half of *this* building was a restaurant and club now. We'd have rather fought absolutely anywhere but here, but this was our best—and maybe our only—chance to catch the Bratva captain and his soldiers all in one place.

Zmey yelled something Russian at Svyatogor, his words a shiver-inducing crackling hiss. Svyatogor just laughed as his iron club whirled through the air and back to his hands. As big as it was, it looked small in the Russian giant's grip.

"*That is so cool!*" Shell enthused, and I had to agree. I gripped Malleus hard. Svyatogor had made it crystal clear that I wasn't to directly touch Zmey once he'd changed or let him touch me under any circumstances.

"Shell? How are we doing?"

"*Grendle's got blondie down, Artemis and Lei Zi have got the rest, Riptide is almost ready—*"

Zmey charged, arms wide, the cement beneath him cracking and bubbling. "Rip, now!" I yelled. Lei Zi had left the order to me since I'd be closest.

Ready or not, Riptide cut loose with all the water he'd gathered behind us. Twin jets blew past me and Zmey disappeared in a back-blast of explosively superheated steam.

The expansive force of water-to-steam off his body threw Zmey back again, the vapor cloud filling the open warehouse space hiding him from sight except as a shining infrared beacon to my super-duper vision. Even *I* could feel the superheated water vapor, burning points on my skin as I held my breath. Then the steam cloud retreated, pushed back and up under Riptide's control, and I gasped as cooler air washed over me.

Zmey had fallen to his knees. He rose again, still roaring, but I could feel the difference—he'd lost a lot of heat in explosive energy-transfer to Riptide's jets. *Now*. I launched and swung, smashing him down again—

His flailing hand swiped me in passing, pouring blazing agony on my leg. "*Hope!*" Shell shrieked with me as I flew *up*, somehow keeping hold of Malleus.

"*Astra, withdraw!*" Lei Zi shouted as Riptide hit Zmey below me and Svyatogor pounded him again with his dancing club.

Pulling back to just under the ceiling, I fumbled with the catches of my leg armor. The Vulcan-forged ceramic armor had blackened and cracked where Zmey's hand had just brushed it. Under it, my leg felt dipped in fire.

Blinking, I squeezed my eyes shut to clear the tears. The pain was a *good* thing—it meant my nerves hadn't been destroyed—and under my blackened uniform my calf presented only cooked red, no blistering or blackened flesh. I let the broken armor piece fall and scanned the scene below me.

Lei Zi, Artemis, and Grendel had accounted for Zmey's soldiers. Except for blondie, who had needed Grendel for the beat-down, the Bratva members were mostly street-villains. Blackstone's intelligence had been solid.

"*Are you okay?*" Shell whispered in my earbug—a totally pointless question since she had to know *exactly* what I was feeling through our neural link.

"My leg is on fire," I gasped, voice a shaky whine. "Other than that, I'm peachy." And Zmey hadn't even touched me *directly*. Lesson learned. The air rang with another hit from Svyatogor's dancing club.

"*You have* got *to get one of those return-to-sender things.*"

I controlled my breathing, tried to match Shell's nonchalance. "Svyatogor told me it's enchanted? Made by one of their Baba Yagas? He called her his 'little Babushka'."

"*Hey! Maybe Ozma can do something with Malleus?*"

Another air-shaking impact in the thickening vapor clouds. Every time Zmey tried to close with the giant Svyatogor—who could have made three Grendels and was a big and relatively slow target—Riptide punched him back into the wall with another explosive reaction of brick-cracking heat and cold water. Despite being heavy brick, the wall didn't look like it could take a lot more of it.

"Lei Zi?" I called through my earbug. "It might be a good idea to have Variforce buttress the north wall? He can just ask Watchman where the hotspot is."

"*Good call. On it.*"

I relaxed a little. Zmey's near-blinding furnace heat had started to dim with each hit, so the precaution might not needed, and it was possible that Variforce's variable-property fields could even handle the energy-transfer from direct contact with the Hell's furnace that Zmey was now.

Then the Russian mob boss *divided*.

"*There he goes!*" Shell gasped as he split into three, even though we'd known it was coming. The two new Zmeys flanking the original broke right and left past Riptide's latest water jets, charging for Svyatogor, Artemis, and Grendel. I dove without thinking.

"*Astra fall back!*" Lei Zi cut in.

Not insane, I led with Malleus—brought it down hard on the left Zmey's back to crush him to the floor. Mere proximity to his sprawled limbs washed me in searing heat, his reaching fingers missing me by inches as I hit the ground and leaped up again.

"Astra! Fall! Back!"

Jacky had retreated into mist again, effectively invisible in the oven-hot and steam filled building. Grendel had been braced to smash his own Zmey with what was left of the table, but we'd drilled together enough that he dropped it and caught my grab for our double wrist-grip as I flew past and took us *up*. Water jets strong enough to carve rocks blasted past below us as Riptide shifted targets.

The nearly concussive explosion of superheated steam wasn't so concussive this time. "Lei Zi!" I yelled over the near-deafening crackle and roar. "The Zmeys are cooler! They're cooling down!"

"*I know!*" Below us, Svyatogor battered the Zmey reaching for him with an air-shaking hit from his club.

"Astra."

I looked down at Grendel. He was reshaping himself—I could feel the skin around his wrist thickening under my grip, taking on texture.

"Drop me."

"What—"

Below us, Blondie was getting up from Grendel's beat-down. That put three Zmeys and Blondie against Svyatogor and Riptide and we were losing the ground-fight. Grendel look up past our linked arms to give me his toothiest grin. "You take the Ajax, I've got Zmey."

A few months ago I'd have asked Grendel if he was *sure*. Now I just let go and dove, dropping so fast I beat him to the ground.

Blondie didn't see me coming and I smashed into him sideways, maul-first, to punch us both through the warehouse wall opposite the hole Svyatogor had made coming in.

"I've got him!" I shouted as we hit the street in a rain of bricks. The street outside was empty of civilians, lit by flashing police lights.

The blond guy agreed. He yelled something Russian as he twisted and his elbow came up, and my vision exploded into sparks of light. I rolled desperately to get beyond his reach, but he caught me again with something and—*the breeze smelled of spring and I looked up at the waving branches above me. Flashes of dappled sunlight through the blossom-heavy branches touched my face and I sighed happily. Sitting up, I—*

"Hope! Hope!" Shell stood over me, slapping me with virtual quantum-ghost hands that *felt* like she'd picked up bricks for extra weight.

"What?"

"He kicked you in the *head*! Get up!"

I looked around. Above the red and blue strobe of the police lights, camera-flash lit the night. Ten feet from me, between us and the police barricades, blondie hung suspended in layers of Variforce's fields—a fly trapped in golden amber. Not that he was frozen; he fought hard and I could see the fields holding him flex and strain as Variforce laid more down.

"Right. Thanks Shell." I stood up, bent to lift Malleus from where it lay on the street as the crowd behind the barricades cheered. My head felt like he'd almost kicked it off and everything had a slight halo around it, but it was my turn.

The fight was over when we stepped back through the hole after handing blondie over to the police, unconscious and fitted with Blacklock shackles. Steam and smoke choked the air.

"Well, that was fun..." With no need to worry about distracting me, Shell had decided to hang around virtually. Her clean athletic shirt and cutoff shorts didn't match the burned out and drowned space around us. Her shirt read *"If you can't take the heat, stay out of the kitchen,"* red on black.

"Really?" I gingerly worked my head side to side, testing my range of pain-free motion. "Define 'fun.'"

I wasn't exactly needed; Artemis and Seven, who must have entered after I "left," were securing the street-villains that had been their targets. Svyatogor and Grendel shackled the Zmeys where they'd laid them all out a good thirty feet apart. We wouldn't move them until we had separate wagons for them—Svyatogor's briefing on the Russian mobster had included the important point that, once separated, his "heads" couldn't rejoin without physical contact and each head was individually much less destructive.

"Hah!" Svyatogor's laugh boomed out. "The little ghost-girl is right! Thank you for allowing a fight of heroes."

Shell jumped. "You can *see* me?" she squeaked, wide-eyed.

"Of course! My wise Babashka has touched my eyes with *rusalka* tears and I can see all spirits."

Her mouth formed an *oh*. I just laughed: magic—it wasn't the first time.

Grendel looked over at the happy Russian giant, shook his head. New skin was already replacing the blackened and charred layer of ablative hide he'd formed before attacking, and Rush had brought him some new pants along with the shackles and the somnolence cap needed to keep his Zmey unconscious.

Lei Zi just laughed, a rare show of amusement at the part of the conversation she could hear. "I'm glad we could provide you some entertainment, Svyatogor. These will hold?"

"Dah!" He patted his own Zmey in friendly fashion. "And this time we will keep him separate! As far separate as the soil of Mother Russia allows! Perhaps we will put one in orbit."

"Good, because our rides are here."

Chapter Two

International cooperation is very important; after all, supervillains don't care about borders and are perfectly happy to go where the money is. Smart countries observe extradition treaties and aren't twitchy about allowing foreign capes to visit in pursuit of villains from their own rogues galleries. Of course it's smart to team them with someone local, someone who knows the territory and the local police.

Astra, *Svyatogor-Sentinels Teamup Interview*

Returning to the Dome meant a trip to the infirmary so Doctor Beth could wrap up my Zmey-burned leg and check me over. Blondie's kick had almost certainly given me a concussion (it wouldn't be the first time), but my superhuman toughness meant it was already healing up; the blurry halo effect had gone away, leaving only a pulsing but not please-kill-me headache, so it wasn't a big surprise when Doctor Beth told me not to hit anything with my head for a while and let me go. Collecting my lollypop, I went upstairs to Blackstone's office.

He looked up at my knock on his open door. "Come in, my dear. Have you been to see—ah, I see you have." I removed the lollypop from my mouth and dropped it in his wastebasket before sitting down. Orange was not my favorite flavor.

"Very good work, tonight." Of course he had watched from Dispatch. "And your 'public appearance' there at the end didn't hurt us. Shots of your little street-fight are already circulating online and being used to frame the news stories..." His smile faded as he studied me. "And you aren't happy about it. May I ask why?"

"I saw the tree." I had to keep myself from sinking down in my seat like a guilty child.

It took him a second to understand, but there was only one tree I'd ever talked about. He touched his epad and his office door closed behind me.

"Kitsune is back in your dreams?" he asked carefully.

"No—no. I'd have said something if he was. But I've been dreaming of the cherry tree. More and more often, almost every night now."

"And this wasn't cause for concern?"

"*He's* never been back." It had been months, but I hadn't seen so much as a sneaky white fox's tail since our defense of Littleton. "I just go to the tree. It all feels as real as it ever did, but no Kitsune. And— It's even kind of nice. Restful. I don't have any nightmares, the nights I go to the tree. But I'm more awake there every time. And I stay longer."

Blackstone sat back, stroking his goatee. "Have you talked to anyone else about this?"

"Shell and Shelly know, of course. I've had Chakra check me out to see if somebody is screwing with my head, but nope." Chakra was also pretty sure I wasn't wandering outside my own head at night—apparently Out Of Body experiences left distinct traces on one's chakras. "And I went to Ozma last week."

"Really? When?"

"Tuesday. We had tea in her lab, and she tested me."

"How?"

"Thoroughly."

Blackstone chuckled. It *had* been a little surreal; Ozma had put on her green lab coat, looked at me through gold-rimmed glasses with multiple swing-down attachments, hit me with an array of tuning forks, made me close my eyes and randomly pick up assorted objects, and finally said...

"She couldn't find anything wrong either. But she admitted that her magic is fairy magic—that it's mostly concerned with forms and appearances."

"What does that mean?"

"That something magical *might* really be going on in my head, but that she's more like a supernatural brain surgeon and I might need a supernatural psychiatrist. She says that my problem might be meta*spiritual* instead of metaphysical."

"And what does *that* mean?"

"I have no idea." I rubbed my face, forgetting to feel guilty. I really had no idea what it meant; magic gave me a headache and there were so many kinds of it. There was Jacky's grandmother's voodoo (which might or might not be a breakthrough), Chakra's tantric magic that bordered on psychic power, Ozma's Oz Magic, the *old* magic of Svyatogor's Baba Yaga. Each magic "tradition" with its own rules, each equally valid, like alternate laws of physics.

Blackstone thumped a finger on his chin, considered what I'd told him. Part of me wanted to leave it at that. The cowardly part. But...

"I'm not here about the dreams. When I almost got knocked out tonight—sir, I saw the tree. I was back there." And it had been *real*, in all its coherent clarity and opposite-of-dreamlike reality. "I'd have stayed if Shell hadn't virtually slapped me silly."

"I see." For just a moment, he looked sad. "And why didn't you come to me with this before, Hope? I had thought ... Well." He waved it away, but I felt awful.

"I haven't even told my parents."

"Why not?"

I was twenty years old, I was *Astra*, and I wasn't going to cry. I kept my back straight, looked at the show-posters behind his desk. "It's like... It's like the doctors again. When I was young."

I wasn't phobic about doctors and hospitals anymore; repeat-exposure to Doctor Beth—not to mention my own hospital trips since becoming Astra—had seen to the wearing away of *that* fear. But for years, doctors and hospitals had been all about chemotherapy or tests, bloodwork to see if my childhood cancer would come back. Those had been years when I'd felt like my own body was a time bomb, ready to start ticking again at any moment, and my parents had walked around trying to act normal and *not scared to death* for my sake.

A few weeks into my training as Astra, I'd realized that my breakthrough had forever removed that particular fear; I couldn't even catch a cold anymore, and while I was *far* more likely to die hard somewhere than I'd been before my breakthrough, I was safe from the big C. I'd laughed and cried hysterically.

And now I had another time bomb inside me, inside my *head*. Blackstone blinked at the apparent non-sequitur, and then his eyes widened.

"I see. I do see. Hope…"

I shook my head. "I know it's not the same. Not really."

And it wasn't. So maybe Kitsune had opened a connection that had stayed open, a connection to Somewhere-Not-A-Dream, and it was growing stronger—it wasn't going to *kill* me. But I didn't know why I was going back to the nicest place I'd ever hung out in between sunset and sunrise. I didn't know what was happening and it was *magic*. It was unknown and therefore dangerous, and I had no control over it.

"We will fix this, Hope," Blackstone said, pulling me from my spinning thoughts. Seeing the bright compassion in his eyes, I swallowed as my throat closed.

"Really?" My voice sounded small even to me, barely a breath, and I flushed. Blackstone's mouth tightened.

"Yes. The DSA and national and international intelligence agencies are already looking for Kitsune." His brow furrowed, but he made no comment on how hard it could be to find a shapeshifter. "And I have contacts in the State Department who can lean on the Japanese government. Since he's their problem originally, they may have incentive to help us. We'll find him, he'll cooperate, and we'll fix this.

"Meanwhile, and I hope you take this as I mean it, for now you're benched."

"I know." If I could suddenly go wandering back to the tree from a hard enough hit, what was next and when would it happen? In the middle of a fight again, when lives depended on me? "That's why I came to see you."

"Good. We'll announce it as a purely medical benching, to be lifted when you're 'medically safe.' After all," he chuckled, making me smile. "You did get a boot to the head tonight. It's on video."

I needed that smile; it gave me the courage for what I said next.

"Since I'm benched, may I take a day? A whole day? I'd like to go see Doctor Cornelius."

"And that's something you don't see every day."

Detective Fisher had joined the after-party, since that was what the after-action briefing had turned into. The scruffy CPD detective had come with Captain Verres to report on the Superhuman Crimes Department and CPD Superpower Response Unit parts of the operation, and now he watched the proceedings with a Willis-supplied drink in his hand.

"Yup," Captain Verres agreed. Svyatogor made even big bad Captain Verres look small, and the Russian giant's kick-stamps shook the reinforced floor as he crossed the cleared center of the team lounge twirling his huge iron club.

I couldn't tell if the captain was impressed or laughing at us, and didn't care either way. Maybe it was a Catholic thing, but even if nothing was solved, even knowing I was going to consult Doctor Cornelius, I felt a hundred pounds lighter for confessing to Blackstone.

Verres wasn't laughing. "I wonder if we could make it part of our hand-to-hand training. What is it?"

"Combat Hopak," Shell said. Because of our guests, she'd attended the meeting in her sleek chrome-girl Galatea shell. "Built on an ethnic Cossack dance."

The Powers That Be had deemed the whole operation an outstanding success. The two-ring containment approach had kept the high intensity takedown of the Bratva cell from spilling out into the streets—with my notable exception—and we'd even kept the damage away from the occupied half of the building. Svyatogor, our on-loan Russian police cape and Bratva expert, had declared a celebration.

And Svyatogor didn't have the floor to himself; Grendel kick-stamped right behind him, dreadlocks flying, drawing on his mastery of the ancient art of hip-hop to match Svyatogor's moves in spirit if not in execution. Half of the room clapped in time, not that the two of them could hear us over the boom of their stamping feet.

There were days when I just purely loved wearing the cape.

"You're recording this, right?" I leaned back to whisper to Shell. The black-haired and mustached giant should have looked ridiculous laughing and prancing in his baggy trousers, but he didn't; egging each other on, he and Brian looked like two war-gods celebrating. Or a god and a monster anyway, maybe Gilgamesh and Enkidu (and my old lessons from Ajax were showing).

"Duh." Shell laughed. "We are going to get *so* many site hits on this. Quin would absolutely kill me if I didn't post it."

The swirling music ended with general applause and they took their bows before surrendering the floor to Quin. Svyatogor dropped into a chair beside us (reinforced, we were used to big company), and Brian wandered off to exchange commentary with Crash and Tsuris while Ozma listened benevolently.

It had been Lei Zi's decision not to involve the rest of the Young Sentinels in the operation—Crash and Megaton weren't old enough for police ops yet, anyway—but she'd insisted we all sit for the briefing; tactics training for the future. We were all in "uniform," of course; who knew how much of the party footage Quin would want to use?

Speaking of Quin… "Wow!" was Shell's assessment of The Harlequin's moves as she called for her own music and showed what a former Cirque du Soleil acrobat could do. Her high-bouncing acrobatic dance routine was anything but improvised and Svyatogor's cheering drowned out further comments.

With all eyes in the room on Quin, Rush appeared in the empty chair at my other side and leaned in to be heard. "And how are you doing, kid? I saw that kick in slow-mo."

I shifted and winced. It must have looked spectacular from his hypertime-accelerated perspective.

"The headache's gone, but I won't be dancing."

Truthfully, it was the *leg* that still bothered me. Doctor Beth had cheerfully informed me that a normal person on the receiving end of Zmey's touch would have been looking at a charred stump of a leg. I just had what felt like the world's worst sun burn and an ache that went to the bone.

"And that is a shame!" Svyatogor clapped my shoulder. "Dancing is good for the spirit, a celebration of life! We live!"

And that made me wince again; not all of us were alive—two of the Russians Artemis had dropped in the action's opening had died when the Zmey fighting Grendel had stood practically right on top of them. They'd basically *cooked* in that steaming hell before Seven could get to them.

The big hand on my shoulder tightened.

"Do not be tender hearted, *devochka moya*. No innocents were hurt today, and no man we found in that place deserved your pity."

"*What he said*," Shell seconded inside my head as Rush nodded agreement. "*I read their files.*"

I sighed. Bright side, we'd stopped the Bratva from moving into Chicago. The fight had been the culmination of months of international cooperation, and the Russian mob's attempt to move in on the Chicago Mob was yet one more of the follow-on effects of our takedown of Villains Inc. They'd brought their own drug suppliers, taste for violent extortion, and sex-trafficking.

I tried on a smile. "At least now you don't have to fight them back home, right?"

That earned me another booming laugh. He patted my shoulder one more time, reached for his beer.

"My dear, you are the *ne plus ultra*, the very epitome, of women! You are strong, enduring, with a heart full of the love of others. You should have been a Russian! But you are an American, which means that even with all of your experience, you are a little blind."

I blinked. It was the first time I'd ever been called *that*. His big dark eyes suddenly looked a lot more serious.

"You see good and evil as forces that can always be divided up into sides. For good to triumph, all it must do is identify evil and fight to win. If only it were so simple!" He wagged his thick finger, no longer smiling.

"I quote the great Soviet dissident, Aleksandr Solzhenitsyn. 'If only there were evil people somewhere insidiously committing evil deeds, and it were necessary only to separate them from the rest of us and destroy them. But the line dividing good and evil cuts through the heart of every human being.'"

He looked at his finger, spread his huge hands and dropped them.

"It loses something in translation, but Solzhenitsyn did not mean that there are *not* evil people doing evil things. Only that we will never be rid of them all. Often they will be unrecognizable, and sometimes they will be us."

"So someone will take their place?"

"Of course. Which does not mean that we should not catch or kill as many of these monsters as we can—any act which lessens the suffering of others is loved by God." His smile returned. "But these are much too heavy matters for tonight!"

After that it was a contest of comparing Chicago and Moscow winters, toasts to international cooperation, and more dancing until Shell finally pulled me away with our pre-arranged "errand" excuse and I flew home. I'd have to be back to the Dome in the morning, but going home had become the thing I just did after every public fight unless there was unfinished business that kept me away.

The house was dark, the parentals already asleep; I'd called before news of the fight had been broadcast so they'd known not to worry and that I'd see them in the morning. Changing for bed while Shell briefed me on the Oroboros' and *Shelly's* take on what our win today likely meant for the near future, I let Graymalkin in my room. Just before I turned out the light I remembered the one question I'd saved to ask later.

"Devochka moya?"

"*It means 'My little girl.' He thinks you're just so cute.*"

"Great. Now I'm going to have to kick his butt before he goes home to Mother Russia. Goodnight, Shell."

"'Night, Hope."

Chapter Three

One of the most corrosive beliefs given new life by The Event is Ontological Nihilism, the belief that reality itself is arbitrary, illusory. And indeed, what are we to make of the impossibilities around us? In the face of breakthrough powers that give reality to every religious belief, folk superstition, and speculative "science," can the universe possibly be rational? And if it is irrational, how can it contain any true meaning?

Doctor Mendell, *Nihilism and the Age of Uncertainty*.

An easy breeze stirred the flowering tree, plucking white cherry blossoms away to fall like snow and pushing the long grass surrounding the hill into green waves punctuated by bright spring flowers nodding in the sun. Alone, I decided to explore and my path took me away from the tree and through the lower hills where the seasons changed from one wooded hill to the next. Stepping along the stream, I wandered into autumn to enjoy the jewel-like red maples and yellow gingko trees. Kicking the leaves and breathing their spicy scent, I kept going until I found a little glade by the stream where I could lie down to listen to the water.

When the lazy laughter of the stream turned into my chiming alarm clock and the spot of warm sunlight through leaves turned into Graymalkin sleeping across my leg, I stretched and brushed leaves—my hair, really—away from my face and sat up with a sigh.

"Morning!"

Shell popped into virtual existence by my bed, looked the scene over. "Aww. Wish I could give him a good scratching."

"After-mass dinner on Sunday, you'll be here with your shell on." I scratched Gray's ears for her; his flipping tail told me he was awake, but he played asleep, too lazy to do anything but imitate a furry lump until I removed the leg that was part of his bed. "So what's up?" She didn't usually pop up until I was headed back to the Dome.

"Did you *dream* again?"

"Yeah." I ran fingers through my bobbed hair.

It had been as clear as the others and, just like with the rest, so peaceful that I couldn't even panic about it when my eyes opened. At least I was thinking more while *in* the dreams, even if I still fell into the same Zen-like acceptance while I was there.

Was that a bad thing, or a good thing?

"Aaaand?"

"And that's it. Still no sneaky white fox." Sliding my legs out from under Graymalkin earned me an aggravated look. I scratched his ears in apology and when I didn't say anything else, Shell shrugged and told me what I didn't want to hear.

"Blackstone got you the appointment with Doctor Cornelius, for this afternoon. He wants you to take Ozma with you after our publicity photo shoot with the team and Svyatogor."

"Joy." I kept scratching Gray, and under my working fingers he rolled over on his back for a quivering morning cat-stretch that doubled his paw-to-paw length. Curling in to tuck his nose under his tail, he went back to sleep. I wished I could. "Talk on the way?"

"Sure. And I got you that training match you didn't say you wanted with the big guy. *After* the photo shoot. You know, just in case. Hope?"

Swinging my legs off the bed and standing, I did a vertical imitation of Gray's stretch. "Yeah?"

"I'm glad you told Blackstone."

The parentals were waiting in the kitchen when I came downstairs, Dad dressed for work, Mom dressed for a morning deadheading the roses that surrounded Corrigan Manor—her name for our old Oak Park Victorian whenever she got exasperated with how big a money-pit of a house Dad had talked her into moving the family into. That had been twenty years ago; she'd gone into labor with me in this house.

Being only one year shy of being able to legally drink meant that my parents didn't wait up for me anymore. No, they just waited patiently for me in the morning after nights when I came home; thumping down the stairs in t-shirt and shorts—I'd be flying out later but I never wore the uniform at home—I gave them a smile that felt real because it was. Eggs, sausage, toast, fruit, orange juice and coffee, Mom's start-the-day breakfast never changed and just the smells made my morning good.

I came home for the breakfasts, really.

Okay, that and to reassure my family that I was alive and well.

Dad looked me over before I got to the table, frowning at the white bandage wrapping my left calf. After a night to heal I'd had high-school sports injuries that felt worse and I didn't really need the bandage, but the skin beneath it still presented an ugly mottled red and white.

He folded up his paper. "Good morning, daughter."

"Good morning, father." I slid into the chair beside him with a quick passing kiss. Mom took the cover off my eggs, nudging the toast plate towards me.

"And how are you feeling?" I hadn't been limping, but he knew that didn't mean anything since I could have walked across the kitchen carrying as much weight as the old floors could stand; I would never limp under my own negligible weight.

"Singed. A bit like Mom's toast." I snagged two slices and reached for the jam. I didn't say anything stupid like *I was never in any real danger*. They wouldn't buy it, and then they'd never believe me when I said it and actually meant it.

"I'm sure that you were careful," Mom observed, scooping a knife full of strawberry jam and moving the jar where I could reach it.

"Shell would yell at me and then Lei Zi would rip my head off and ground me to the Dome for retraining if I wasn't."

Dad choked on his toast. "*Shell* would?"

"She says being a quantum-ghost means she has a decent chance of outliving the solar system, so she wants to make sure *I* do too—" Wincing on the last word, I crunched on my own toast and tried to pretend I hadn't said it. "Anyway, it was the kind of fight Atlas liked. They never saw us coming, and we had them outnumbered three to one."

Mom cooperated with my change of subject; it wasn't like we could brainstorm a solution to my "problem" anyway. I'd had plenty of time to think about it since Doctor Beth had confirmed last month that, based on nearly two years of observation and measurement, I wasn't aging anymore. Not a big surprise, stronger Atlas-Types just didn't, but I was also the youngest known Atlas-Type and we'd been hoping that I *would* age—or at least continue to physically mature into fully developed adulthood before I stopped.

Nope. I hadn't been doing much of that before my breakthrough, and I was doing zip now. If I didn't die hard I was going to outlive almost everybody I knew, and I was *devochka moya* for *life*.

Just...yeah, no words.

"So, what are your plans today?" Mom asked.

"The usual after-action stuff. I get to review and submit my action report. We did the team review yesterday, so we get our one-on-ones this morning. Quin wants to get some public relations pictures of us with Svyatogor before he goes back home. I get a sparring match with him before he goes."

And then I slip away to California.

"Are you up to it, dear?"

"Sparring, yeah. Doctor Beth has to clear me for duty before I go back into the field, though. Even to just patrol." I let them assume it was about the leg, or the hard hit they had to have seen last night, and the toast tasted way too dry in my mouth. Seeing them relax a little made me feel worse.

I'd thought this would get easier for them, and it didn't look like it was ever going to. Swallowing, I smiled.

"So, what are you guys doing?"

Breakfast got better after those first awkward minutes. It always did. Dad owned his architectural practice and had no scheduled meetings, and Mom could deadhead the roses anytime, so we stayed in the kitchen until the last piece of bacon was eaten and I got them to laugh at my recounting of last night's after-party.

Mom surprised me by handing over an engraved invitation to the Silver and Green Ball, Mrs. Lori's annual charity ball and international art auction. She also passed on verbal instructions from the *grande dame* of Chicago society to show up as Hope Corrigan rather than Astra. Just in case I couldn't read the name on the invite.

I loved Mrs. Lori, but I'd always had the completely unfounded fear that she would rap my knuckles or switch my hiney like an old fashioned parochial school nun (not that she'd ever threatened too—just because of the way she *looked* at errant young society girls). Now that I was infinitely stronger than her she made me a lot less nervous, but she remained convinced that I should train and fight crime less and do the charity-circuit more. Her argument was that there were "dozens" of Atlas-Types and only one Hope Corrigan Also-Known-As-Astra.

"Could you tell her I'll try?"

Mom accepted that and I got away without further commitments. Trading kisses with the parentals, I headed back upstairs to "dress for work."

"*You* will *go to the ball, you know*," Shell giggled in my ear as I changed. "*Blackstone's afraid enough of Mrs. Lori that he won't schedule anything conflicting for you.*"

"Yeah, well maybe we'll get lucky and aliens will invade."

"*They wouldn't dare. The old dragon wouldn't stand for it.*"

"Be nice!" I swallowed my own laugh and clipped on my cape. Mrs. Lori was kind of a dragon, and not the cute kind like Kindrake's flight of rainbow drakes.

Mmm. Kindrake and her friends at the ball... I shook the image out of my head; first, Mrs. Lori wouldn't invite just *any* cape to her events—of the other Sentinels only Blackstone and Chakra usually rated one—and second, Kindrake was still in St. Louis finishing her CAI recertification.

The final fallout of our brawl with Powerteam three months back had been our exoneration and the reality-show team's complete decertification. They were recertifying now, but Kindrake had left them to do hers elsewhere. Once she was done, we planned on thanking her for her assist in Littleton (which Never Happened) by bringing her back here for cross-training exercises while she applied for a place with the Hollywood Knights.

Weirdly, Powerteam's viewer ratings had gone up, which was just wrong on so many levels. Somewhat selfishly, I wanted Kindrake to do well just to spite Powerteam, but Kindrake was nice once you got past her Artemis-wannabe attitude and I did think her whole goth-girl thing would make a good contrast to all the glamour heroes in LA.

"So besides our morning schedule, what else have we got?"

Since a medical benching meant no serious training, the answer to my question was "Next to nothing." The daily briefing for the Sentinels and Young Sentinels took half an hour—a *military-time* half an hour, which meant exactly thirty minutes. My own one-on-one action review with Lei Zi took ten minutes. The Harlequin made sure the photographer got me holding Malleus in full view in the photo op; I couldn't do anything about looking small, especially in any picture with Svyatogor in it, but at least I could look like a serious problem. Then I got to fight him.

Astra vs. Svyatogor was pretty much a wash. Facing off on our hardened training room, I dodged his thrown club and got the first point before it returned to him. He held onto the club and block-hit me hard for the second point, and I got in the third point after some fancy air dancing only because Svyatogor, giant A Class Ajax-Type that he was, couldn't *quite* make himself go all-out on me.

Could I have taken him for real? I had no idea, but he knew he'd been touched hard. When he got back home he wouldn't just be talking to his comrades about how *cute* I was. Anyway, the match took my mind off my impending trip until it was time to go.

Ozma called to let me know she'd meet me in the flight bay. With the expanded team and *two* Atlas-Types to provide fast lift, Blackstone had made an agreement with NASA for us to house a pair of their ground-to-orbit Atlas Lift pods. A GTOAL pod was basically a five-man carrier (the fifth being the Atlas "lifter") with separate payload space. Stripped down, they were only meant for direct docking to other spaceships or stations and we kept them ready for emergencies. In return, we got to use them for in-atmosphere trips when we really needed speed—we could lift with them from the Dome in under two minutes.

She arrived in the bay with Nix on her shoulder and wearing her art-deco robes and silver wire coronet, Grendel following with her "luggage," and I was surprised to see Riptide flanking him.

"*Think she's trying to impress someone?*" Shell whispered in my ear. I kept the grin off my face (with Ozma's robes, Grendel's preppy vest and tie, and Riptide's street-hood leather duster they made a colorful and mismatched sight), but I couldn't resist bowing her majesty through the hatch at the rear of the pod. Her smile recognized my brief amusement and her nod played along, something I really needed.

"Buckle up," was all I said, giving grumpy Grendel a pat on the arm as he squeezed inside behind her. When Shell told me they were ready, I flew to the top of the pod and buckled into my own external lift harness. Shell opened the bay doors, and I maneuvered the arrowhead-shaped pod up and out with the ease of hours of practice.

"*Safe flight, Astra,*" Blackstone said in my earbug as I cleared the doors—as formal as always, but knowing he'd been watching my departure helped.

"We'll be back for dinner, sir. Unless the Hollywood Knights have a good table tonight."

"*See that you are.*"

Chapter Four

Orb is one of the strangest breakthroughs I know. She's blind and deaf from birth, and her floating silver sphere sees and hears for her. But she's told me her "sight" spans the full electromagnetic spectrum, plus her sphere's fine-grained pressure sensitivity lets her map three dimensionally with sound waves. Add to that her total control of the sphere's location, motion, and topography—she can form it into a nearly indestructible shield, or a floating blade with a monomolecular edge that can cut me with little effort. So my question is, what kind of weird breakthrough produced that thing? And what does the world look like to her?

From the journal of Hope Corrigan

Lunette's looked just as downscale and seedy in the daylight as it had the last time Shell and I had visited the superhuman nightclub. Papers blew across the empty walk outside its industrial-steel doors, and without darkness to cover them the squat building's white stucco walls were gray and dingy.

The fenced-in and nearly empty parking lot gave me plenty of room for the pod and Orb met us at the doors, standing below the crescent moon that was Lunette's sign. Her crisp white pantsuit was a perfect contrast to Ozma's jade robes. Her golden hair, done up in its signature hard-set and eye masking conch shell doo, gave Ozma's golden locks serious competition. As always, she looked too classy for the club she owned.

She ignored Ozma and her party. "Astra. It's good to see you." The silver orb hovering above her shoulder rippled in micro-patterns as it projected her voice.

"You, too." I smiled, uncertain if she "saw" it. "How've you been?"

"Busy."

I certainly knew that; Orb Investigations had become the premier superhuman investigations agency in California since Orb and Rafael Jones "adventured" with us in the Villains Inc. case. Her orb's sensory powers let her detect and analyze anything physical, while Rafael—now Doctor Cornelius—could do the same for anything metaphysical with his Agrippan magic. They consulted across the country, and I was lucky they were available to see me.

Finally nodding at Ozma and the boys, she pulled the door open and led us through the empty club. Shell popped in beside me, looked around as we crossed the open dance floor. "You'd think they would have upgraded to a better office."

"Hush," I whispered automatically; of course Orb didn't notice—Shell's body was virtual, after all.

Orb led us to a door at the back of the club, drawing a red curtain aside to usher us into a private room where Doctor Cornelius waited for us beside an ominous and intricately drawn magic circle.

"Astra." He nodded, smiling. "Good to see you and Shelly again." *He* always saw her just fine. "And Ozma, good to finally meet you."

I tore my eyes from the circle. "The same. You're looking good."

He did look good. The first time I'd seen him I'd recognized a strung out meth-head; the last time I'd seen him hadn't been long after he'd spoken one of the three Deccanic "Words of God" in his head to spontaneously heal Orb's fatal injury. That spoken Word had also raised Jacky from an undead vampire into a fully alive one and cured my PTSD as a *side-effect*. The effect had extended to him, and he'd looked a lot better then; now any lingering evidence of his hard years were gone and his eyes sparkled in his darkly handsome patrician face.

Ozma just gave him a regal nod and stepped over to a prepared side table; accepting a box from Grendel—the magic box that looked like an empty ornamental box made of gem-dusted gold wire filigree—she opened. Riptide watched Doctor Cornelius and Ozma with arms folded and an *I've seen weirder shit* eye.

"Did you ever speak the last Word?" I blurted without thinking as Orb closed the door behind us and Ozma pulled stuff out of her empty box.

His smile turned into a deep laugh. "Have you read about the Everglades Deadzone? All the Words are gone from my head. I am only myself, now."

Shell started. "Really? What did you kill?" The final Word had been the word for *Death*.

"Besides many square miles of glades? Something that badly needed to be dead. Shall we get started?" He nodded to the circle.

He had drawn the circle on a single piece of polished black granite that floored the center of the workroom, at least fifteen feet on a side. Russet-red banners had been hung around the circle on eight freestanding frames to give the room an octagonal shape. The room's walls were purest white.

I swallowed. "What do I do?"

"Change into this. Leave everything else." He held out a small white bundle. "Then stand inside the circle."

When I reached out he dropped it into my hand, carefully not touching me. Unfolding it, I found myself holding a plain white cotton shift.

"You can change in any corner," he said. He was right; there was plenty of room behind the banners.

"What's this for?"

"I spoke with both Chakra and Ozma after Blackstone called." He nodded to Ozma. "Since both of them are sensitive, in themselves or in the tools they can use, and neither found traces of psychic or supernatural influences, we're going to look deeper. This—" he waved at the bewilderingly complex white circle again "—is specifically tuned to you and only to you. Everything you're wearing brings its own signature and nature with it, and taking any of it into the circle with you will interfere with what we are trying to do."

"So, you need a clean testing environment?"

"Exactly."

I took a breath. Okay, I could do this.

I picked a corner and stripped out of the uniform, setting my earbug on top of it, and slipped on the sleeveless tunic. It covered everything important, but it was so light it barely felt like it was there. Which was the point, I supposed; barely there, it wouldn't get in the way. At least it wasn't as bad as an ass-flashing hospital gown.

Leaving everything piled in the corner and coming back out, I started to carefully step into the circle when Doctor Cornelius cleared his throat. He looked at Shell.

"I'm going to have to ask you to remove yourself as well, young lady."

I cringed as Shell started to protest loudly—then shut up. She could work it through, too; if she was present virtually, it was through our quantum-link and that brought her into the circle with me.

"Fine," she huffed. "But I'm turning her earbug *way* up."

"Understood. Astra? The lines are painted, so you don't need to worry about scuffing them."

Painted? Now I could smell it, under the aroma of musk and some kind of fragrant dried plant (not a controlled substance or something otherwise psychosomatic; I could recognize those from my training with Fisher's team). He must have spent the entire morning carefully tracing and then painting the circle with fast-drying acrylic—it was *complex*.

The circle's circumference was two thick and close-spaced concentric rings, then a ring of Latin and mystic symbols, then a thinner inner ring, then a hexagon. A nest of crisscrossing inside lines touched all the hexagon's corners, three of the lines thicker to form a triangle framing three touching circles enclosing more symbols that I assumed described me somehow and an empty double-lined and word-ringed circle at the center. All of it was meticulously drawn, laid with a drafter's precision that had to require special tools.

Doctor Cornelius directed me to stand in the center. I'd never seen anything this elaborate before—even the wards he made for the Dome last year didn't look like this—but I recognized the russet bundle he pulled out of his black coat. Seeing it made my palms go damp and my heart beat fast; the last time he'd used that stuff, a *thing* from somewhere worse than Hell had showed up and tried to kill everyone. It had "temporarily" killed Orb and Jacky, and had nearly killed me.

Orb made a noise and Doctor Cornelius looked up. He gave me a reassuring smile.

"Don't worry. This time there's no tether to the lower regions left behind to trip, so no qlippoths today I promise you. This is *my* workplace." Standing beside Ozma, Riptide folded his arms and nodded and I suddenly realized why he'd tagged along with Grendel: he'd heard what happened the first time Dr. Cornelius had done a favor for me, and had come *just in case*.

My heart was still beating fast, but I jerked a nod and tucked my hands down by my sides. Tugging on the tunic's hem, I tried to be still, to pretend it was just a bizarre medical checkup. Ozma slipped on a pair of narrow gold-rimmed glasses, and gave me her own reassuring smile.

I tried to return it. I could do this.

Doctor Cornelius began, reciting in Latin as he unwound the russet stole from the sticks, draping it over his shoulders and connecting the bundle of sticks into his surveyor's rod. And just like last time, the world changed as he spoke, my ears telling me the words of his recitation were going out from us, no longer trapped and reflected by walls. The words grew heavier than the tone and strength in them could convey, and as seconds passed everything outside the circle grew less present, less *real*, though nothing had gone away.

I tried not to breathe, then realized that was silly. The atonal Greek chorus was back, somewhere out of sight but echoing under his words as he went on.

Minutes ticked by, until I wondered how long he could keep going without a pause—the last time we'd been interrupted by the qlippoth, so I had no idea how long it was supposed to take—and then I wondered just how much I could move without messing him up. Was it like lying still for a CAT scan? I really should have asked. At least nothing too hideously ugly to think about arrived, which was a good sign.

I couldn't see Ozma or the boys—only Doctor Cornelius, and Orb who stood beside him holding a silver bell in her hand.

Then I felt the breeze, air moving on my skin. My first panicked thought was for my too-brief shield of modesty, but the gossamer cotton didn't stir. The air in the room didn't stir, but I felt it anyway.

And I smelled it, too. As Doctor Cornelius' voice rose and fell, I smelled wildgrass and cherry blossoms. The air got wetter and then my tree was there, along with a landscape clearer than I'd ever seen it before. The stream I'd followed last night bubbled up from a spring at the base of my hill, winding through lower dips and hills to a shore. My tree stood on the highest hill of a small island, one of many islands off of a circling coastline, part of an inland sea or great lake. The scent of saltwater said sea.

I could barely see the magic circle, and Doctor Cornelius stood in the grass watching me as I turned about. Time was only my heartbeat until I saw him raise his hand and heard Orb's bell ring, bright and pure. With each clear strike of her musician's hammer on the bell, the tree, the hill, and the sea faded until I stood inside the circle again.

Along with a light dusting of cherry blossoms.

He bent down and carefully picked one up to examine it. "Well, that is interesting."

Back in uniform and at a club table in the main room, I wrapped my hands around the warm cup Orb brought me. The coffee was mud compared to Jacky's or even Willis's, but it was real.

"What was that?" Shell asked.

She'd come back and now she sat beside me. I could tell she was worked up—her black athletic shirt, read *What the Freak?* All she'd heard through my earbug in the corner was minutes of Doctor Cornelius' reciting and then the bell. She'd actually turned her gain and filters up enough to hear my heartbeat speed up and then drop off, but even checking my sense-memory through our neural link after the fact hadn't told her anything; I hadn't *seen* any of it, not through my optic nerve anyway.

On my other side, Ozma was pulling little bottles and dishes out of her empty box. As freaked as I was, watching her pull stuff out of a box you could *see right through* didn't get to me at all. Or maybe I'd just gotten used to Ozma.

"That was nothing," she told Shell, who must have been relaying through Ozma's own earbug. "There was nothing in the circle with Hope. She went somewhere else."

"But she didn't *go* anywhere!" Shell protested. Grendel rumbled his agreement and Riptide nodded.

"You can go somewhere else and not leave," Ozma said like it made perfect sense. "But it might be more correct to say that another place came to her. Doctor Cornelius?"

"Yes." He had found an orange somewhere and sat peeling it into a bowl.

I had a dizzying moment of *déjà vu*. As relieved as I was that it was over, the fruit actually made me smile. "The orange?"

"Indeed, the orange."

Shell scowled, but she remembered Doctor Cornelius' fruity metaphor for the structure of reality.

"Reading about your interactions with this Kitsune person," Doctor Cornelius mused as he peeled, "and from what I saw in there just now, I would say that you have been brought to the attention of a more real portion of reality. Closer to the center of the orange."

"Why didn't Chakra or Ozma find anything?"

"That would be because *you* haven't changed. Does the fact that I can see you, even call you and speak with you on your cell when you're somewhere else, change you?"

I couldn't help the laugh. "That depends on what you say to me."

"Point. But nobody looking at you would see anything different forensically, even metaphysically. Ozma?"

While he'd been talking, Ozma had gotten out a small golden bowl and dumped a handful of the gathered cherry blossoms into it. Now she popped the top off a wax sealed bottle and carefully measured out crystal grains onto a fold of wax paper.

"Sands of time," she said to everyone, capping the bottle.

Doctor Cornelius didn't ask and I couldn't tell what Orb was thinking, but I just couldn't let that go. "The sands of time are *real*?"

"Real enough. To be more precise this is time squeezed from sand, like juice from a grape. You can extract time from anything, but sand is easiest."

"*Why?*"

"For measuring doses." She gently shook the paper over the bowl, letting the sand fall over the petals. "You cannot extract time from just a portion of an object. You could take time from a hundred pound rock, but then you would have a hundred pound piece of time. Add it to something as small and light as this, and you might get interesting results but probably not the ones you want."

That was typical of any explanation from Ozma—I would understand every word, but all of them together would make me wonder if I'd heard her right. It was like when she told me "Yellow is bright, brightness is an energy state, energy is speed, so yellow is fast." I'd learned that when I asked about the Yellow Brick Road, and of course it was obvious. To Ozma.

The sand falling onto the pink-white petals dissolved, or faded away, or whatever its disappearing meant. The petals didn't change, and Ozma sat back.

"Doctor Cornelius works from a different model of reality than the one I possess, but I agree with his conclusion. The petals you brought back with you originate from and remain part of a domain in which time is more eternal than sequential. They are always blooming, always falling, always waiting to fall. They are not dying." She put away the bottle, not at all perturbed by the fact that she was looking at something that shouldn't be here.

"But—they're from my dream!"

"You've always known that your Kitsune visions were more than mere dreams, Hope. We've just been assuming they were less than real. Doctor? The Wizard might have been able to tell me more, but I am not familiar with many places outside this world and Oz. Do you know where these are from?"

He shrugged thoughtfully, nibbling on a piece of orange.

"Considering that a kitsune is a Japanese fox-spirit, and based on what I saw, I would have to say that the tree these fell from sits somewhere in what Shinto belief calls the High Plane of Heaven. I would call it a part of Briah, the Iconic Realm."

"Heaven—" There was no way I'd been meeting that fox in *Heaven*.

He chuckled. "Don't get theologically confused, Astra. The Iconic Realm incorporates all spirit realms, both afterlife realms and godhomes, all manifestations of the divine shaped by humankind. The High Plane of Heaven is the Japanese equivalent of Mount Olympus or Asgard. It's the dwelling place of their celestial spirits."

"Okay. I think?" That sounded a *little* better, anyway. "So what does it mean? What's happening to me?"

"Just on a guess, I'd say it looks like a tree on the High Plane of Heaven really likes you."

"*What?*" Shell didn't quite screech, but Doctor Cornelius smiled.

"This is pure conjecture, understand. You already know Kitsune is more than just a shapeshifter. What if he has access to the High Plane of Heaven? Say that he wanted to pass you a message, so he went to that place you're always seeing, the tree, and opened your sleeping awareness to it? Do you follow so far?"

I nodded slowly, not at all sure I really did but hoping it would make sense.

"Shinto is an animistic religion—Shintoists believe that all things in the world have spirits, kami. The only real difference between the kami in a rock, a person, and even a god, is its degree of power and awareness. Objects in which kami are more than normally aware are considered sacred and made the center of shrines. Trees certainly have their own kami, even here, and in the High Plane of Heaven they are almost certainly as or more aware than we are."

"So when you said I'd 'come to the attention'—"

"Yep. You said you haven't seen Kitsune there since whatever happened that you can't tell me about, but the tree is always there. I think it likes your company, so it's talking to you. When you sleep, your awareness of the physical plane fades and it's able to get your attention."

"So Hope's being haunted by a *tree*?"

Big bad Grendel and been-there-killed-that Riptide looked almost as freaked as Shell; how were they supposed to protect me from an otherworldly *tree*? Despite everything I had to laugh. "Don't worry Shell, you've got dibs. So, does that mean that I'll just keep dreaming about it? That's not so bad."

He put the orange down. "Maybe. Orb, what did you see?"

She'd been so quiet I'd almost forgotten she was there; now she gave me a look which of course I couldn't read under the mask of her hair.

"You went away, Astra. Physically. For less than a second, a hundredth of a second, when the cherry blossoms appeared. You brought them back with you."

Chapter Five

"Unless you're stopping a supervillain In-the-Commission-Of you need papers and a judge to hunt down and bring in the Bad Guy. Work without it and you're just a super-vigilante and part of the problem. Not glamorous, I know, but nobody remotely sane would have it any other way."

Astra, Hillwood Graduation Guest Speech.

"When did my life become a fairytale? Because you know, I really should have noticed."

I'd waited to whine until we got ourselves settled at Restormel. The Hollywood Knights were filming their next movie in Hawaii, but Rook had offered the hospitality of their headquarters while we were in LA. Since Ozma had decided to stay at Lunettes and consult with Doctor Cornelius, I had flown the rest of us and the lift pod to the tower.

"Fairytale?" Riptide opened the fridge in the en suite entertainment and conference area and whistled. Plopping down into the biggest lounge chair, I refused to be cheered by the stocked bar or the beautiful view from the tower's bay windows.

"A fairytale. I've got to go find a friendly fox, and ask him to go talk to a magic tree!"

"Are there trees in fairytales?" He opened a beer and offered it to me. Yeah, right.

I covered my eyes, rubbed them. "There was in the original Cinderella. The blood-soaked version with the sisters mutilating their feet and the stepmom getting her eyes pecked out? She sang to it."

"The stepmother?" Grendel asked.

"Cinderella. I think."

"I like your mother. She's not in any danger, is she?"

I opened my eyes, but Grendel wasn't smiling. At all. "Do I *look* like Cinderella?"

"Well she was a blonde," Shell quipped. Pure reflex; she didn't look happy at all. "At least according to Disney. And the talking animal really should have been a clue." Riptide and Grendel both laughed. They couldn't see her, but they were perfectly used to hearing her through their earbugs. What they also didn't see was *Shelly*—she "sat" beside her twin. Once Restormel's Willis had left us alone, Shell had started relaying her so both of them could be here virtually.

Seeing them side by side was deeply weird. Shell wore virtual cutoffs and an athletic shirt, looking maybe twenty and wearing her now-black hair in a short bob. *Shelly* looked her seventeen biological years and sported her original long red hair. She also wore the tailored office suit she was almost certainly wearing in her office at the Institute, a continent and a gulf away.

I sighed, let myself wilt. "Nobody's taking me seriously."

Did I have a right to my attitude? *Yes*. Because it wasn't just a problem of nocturnal wandering anymore. Ozma agreed with Doctor Cornelius' diagnosis; my recent visit to an extrareality pocket (Littleton, which I could neither confirm nor deny for him) had weakened my "tether" on reality.

This wouldn't normally be a problem—and *wasn't* for anyone else—but Kitsune happened to have previously introduced me to a powerful if vegetable kami on the Plane of Heaven. Apparently it wanted to deepen our acquaintance, and judging from the cherry blossoms, there was a very real possibility that some night soon—based on the rate of increase in dream-regularity and something Dr. Cornelius called *resonance*, probably less than a month but likely no sooner than two weeks—I was going to go to sleep and fall into an unknown extrareality realm.

"I am *not* going to disappear down some cosmic rabbit hole and leave Dad and Mom wondering whatever happened to me."

Riptide shrugged. Taking a sip of his beer, he checked the label.

"That's some fancy stuff. No worries, *chica*. Our *bruja* and *brujo* will find some way to fix you up. Or we'll find Kitsune, get him to do it."

"What he said," Grendel seconded. I scowled, sighed again. Shell and Shelly shared a look.

"We've got a solution for now—"

"—at least we think so."

"We're working on it and you'll know when you go to sleep tonight."

"But we've been looking for Kitsune since you told us about getting more dreams—"

"—and he's not on anyone's radar—"

"—even with the DSA, CIA, Interpol, pretty much *everyone* looking for him—"

"—we're not going to find him that way," Shell finished.

Their worry was pushing them into quantum-linked gestalt and making me dizzy; Riptide and Grendel didn't even notice them swapping lines but I sat up, closed my mouth. *Great pity-party, Hope—way to scare your friends.*

"If I'm good for now...could you let Blackstone know what's going on, Shell?"

"Already done."

Riptide finished his beer. "Well I don't know about you guys, but all this luxury is making me itch. I'm going to head down to the barrio, get some real food, see how it all looks on the ground."

"Are you sure—" I shook my head.

We knew it wouldn't look good. A year and a half after the Big One, you almost couldn't see the scars the quake had left in the city's downtown. The holes in LA's skyline were almost filled (even if most of the new buildings were shorter) and most of the broken-up roads and wrecked utilities were fixed up or at least patched and workable. But flying in, I'd seen the empty and bulldozed spaces where older apartments and homes had been shaken down and gas-line fires had spread to burn out whole neighborhoods.

Real recovery depended on local economics but a lot of companies were leaving California, taking the jobs and the taxes needed to rebuild with them. Southern California was actually still losing population as residents looked for opportunities elsewhere, and Riptide's old surf-and-biker gang territory had been one of the worst hit. To make the "quake-blight" worse, parts of LA were blowing up into open street warfare. The local gangs, cartel-members, and refugees from Mexico's civil war were killing each other over the territory that was left.

"I feel like some real Mexican food," Grendel spoke up. He hadn't said much all day, just loomed like he was the Army of Oz. Which he was, half of it anyway. "Or Tex-Mex, or whatever you call it." They both looked at me.

"I think I'll stay in, guys. Besides—" I couldn't help smiling. "You'll have more fun without me. Just—don't start the fun. Okay?"

"Do you think anything will happen to them?" Shell asked when the door closed behind the two.

I headed for the fridge. "Nope, I think they're going to happen to someone else." The fridge held *two* brands of sparkling water along with the fancy micro-brewery beer Riptide had found; I was pretty sure the multi-bedroom suites the Hollywood Knights had given to us had been designed specifically for visiting teams.

Sitting back down, I considered calling Julie; staying in LA meant missing the shopping expedition the Bees had planned for tonight—nine high-end boutiques along and off Miracle Mile in one evening to update our wardrobes. (And take lots of notes; the Bees were still dedicated to their post-graduation assault on the fashion world, and the first step was their own boutique.)

Lowering my bottle, I found two sets of green eyes staring at me. "What?"

"They're going to *happen* to someone—" Shell repeated incredulously.

"—and you don't *care*?" Shelly finished.

Didn't I? I poked the spot in my head that usually exploded into panic at the thought of "negative public events," and realized that I really didn't. Grendel was level-headed when he wasn't in full berserker mode, and after all of our training together he knew how to avoid it. And Riptide enjoyed his bad-boy street villain posing, but he knew just what he could and couldn't do; he'd step right up to the line and sneer over it, but whatever happened he wouldn't start it or escalate it. He'd just finish it.

Not my circus, not my monkeys.

Green eyes narrowed and Shelly opened her mouth to protest. "Hope," Shell interrupted. "There's a call for you. It's *Veritas*."

"*I'm glad you could talk to me,*" Veritas said five minutes later. Taking one of the bedrooms, I had asked Shell to do a complete signals check to ensure we couldn't be monitored and then route Veritas' call through our quantum-link. I was talking to him inside the 21st Century equivalent of the Cone of Silence, and anyone managing to overhear anyway would only get my side of the conversation.

Paranoid? Just because the man who played *Second Spook to the Spookmaster* (Shell's words) wanted to speak to me?

Keep it light. "What can I do for you? Should I complain? You never call, you never write..."

"*I'll send a Christmas card. I understand you're looking for someone?*"

"Yes sir, I am." Someone? So he didn't trust his own secured line, or he was just that paranoid too. Should I be worried I was starting to act like him?

"*Blackstone's friends won't find him, because his friend's friends don't want him found. They will tell him they'll do their best, and they will. But nothing will happen.*"

My heart sank, even as I tried to figure that out. "Why?"

He didn't answer, and it was only my super-duper hearing that told me the line remained open. He was even calling from somewhere shielded for sound and I couldn't hear anything but his breathing and his calm and steady heartbeat as I waited, feeling cold.

"*Damn it,*" he finally said. "*Hope, how much do you know about what's going on with Japan?*"

"Japan's our ally?"

"*Wrong. Lesson one, there's no such thing as Japan, outside of a geographic and cultural distinction. An island can't be someone's ally.*"

"Um, okay?"

He blew out a breath. "*The same goes for us. The United States isn't anyone's ally. A country isn't a person; people are allies or enemies. At best, a friendly country is one whose people don't dislike us on principle and whose leaders consider cooperation beneficial. Our leaders have signed treaties with Japan's leaders, committing our countries to alliance in the League of Democratic States. But Japan's leaders are responsible first for doing what is best for the people of Japan. Do you follow me?*"

"I think so?" Beside me, virtual Shelly mouthed *What the hell?* I mimed slapping my hand over my mouth and glared at her.

"Kitsune infiltrated Littleton and the Institute to gain access to certain files that you are aware of. Files that might give a nation's leaders guidance in making certain near-term decisions. Hope?"

"I'm here," I breathed, feeling dizzy. *Now* I was beginning to follow.

"Because of the Villains Inc. business, we assumed that Kitsune was just a high-end thief. He has left his calling card behind at other jobs. After Littleton, the likelihood that he works for someone in the Japanese government approaches certainty. The files copied were historical, detailing potential events for Asia based on past probable futures."

"But you said that allied heads of state had access to the files!" He had, right? I tried to remember our conversation back in Littleton.

"No, I said they knew *about the files.* The team you met down there prepares and disseminates position papers for the leaders of the League based on their analysis of them."

Shelly nodded confirmation, but I couldn't believe it. "But that would mean that the prime minister of Japan..."

"Yes. And now you know why they aren't going to help us get Kitsune. He's their asset. If they know where he is, they won't tell us. If they have him, they won't turn him over."

I dropped to sit on the bed.

"And if you go and look for him yourself..."

"If he's in Japan, *they* either won't let me into the country at all, or will make sure I don't find him."

"I'm sorry." And he really was; I could hear it in his voice. "What do you plan to do?"

"Do you think I should tell you?"

"No." He gave me another minute of silence, but didn't hang up. I pulled my mask and wig off, running fingers through my hair, and waited; I couldn't think of a thing to say.

"May I offer an observation?"

"Okay."

"Things that governments cannot admit to, did not happen."

"Sorry, I— What?" I replayed his words twice in my head and they still didn't make sense.

"If someone was to find Kitsune in an inconvenient location, and remove him to a convenient one, another government could not admit to his having been in that inconvenient location, or protest a removal which obviously never happened. Do you follow me?"

"I—" My eyes had to be wide as saucers. "Yes. Thank you."

"Since this conversation is one of those things which never happened, you have nothing to thank me for. Make sure it's that important, Astra. Our government cannot admit to certain things either. Good luck."

"Th—thank you." The Shells stared at me and I stared back. This time the connection went away.

"Holy *shit*," Shell gasped. "Did Veritas just give us the green light to hunt down and *kidnap* Kitsune?"

"It's called a forceful extraction, when governments do it." Shelly corrected absently. They weren't in synch now...

"Yes, I can find him," Ozma said.

She had finished consulting with Dr. Cornelius and arrived at Restormel. The rooms had met with her serene approval, but she'd barely accepted a water from Nix (in a glass—she'd never ever drink from a bottle) and didn't ask where Grendel and Riptide had disappeared to. Glass in one hand, she sat correctly upright (quite a trick with the suite's body-swallowing lounge chairs) and argued single-mindedly with the Shellys.

"So let's find him!" Shell exclaimed. Ozma wore her Seeing Specs so she could see as well as hear the two of them. "A grab would be easy."

Shell was in favor of crowd-sourcing a kidnapping—tapping a few accounts and putting a bounty for discreet delivery up on the dark net (*somebody* greedy and untrustworthy had to know where he was). Shelly was more cautious. I'd begun noticing differences between Shell and Shelly, and wondered how much of it was her few extra months of experiences that hadn't been part of Shell's backup (which included dying—again) and how much of it was being in a physical (and vulnerable) body.

"How would we find him?" I asked more cautiously. "The *DSA's* best efforts came up short in Littleton, and they were actively hunting him in a small and heavily screened population. Now he could be anywhere in the world. And anyone. That doesn't help."

My observation didn't phase Ozma; she touched her cheek, looking thoughtful. "Does Kitsune have any living family? Close relatives?"

"No." I shook my head, remembering Fisher's background file on him. "He lost his older brother and two sisters in World War Two, and his wife died in the eighties, I think? His daughter and granddaughter were his only remaining family when they were killed."

"And no other living relatives back in Japan," Shell confirmed. "The war hit his home village pretty hard."

"Then I can find him. The misfortune of his family line may now be our good luck."

I blinked. "How?"

"Simply put, the bones of his ancestors can lead me to him no matter what form he takes. If there were more than one of his line left then it would be problematic, like a compass seeking two magnetic poles."

For an Ozma-explanation, that actually made sense. And couldn't have been worse. "The bones of his ancestors are in Japan."

"Then we will go to Japan and get them."

"Um," said Shelly. "About that..."

Five minutes was all it took to bring Ozma up to speed on the problem. Which did not perturb her in the slightest.

"Then we will not seek permission. We must go, so we will go. And we must go soon. Between the two of us, I and the esteemed Doctor Cornelius have established that once Hope is drawn into this other realm we will not be able to follow her. Not even the way we went to her in Littleton. She will be lost to us and—"

"Stop!" I held up my hands. "Shell and Shelly have already explored the possibility of sneaking into Japan." And of our smuggling Kitsune *out*. "We can't just get our passports and catch a plane from LAX. The Japanese government needs to approve applications for entry by visiting breakthroughs. They can deny us entry for any reason or no reason at all." Blackstone *might* be able to use his contacts to leverage approval, but that would take time.

"And we can't just sneak in," Shelly added. "Their national security agency is good—we don't know all the details, but they'd probably spot you for your magic and they may even have ways of detecting cape-type powers like Hope's coming in through customs."

"I see." Ozma's perfect brow furrowed.

Nix raised a tiny hand. "Couldn't you just pay someone there to…"

Rob a grave were the words she was looking for, and I smiled at the earnest doll. "Send us a bone or two in the mail?" I could just imagine it: *Oh hi, we got your number, and could you just mail us an ancient bone or two? Really? Expedited shipping would be great, we appreciate your skills in breaking several international laws and trafficking in human remains for us.*

The Shellys looked thoughtful. "How much time do we have? Enough to locate a reliable local resource? Or send someone less noticeable?"

"I would still need to go," Ozma said firmly. "Our Hope may not have more than days, and I would need to be assured of receiving the correct material." And then of course Kitsune might actually be in Japan.

Mom and Dad would always wonder what had happened to me.

I closed my eyes, opened them. "I can get us into Japan," I said, startling Shell and Shelly. "And I can get us out with Kitsune."

Chapter Six

The more rules and regulations, the more thieves and robbers there will be.

The more prohibitions you have, the less virtuous people will be.

Good Government is not intrusive, the people are hardly aware of it. The next best is felt yet loved, and then comes that which is known and feared. The worst government is hated.

Lao Tzu

Going supervillain takes *planning*. And that was what we were doing; it didn't matter that Veritas had practically signed off on it—we were planning on violating the territorial sovereignty of an allied nation, and in a big way.

I set some rules.

Rule Number One: only Ozma, the Shellys, and me, were doing this. We weren't widening the circle of people involved in any way that could get them in trouble later.

Rule Number Two: we were only going if we could come up with a foolproof way of *not being recognized* once we were in the country. Just thinking about what we were doing made me sick to my stomach, and not for the reasons Shell thought.

I wasn't Miss Stick-Up-Her-Butt Law and Order, but I knew I sounded like it most of the time. I didn't paint inside the lines because I had a particular respect for the law; I'd grown up in *Chicago*, and my family was *connected*. Even if we didn't take advantage of the political machine I'd heard enough over the breakfast table, and overheard more than enough attending society's endless round of charity events, to know the true character of a lot of the people who made and used those laws.

But there was a reason why I was always on Shell's case over casual hacking and snooping, and why I kept dragging Jacky back up to Chicago at the slightest pretext to play Artemis instead of the shadowy vampire-enforcer of New Orleans.

Atlas and Ajax had drilled it into me from day one—superhumans were powerful and *scary* to everyone else. Beyond the profitability of playing to the whole superhero image, the reason for the colorful costumes and silly codenames was simple; we could only be trusted if our deeds were done in the daylight, if we could be seen and held *accountable*. And we had to keep that trust, with both governments and the public, or none of it would work.

Which meant acting inside the law, being *seen* to act lawfully at all times—otherwise people started asking questions like "Who watches the watchers?" We watched ourselves and each other, it was the only way it could work.

And sneaking across another nation's borders in pursuit of a fugitive was definitely painting outside the lines. I wasn't sure how many laws it broke, but if we got caught violating Japan's sovereignty it would be…bad. The Sentinels had built their reputation for more than a decade and they'd survive, but Blackstone wouldn't even have to kick me off the team—I'd just resign. It might be the beginning of Ozma's supervillain career, and while Shell would be safe enough, *Shelly* would certainly lose her security clearance because of her quantum-link. She'd have to leave Littleton, even if she wasn't directly involved in what we were about to do.

Assuming I didn't do jail time, I could always become a payload lifter for the Lunar Territory and help to build Armstrong. Living part-time on the Moon would be cool and certainly contribute to the future; Armstrong's population was set to hit a thousand this year. One thousand colonists living on the Moon.

But I'd be done wearing the cape, so if we were going to go supervillain there were rules.

Shell took the job of arranging our covers and finding out where we needed to go once we got there. Ozma started making lists, itemizing stuff she'd need from her lab in the Dome. When the boys got back, we listened to the story of their night out (the part of me not focused on *my* problems had been a little worried it would involve police, and it had but only for the cleanup).

Since my part of it didn't start until we were going, that left me no excuse not to call it a night.

Changing into the white sleep-shirt and shorts that came with my field pack (Vulcan-made of course, in case I had to wake up and fight somebody), I climbed into bed. Knowing I might wake up somewhere else for good, if it wasn't for Shell's whispered *"Don't worry, we've got you covered,"* I wouldn't have been able to close my eyes.

To sleep, perchance to dream...of an undiscovered country. That's not where I woke up.

I "woke up" on a cloud-soft bed. Circular, slightly concave, and with no sheets above the form-hugging pad, it occupied the center of a featureless and equally circular white room. When I sat up, still wearing the sleep-set I'd laid down in, the walls brightened.

It said something about my experiences that waking up not knowing where I was didn't instantly freak me out.

A deep, mellow chime rang and faded. Rang again. Not sure why it reminded me of a caller tone, I answered.

"Hello?" I said to the walls.

"Are you decent?"

I knew that voice and felt the smile stretching my face. "I try to be?"

"Good enough." The featureless wall presented a door-shaped outline, becoming a door panel that pulled inward and slid aside. I folded my legs under me and scooted around to face the door as it opened for Mistress Jenia, Western Warden of the future Confraternal Unity and quantum-ghost. "Be well, Hope Corrigan. And welcome again to my home."

"'Be well?' Is that a future greeting?"

"Yes…and an in-joke for students of cinematic sci-fi history." Her floating mother-of-pearl throne drifted back from the door, allowing me to climb off the bed and exit past her into her cloudhome's main room. The long bay windows looked out on a sunset-painted cloudscape. Late evening light painted the white of the walls, my nightwear, her throne, and her translucent robes with gold, and added shadows to her rich chocolate skin. The soft light only gilded the lily of her ageless beauty.

She waved an elegant hand to take in her home. "Ozma and Doctor Cornelius were of the opinion that, so long as your awareness of the real world doesn't entirely fade with sleep, your point-of-awareness will not be drawn to the other world you are avoiding. If so, even a virtual-reality awareness…"

"Should anchor me here while I sleep?"

"We hope. It should help at least until the pull of the tree grows too strong, which shouldn't be for some time yet. Shell could have done it, but her system isn't specifically built for sustainable omni-detailed virtual environments and you would have spent your night in a sort of high-definition CGI cartoon. Hardly restful, so she called me. Drinks?" A table rose out of the floor beside her throne, stocked with ice and bottles.

I accepted a crystal bottle of sparkling pink something. It fizzed in my nose and tasted vaguely fruity. "Please tell me you're my Ghost of Christmas Future, come to tell me how this all turns out."

"Hardly. You must remember that the probable future the Teatime Anarchist brought me back from is no longer probable. The history of the Sentinels alone has deviated significantly in the past year, starting with the fact that Blackstone is still alive…"

"What… Oh." I could see where she was leading. "Then you never heard of Kitsune, in your potential history?"

"Correct again. I believe that in my future he lost his game with the Chicago mob and Villains Inc., cutting short his criminal career and ending his participation in history. And of course he never then met you. I think actual history has worked out much better there, don't you?"

"So, can you tell me anything?"

"About your immediate goals? No. But I do have some words for you." She turned her throne to watch the sunset, the windows darkening to allow comfortable direct viewing. "Be very careful. There are some times and places where radical change does not have much influence on future world events. Japan is not one of them. Not now."

"So I can break the *future*?" My voice rose at the end, and I put down the drink. "What do I need to know?"

"You are aware of the ongoing Kyoto Convention? Delegates from most of the Chinese Secession States are now in Kyoto trying to hammer out an agreement of unification, and Japan's government and people are incredibly conflicted over the China Question and their own role as a nation."

"What's the China Question?"

Her elegant hands smoothed her robes. "Very simply, what will China become, going forward? A collection of allied but independent Chinese states, much like Europe? Or a single federated state, much like the US but with a weaker central government overseeing semi-autonomous states?"

"And why does Japan care?"

"Japan cares because, even without the breakaway states that will not return, China is a nation of over one billion souls. Reunification, under any reasonable circumstances, will eventually return China to its preeminent position in Asia. And even with all the material aid Japan has given to some of the Secession States, China has a good memory and has not forgiven Japan for its 19th and 20th Century barbarities. So Japan is torn. It would rather see a collection of allied but autonomous states than a single nation-state—but not if those autonomous states can't create and maintain internal peace and suppress warlords and rogue states. Unrest and conflict on the continent is dangerous to Japan as well, and very bad for business."

I nodded, focusing on the clouds sailing above and below us and trying to keep in mind Veritas' recent speech about nations and people.

"So what happened in your probable history?"

Mistress Jenia sighed and smiled. "The Kyoto Convention resulted in the United Chinese Republics, a national federation. Beijing held out for a few years but eventually reformed itself politically and signed on with them, and the United Chinese Republics joined the League of Democratic States to become equal in power to the United States of North America. All was sweetness and light until the Last War, out of which emerged the Confraternal Unity."

"*China* becomes a liberal democracy?"

"Don't laugh. Liberalism as a political strain appears throughout history, and not just in the West—it merely came into its own in Europe and America. Successful revolution requires an ideology, and the thinkers and statesmen of the Secession States are going far back into China's intellectual history to find cultural refutations of the People's Republic's authoritarian statism. They will bury Maoism with a Chinese shovel."

"Have they?"

"Have you heard of Taoism? The Way? Lao Tzu didn't say much about government, but what he did say can be read as a libertarian refutation of the totalitarian People's Republic. They are building on that, and on Confucius' principles of meritocracy and respect, to build a culturally authentic ideology of Chinese liberalism. Of course they are opposed by One Land."

One Land. *Tianxia*. I shivered. We'd faced members of *that* terrorist organization in the Whittier Base Attack, part of The Ring.

According to Blackstone, a jihadist was to the average Muslim what a One-Lander was to the average Chinese. Tianxia meant "Under Heaven" and was the name for their movement, but *Yi Guo!* was their battle-cry—*One Land!*—and the name they used in English because it made more sense to westerners that way. One-Landers believed that Beijing retained the Mandate of Heaven, and claimed everything within China's widest historic boundaries. They were nationalist nut-jobs who wanted to restore China to "Unity, Purity, and Power." Murderous, whatever-it-takes nationalist nut jobs.

Turning away from the windows, I shook my head. "I'm really not sure what our trip has to do with what's going on in China."

"Japan is a charter member of the League of Democratic States, and the League has committed to recognizing whatever resolution Japan favors. Japan's decision will depend to a great degree on its sense of solidarity with the League's principle power, the US. If your mission..."

My heart sank. "If our trip blows up into an open violation of Japanese territorial sovereignty, that would be bad?"

"Depending on how you are discovered, it could be very bad. You are, after all, an officer in the United State's armed forces."

"A state *militia* officer." Not that other governments cared about the distinction. I slumped. "So I shouldn't go, then."

"I didn't say that. Losing you into some extrareality realm would have its own repercussions for history. In the end, even with all the future-histories in the Oroboros' files, I cannot say which outcome would be worse." Looking up at me, she laughed ruefully and shook her head. "History is an emergent phenomenon, and with all my quantum-brain power I can't do more than guess. I wouldn't bet dinner on my conclusions."

Great. So all the quantum-ghost of a future head of state and librarian could tell me was that my actions were *important*. I sank into the mother-of-pearl chair that appeared for me.

"Do you mind if I whine just a little?"

"Not at all. You were over that habit by the time I knew you, but Jacqueline still teased you about it even then."

"Jacky?" *That* made me smile. With all the stuff Jacky got into in New Orleans—her twenty-four hour coffee shop, her supernatural detective agency, and keeping Acacia alive and preventing the Master of Ceremonies from going full godfather—I worried. Just a little, and she'd laugh at me if she knew. "What year did you say you're from?"

"Let us say, awhile from now."

I took a breath. "And you knew me—know me then?"

"Yes. Very well."

"Will I still be the same?"

"Yes. No." Her lips curved up, her thin but unlined skin making her look sixteen and one hundred and sixteen at once. "Your smiles are not as wide, then. But your eyes are as kind."

She floated her throne over to me, close without touching, and the look she gave me was somehow both stern and so fondly maternal I had to blink suddenly swimming eyes.

"Of course that was a potential Hope, the most *probable* future Hope the last time the Teatime Anarchist made that journey and brought me back with him. Certainly you are being shaped on a different forge of experience now, and the anvil of time will beat you out differently than it would have before. More lightness, less dark I think, although I suspect your heart will stay the same—it did through every possible incarnation that the Oroboros ever saw."

I didn't know what to say.

Mistress Jenia was a good hostess; once the sun set, she turned her cloudhome so we could see the blue moon rise. To me, it looked like a promise—just looking at it made me feel better, like whatever happened we'd survive to do *that*. And that beautiful second home for humanity was only going to be the first of many—Jenia told me about the Martian and Venusian terraforming programs and the extra-solar colonization arks that would be planned.

I curled my legs up under me, and as we watched the blue moon she told me more weird stuff about the future—not other things we would do (which might not be true anymore, anyway), but things we'd learn. Like, we'd learn the stars weren't huge thermonuclear engines like we thought, but nodes of plasma discharge powered by galaxy-threading electrical currents. We'd learn that gravity itself was simply an electrostatic dipolar force (whatever that was), that plasma fields did more to shape planetary orbits and galaxies than gravity, and that the universe was a lot younger than we thought.

More weirdly, gigantic orbiting optical and radio telescope arrays, interstellar probes, and interstellar-range teleporters would tell us that we were alone; against all predictions, in a century of looking, listening, and searching no life would be found anywhere else in the Universe. Future theories would include abiogenesis as a cosmically unique event, colonization from another universe (maybe an extrareality more real than we'd thought), and Intelligent Design.

"Arguments do get rather circular," she laughed. "Scientists say 'It happened, and we don't know how or why.' Theists say 'We know how and why.' Atheists say 'We know it didn't happen like that!' Eventually the scientists walk away and think up more experiments."

She favored the colonization theory herself (called Hyperion Theory for the name of the hypothetical originating extrareality realm), since it explained both our apparent uniqueness in an otherwise empty universe and the reality-shaping nature of breakthrough powers. According to Hyperion theorists, life itself was a "supernatural" intrusion into a realm whose native natural laws favored unliving physics and chemistry. We were all more than *just* physical, with breakthroughs somehow connecting more strongly with our universal "higher reality."

Of course there could still be extraterrestrial life out there, halfway across the universe, but real aliens? It looked like the Server of Ganymede came from somewhere as much part of our own universe as John Carter's Barsoom. Or Littleton. In the physical universe that we knew, there was only us to count the stars.

We tripped from deep topic to deeper topic and it felt almost like a college night in Polevsky Commons with the Bees, staying up with pizza and philosophy and debating the whichness of whatness, of life, the universe, and everything until the small hours of the morning. Without my breakthrough that would have been my whole freshman year, and I'd still managed to get in a few of those unsleep-over nights with Julie, Megan, and Annabeth. Mistress Jenia (who felt in weird ways like Ozma) kept me entertained until Shell whispered *Wakie wakie...* in my ear and the night was over.

Chapter Seven

"Since the internet is forever, you need to be careful what you say; a minor interview with a fan club spilled my nickname for Artemis and her nickname for me into the world, and now people (the ones who don't try and 'ship us as a couple) ask how Little Miss Sunshine and a "bloodsucking fiend of the night" can be such super-friends. I tell them Artemis puts up with me. She tells them she's trying to keep me alive."

Astra, Power Week Interview.

The fix was in; somehow during the night Blackstone managed to arrange for Riptide and Grendel to temporarily attach to the LA Guardians, something to do with following up on their Guy's Night Out. According to Shell, they'd bonded over burritos and bad guy beat-downs (Grendel had come back missing a fang) and it had been *good publicity*. That got them out of Restormel before our stuff from the Dome arrived.

The problem was the stuff arrived with *Jacky*.

"No."

Jacky was unimpressed. "Yes. Of the three of us, who is the least likely to be caught?" She mimed going poof with a flip of her fingers. "And who can 'adjust' a memory here or there if we need to make our footprint invisible? You *need* me for this, and we've had this argument before. Think you're going to go supervillain *and* invade Japan without me? Oh, hell no."

I wanted to scream at her, and bit my lip hard enough to almost draw blood, but she was right; if it all went south then she had a better chance than me or Ozma of getting away clean—and the ability to cover our tracks might make the difference between success and failure.

"Besides." She rolled her shoulders and gave me a smile with fangs in it. "If you find Kitsune, you may need help persuading him to cooperate. I'm good at that, too."

I turned to Ozma—we couldn't have this fight anywhere private inside the lift pod's cargo space—but the Empress of Oz ignored us in favor of her inventory; Jacky had brought a crate of stuff packed by Nox, and she was examining each item before transferring it into her magic box.

Shell stayed out of it and Shelly wasn't here (we'd decided that she had to stay out of this, even virtually, in case she was asked questions later).

Snapping open the top case in the stack she'd kept for herself, Jacky handed me a bundle of black cloth.

"Shell needed me to get the designs for these from the Bees and get Vulcan to fabricate them overnight for us. Julie says hi and 'You'd better come back.'" The bundle turned out to be a new costume. I turned it over, let it slide through my hands to puddle on the folding table.

"Please. Please, please, *please* tell me you're not serious."

Virtual-Shell couldn't stop laughing. "Serious as a subpoena. Oh my *God*, you look— Anyway, you kept talking about going supervillain, so we thought 'why not?' Put it *on*."

"This does meet one of the necessary criteria that you insisted upon, Hope," Ozma informed me, ceasing her inventory to take the matching bundle Jacky handed her.

I sighed and started stripping.

I'd recognized the outfits instantly from some of Julie's sketches done during the Bee's villain-rap phase, and they were the same for all three of us. Black high-necked coats, they fit like tailored gloves from the waist up and flared into loose robes from waist to ankles, buttoning up the front from waist to neck. Beneath them we wore black two-piece bodysuits that covered us from wrists to neck to ankles under the fitted coats. Black boots, of course. Wide black sashes around our waists completed the outfit (and with the high priest-style collars made us look vaguely and sinisterly clerical). My coat came with a sleeveless shoulder-hung scabbard.

"How did you get these so fast?" I asked, twisting to settle the sewn-in harness.

"Andrew has every inch of our measurements," Jacky explained, tugging to even out my jacket shoulders. "And Vulcan was able to fabricate everything using a reserve barrel of the polymorphic-molecule goo he keeps in the Pit. They come with these."

The box she handed me held a pair of narrow black shades. Taking them from me, she slipped them on my face. "They're as nearly indestructible as the rest of the outfit, and Ozma says she's got a charm she can put on them so that nobody can snatch them off. *And* they'll stay where they are if someone punches you."

Tightening her own black sash over her Magic Belt (covering the distinctively brilliant white and gem-studded belt certainly made sense), Ozma nodded. "That will be simple enough, and Jacky insisted that they 'completed the outfit?'" She laughed gaily. "If we are to adventure incognito, then they do seem appropriate."

I fidgeted as Jacky turned away to change into her own new villain-wear. Twisting in my coat, I tried to get used to the way the bottom moved almost like long skirts (if you split them up to the waist in front). They belled out when I spun, definitely weren't designed to break away like my cape would if grabbed, and felt like they might easily get in the way.

Once Jacky was ready, Ozma pushed us all together and had us take hands. Raising her royal scepter in her free hand, she waved it over us and chanted.

"Eri emi ipso!" Her magic belt flared bright under the edges of her sash and then she wasn't Ozma anymore.

Well, she *was*...but not. Her golden hair had gone black as night to make her alabaster skin even more striking, and when she lowered her shades to wink at me over them I could see her eyes had gone black and almond-shaped. All her features softly changed, she remained as stunningly perfect as ever. Jacky's transformation was less startling, but only because her hair had already been dark. Weirdly, Jacky was staring at *me*. I tugged a lock of my hair forward where I could see it, sucked in a breath.

"Shell?"

"On it!" Shell waved her own hands dramatically (and needlessly), and a virtual mirror popped up in front of me. I took my new shades off to look at my virtual image. Oh. *Oh.*

"Hope? Hope? Earth to Hope?" Shell was giggling and I didn't care.

The angles of my face were smoother, rounder. My nose had never been a big feature and now it was even less prominent, especially across the bridge where it was a gentle hill between my eyes instead of a ridge. My wide eyes were now almond shaped of course, but I hadn't been prepared for the *color*. My friend's assurances aside, I'd always thought my grey-blue eyes and platinum blonde hair made me look colorless (and deeply envied Jacky her dramatic midnight eyes and locks); but now my eyes were a deep hazel and my *hair*, my bob-cut hair, was a rich dark brown with red highlights, like aged and polished redwood. I was...

"I'm beautiful," I breathed.

"You're different, that's for sure," Shell laughed, and beneath my wonder I felt a spark of optimism. *Nobody* was going to recognize us like this. Maybe, just maybe, we could get this done without disaster.

That was hardly the last piece of magic, or the last surprise.

Ozma passed Jacky and me tiny magic rings that looked like they'd been cut from single pieces of emerald. How did I know they were magic? She actually she picked them up from the table where they'd been sitting unnoticed in plain sight—which shouldn't have been possible since they were *glowing*. We put them on and then twisted them as per her instructions, and in a flash of light we all found ourselves naked. I squeaked and covered myself by sheer reflex.

"Well, that would be fun at some parties." Obviously forewarned, Jacky handed out neatly folded changes of casual civilian clothes. Once we'd all restored ourselves to modesty Ozma had us twist the rings again and, in another flash of light, we were back in our supervillain costumes.

We'd become *magical girls*. Magical Girls in Black. Could it *get* any weirder?

Yes, yes it could. Next Shell showed me The Sword; as big as me, it deserved capital letters. I'd thought the scabbard might hold more than one weapon, but no, it had been made for a blade at least as heavy as my titanium maul. Crossing down behind my back, it bumped my calves if I wasn't careful and the hilt stood out above my head. She had to show me how to sheath and draw it.

"Vulcan originally made it for Grendel," she explained. "All I had to do was modify the hilt."

I swung it and held it out straight, eyeing it along its edge. "But I don't swordfight!"

"So who expects you to *fence* with it? Swing it like you would Malleus—its edge can cut battle armor, but even if you use the flat anyone trying to parry or block your hit is going to really wish he hadn't!"

While I was considering her point, she pulled out her last surprise. A cat. A coffee-and-cream colored cat with darker booties, tail, and ears that hummed almost subliminally to my super-duper hearing.

"Neat, huh?" She did something and the cat turned into a hovering sphere the size of a baseball. "It's a drone Vulcan came up with. He can't make it completely stealthy, so he built in a projection field. It's got a satellite uplink so it'll be off the local grid, and you never know when you might need a scout or lookout. I call it Snoop."

Back in cat form, 'Snoop' regarded us all with regal disinterest and turned to washing himself.

"A.I.?" I asked weakly while Jacky snickered. Shell looked unhappy.

"Emulation A.I. only. It's pretty dumb."

"Anything else?"

Ozma softly chanted to herself. Transforming her royal scepter into a something like a drum-major's long baton, she smiled triumphantly.

Shell shrugged. "Nope, that covers it. Your passports, visas, credit cards and other papers are in your coat pockets. You and Jacky are traveling as Japanese-American cousins in Japan to visit Ozma. FYI, Jacky's the only one of you over sixteen."

They all looked at me expectantly.

They'd met every condition. We were going.

Chapter Eight

"Superhumans are the gateway to the Solar System. Not considering the few breakthroughs who can survive indefinitely in a complete vacuum, there are many superhuman flyers. More than a decade after the Event, we still don't understand how they fly, but many of them display all the characteristics of the science-fiction concept of reactionless drive; they move by will alone, sometimes at supersonic speeds. What this means for space exploration and development need hardly be articulated, but for those who like hard numbers I will try."

Dr. Donald Piers, NASA Ways and Means Conference.

Ozma told Nix she was staying to keep an eye on Grendel—a royal command the tiny doll accepted happily since she absolutely adored the big guy. We packed everything tight, double and triple checking like we were packing full field-loads, folded up the tables, and strapped it all down in the cargo space before we buckled up—a more involved process for me as I locked myself into the Integral Center Flight Frame and Shell closed the pod up.

For in-atmosphere flights I preferred to use the exterior lift harness, but what we were about to do required extra-atmosphere travel and *that* required a spacesuit even for me. Which was why the flight frame (a cross between a harness and an open cage) was *inside* the pod hull, anchored both top and bottom—I flew the thing by standing in the center of the pod and lifting it from inside, pushing against the frame with my shoulders, chest, back, or feet.

Of course I could barely see outside through the pod's small and thick windows, but they weren't designed for piloting. That was what quantum-ghost friends were for; as she closed us up, Shell brought up a full-surround ghostly representation of the outside from the pod's cameras for me to see.

"All internal systems are good, navigation and external cameras are working with full redundancy, Captain. Are you ready to boldly sneak where no one has sneaked before?"

I burst into uncontrollable giggles; Virtual-Shell stood beside me with feet apart and hands folded behind her back, her ears transformed to Spock-ears, and she wore a blue and black Starfleet uniform for the occasion.

"Are we clear with LAX airspace and North America Command?" I asked as soon as I got it under control.

"Aye aye, Captain. We are clear to go." She gave me a wink that said *And they never saw a thing*. Being able to do this meant somebody somewhere would be forgetting our tracked flight-path.

I lifted us, guided by the pressure on my shoulders and the changing virtual view. It had taken me a couple of weeks training with Watchman to get the hang of lifting like this, but now it was like riding a bike and we rose above Restormel and kept rising into the morning light as Shell painted LAX flightpath lines for me to see. I turned us towards the sun and accelerated.

"Our path to orbit is clear," Shell reported. "Turning off our transponder and going radio-silent, clear to turn in three…two…one…now." High enough that nobody in LA could still see our unreflective hull, I turned us west and steepened our climb.

Getting us into Japan was simple; I just had to avoid the attention of their National Defense System. Of course simple didn't mean *easy*; Japan had begun thickening its defense system when China's collapse had put many of their ballistic nuclear missiles in non-government hands, and had worked even harder at it since the first godzilla hit Tokyo.

They'd had to, because while the rest of the world (including New York and Chicago) had seen a few of the monsters wade ashore, the Tokyo Godzilla had been just the first of *many* to hit Japan.

Even with Shell's Big Book of Contingent Prophecy and the Oroboros' own collection of past future files, we had no idea what had changed. In the older potential futures—pre-California Big One and before the Teatime Anarchist ended the time war against his evil twin with mutual annihilation—the godzillas had arrived nearly two years from now. They also hadn't been followed by *more* and *bigger* breeds of monsters. The Japanese called them *kaiju*.

The Oroboros' best guess was that whatever Verne-Type mad scientist had created the 'zillas had been under the control of the Dark Anarchist. (The Oroboros *hated* the name I'd given the evil twin, especially since Shelly used it in all her reports. They weren't too fond of *Big Book of Contingent Prophecy*, either.) With DA as dead as villain-rap music should be, the Oroboros believed that either the Verne-Type who'd made them had been "unleashed" or the creatures themselves were mutating without control. Either way, with only occasional exceptions the new kaiju, to use Shell's phrase, all loved-loved-*loved* Japan.

This meant Japan's network of defense radars was second to none, and their sonar network was even better. If they saw something unknown and potentially hostile coming in, and if they said hello and it didn't say hi back, they'd either drop a crowbar on it from orbit or fire an over-the-horizon missile at it. And that was just the outer ring—if you got through that they scrambled subs or jets depending on whether you were wet or dry. If you managed to hit shore in an urban area, well, that's when the mecha got dropped on top of you, or one of the oversized and heavy-hitting national cape teams like the Eight Excellent Protectors and the Nine Accomplished Heroes.

But they couldn't watch everywhere, so they tended to focus on surface and sub-surface threats. That's what we were counting on. The lift pod had a low radar signature and *no* internal heat-signature. Non-reflective, it was a dark body at night and I could slow us down enough on reentry so that atmospheric friction wouldn't heat us and light us up as we came in. Not coming from the west, it was unlikely they'd spot us at all.

Once we'd come down, I would put on the brakes and drop us just offshore in shallow water—avoiding death-by-missile or breaking our necks, whichever came first. Simple.

The minutes crept by, counted on a virtual clock Shell provided as I kept our acceleration at one gee and kept us inside the virtual painted lines. "Entering orbital path," Shell informed us all. "One ring around the rosy and we're good for entry." I relaxed a little. We were in orbit, floating in zero-gee, and she was saying nothing about non-NASA or Air Force contacts. We'd passed over Japan's high-frontier once going up, and Shell would tell us if someone was talking. Jacky looked bored and Ozma read a huge old book she'd pulled from her little box.

The virtually painted lines changed, dipping down as Shell chanted.

"Begin braking in three...two...one...now!"

Spinning us so the g-force from braking would press Jacky and Ozma back into their seats, I pushed hard, shedding orbital velocity and letting gravity have its way.

"Adjust attitude in three...two...one...zero."

I stopped pushing and spun us again until the attitude lines showed we were coming in belly-down. Feeling the atmosphere start to grab, I held our attitude until our building velocity did it for me. In interest of keeping the lifter's weight down, only the bottom of its hull came with a thick heat shield—and even if we weren't going to come down hot this time, belly-down reentry was safest.

A climbing whistle softly vibrated through the cabin, the first wisps of atmosphere contesting our intrusion. "We're riding on rails now, people," Shell sang out. "Prepare for spin and breaking in five minutes, give or take a few counts. Next stop—" She cut out, *vanished*, along with the virtual map and positioning lines I was following.

"Hope? What's happening?" Ozma closed her book and looked up, and I realized she'd been wearing Seeing Specs so she could see Shell and her virtual screens.

"Shell? Shell?" No answer in my head. *Shell wouldn't leave.* That was stating the obvious. Okay, something had broken our link, a quantum-entanglement interdiction field or something, like the one around Guantanamo Bay. *All the way up here?* Still being obvious. "Shell's gone, and I'm blind."

Jacky started unbuckling, looking around the cabin. "What about the internal controls?"

"Stay in your seat, there *are* no internal flight controls. Watchman uses a VR rig when he flies inside, and it's back at the Dome."

"Can you land us without it?" Ozma asked with the same urgency she'd use to ask if tea would be served on time.

"No." I started unlocking myself from the flight frame. "We're in free-fall, which means when I start pushing I won't know which direction *down* is. I won't know when and how hard to push, and even using the windows I could fly us into the ocean. I'd survive." I didn't have to say "*you wouldn't.*"

"Okay…so what do we do?" Jacky sounded nearly as calm as Ozma. I wasn't panicking, but only because there was a way out. It killed the mission, but we'd go home.

"I need to go outside to land us, and we don't have a pressure-lock. If I pop the hatch we're going to depressurize and start tumbling, and our radar-profile is going to spike. Which means a getting a crowbar or a missile."

"So we can't stay. Got it." Jacky started unbuckling again.

"No. I'm aborting the flight." I'd reached the single control box in the cabin, the one with the big red handle. "When I pull the emergency release, the transponder turns on, the radio starts screaming SOS, and we grow parachutes the instant the flight computer says we're low enough."

Hopefully we weren't already in Japan's airspace.

"Stop!" Ozma actually yelled over the rising vibration and howl. "Jacky, how long can you remain mist?"

"Up to half an hour. Why?"

"Get what you need. Hope, you're leaving. We're leaving with you."

They unbuckled and moved fast—all the Sentinels and Young Sentinels had received zero-gee training. I grabbed my sword and sheathed it while Jacky grabbed her guns and Ozma retrieved her wand-baton. Clutching it and her magic box, she yelled a string of nonsense-words and turned into a green crystal jar.

"Okay, she can come," Jacky said.

"You think?" I picked Ozma up and popped her lid, trying not to think about it. "Get *in*." When Jacky turned herself into mist she also lost a lot of her mass (otherwise the transition from solid to gas would have made her transformations *explosive*). The remaining mist that was Jacky could compress into the jar, and did, leaving me with a sealed Ozma-jar of Jacky and an empty cabin.

Our baggage wouldn't survive the trip. But then again, I wasn't going to let go of Ozma with one hand just to take anything else with us.

How much time? Less than five minutes, but since we hadn't eaten a missile yet there was reason to be insanely optimistic. I went back to the control box and popped and pushed a different button, then took a deep breath and punched through the hatch.

And spun hard in the hammering air.

It took a few seconds of spinning ass-over-teakettle to figure out which end was up and get in front of the tumbling lifter while counting—which was important because of the button. Thirty seconds later the lifter blew up, throwing me ahead of it. I didn't let go of the jar.

It's not often I could say that falling at terminal velocity was a good thing. Rolling over so I could see the blast cloud, I couldn't see any very large pieces; the blast combined with the violence of reentry would spread what bits survived—which wouldn't be soft things like clothes or travel bags or even shoes—over a wide radius. And hopefully Japan's defenders had mistaken the radar-spike and explosion for a meteorite coming apart in the atmosphere.

Turning back over, I looked ahead. No glowing missile trails, no sudden launch plumes in the black water far below me through the gauzy cloud layer. And no radio for me to yell my harmlessness through if one appeared.

St. Michael, defender of man, stand with us in the day of battle.
St. Jude, giver of hope, be with us in our desperate hour.
St. Christopher, bearer of burdens, lift us when we fall.
And please don't let me have just killed my friends.

Somebody heard me, and not the wrong people; the ocean remained unbroken and when I hit the lower cloud layer I hesitantly began flying instead of free-falling, turning my steep descent into a more gradual one towards the coastline glittering under the Moon.

If this had been a movie I'd have submerged and swam ashore, walking dramatically out of the surf (probably wearing something appropriate to a wet t-shirt contest). Movies are stupid; I hugged the waves and angled to the south of the thickest lights, looking for a dark beach. Sliding past a fleet of outbound fishing boats, I found a stretch of sand cut off from the resorts around it by cliffs pushing out to sea, and landed on sandy rock far above the high tide line.

And sat down.

I waited until I stopped shaking and my breathing evened out. It wasn't PTSD (I knew what that felt like)—it was five of the most terrifying minutes of my life, ready to eat a missile at any moment with no warning and literally holding my friends' lives in my hands. When I could trust my hands not to shake and drop it, I carefully popped the top of the Ozma-jar. Jacky rose like a genie from its bottle, filling out and then dropping into solid black-suited flesh.

"Hey," I said.

She looked around at the cliffs, down at me. "'Hey?' I heard the boom, and all you've got is 'Hey?'"

"That was the lifter, not a missile. I stuck around so I'd be mistaken for debris if anyone saw me fall."

"Clever girl." She sat on the rock beside me, nudged Ozma. "So, how long do you think she's going to stay a canning accessory?"

"You said you could stay mist for half an hour, so I suppose she'll un-jar a little before that. She wouldn't want to risk you going…" I mimed an explosive size change with my hands. "*Bawoosh!* inside her. And if I was still in the air after half an hour, something would definitely be wrong."

Jacky nodded, brushed the sand beside her. "So, no lifter. How are we going to leave with Kitsune?"

"We'll think of something."

"And our vacation luggage?"

"We have credit cards in our packets; we'll buy more."

"And without Shell, how are we going to find the Miyamoto family grave?"

"I— I don't know." I really didn't. "We'll manage."

"Yeah. We always do."

We sat and looked out at the water.

"Jacky? I'm glad you're here."

"Don't get sappy on me now."

I smiled in the dark, and when Jacky looked down at the jar sitting between us and scooted over a couple of feet, I burst into laughter. I was still laughing when Ozma stopped being jar-shaped.

"Hey," Jacky greeted her, bringing another burst of giggles out of me.

Ozma nodded silently. "Are you okay?" I asked when she didn't say anything.

"I was quite happy being full, thank you." Her voice was thin, her eyes unfocused, but then she smiled. "After all, that is a container's purpose in life, and if I can't abide a little time as a useful oddment then I have no business turning people into headwear. Are we in Japan?"

"Yes. We made it."

Out to sea, gold light touched the horizon to fade the stars.

Episode Two

Chapter Nine

Defensenet Report, Shibushi Alert: See attached video-report from Defensenet boat Kagoshima 4-7. Observation of high-altitude detonation and confirmation of floating debris suggests independent destruction of unknown transport vehicle, direction of travel unknown.

Defensenet Recommendation: Move Defensenet assets to region and elevate observation until security from incursion has been assured.

DR105-BV [Classified]

A warm summer rain started to fall and we moved under the ridge of the cliff as the sky brightened to gray.

By American standards, Japan didn't have a lot of wide-open and empty places. There were only about one-third as many Japanese as there were Americans, but they all lived on an *island chain*—a *mountainous* island chain at that—so all the territory that wasn't too vertical or forested was either farmed on or occupied.

But growing stuff takes a lot of space and not every inch of shoreline was built on. I had chosen Kagoshima Prefecture, just north of small Shibushi Port and far from the megalopolis that was the Greater Tokyo area. The plan had been to walk into Shibushi, wheeling our bags behind us, and rent a car for the road-trip. Easy, but Shell was our map. Also, we were going to look a lot more conspicuous now, walking into town with no luggage and two of us holding American passports. And although I hadn't gotten shot out of the sky, the lifter's explosion had to have put *somebody* on alert; even a notice to the local police to keep their eyes open could doom us if we stood out. We needed to connect with Shell, but first we needed to get out of Shibushi without attracting attention. And before that, we had to get *into* Shibushi without attracting attention.

I watched rainwater drip off the black-rock cliffs and tried not to feel overwhelmed. Beside me, Ozma sat down and started unpacking her magic box. Laying aside a silver tea set and a water-filled crystal ball occupied by a happily swimming clownfish, she pulled out a small plastic eye-drop bottle labeled *#5*.

"Will we be going soon? If we are, it really is time for this."

Jacky rolled her eyes. "And what's that?"

"Comprehension drops. Apply daily to eyes, ears, and tongue to comprehend and be comprehended."

I stopped half-heartedly adjusting my sword harness, fought the smile spreading across my face. "How do you make *those*?" *Wait for it…*

"I started with a flash drive full of Japanese-language textbooks, dictionaries, and self-study audio files and dissolved it in a universal solvent. After that it was simply a matter of separation and distillation."

Of course that's what it was. Jacky just shook her head, but I snorted a laugh before getting it under control. Okay, still not a fan of magic, but *Oz* magic? It just made my world a brighter place.

"So we'll all be able to talk like native Japanese? Why are Jacky and I still American citizens, then?"

"Because although you'll be able to understand and speak Japanese, you don't know the culture. It's very formal, and if you talk like an educated Tokyo native and don't use the honorifics or bow correctly you'll look and sound unspeakably rude."

I started to protest, stopped myself; my knowledge of Japanese etiquette didn't go beyond basic "san" use, bowing, and introductions—the "boardroom etiquette" Japanese businessmen appreciated seeing when visiting Chicago.

"And *you* know how?" Jacky cocked a skeptical eyebrow.

"Of course. The degrees of social deference and appropriate addresses are all based on older Japanese court-behavior and I can do court in any country in Europe, Asia, and the Indian Subcontinent. I can do court in Siam."

"So you'll come across as an educated aristocratic Japanese blue-blood?"

"And you are both my American cousins. Nobody here expects foreigners to have proper etiquette, so you won't be considered crude once they know you're American. Just don't speak Japanese unless you absolutely have to, and watch the bows. I'll explain on our way to town, and you'll pick it up after a while."

She'd been putting drops in her eyes and ears while talking, and only Ozma could look graceful with her head tilted ninety-degrees sideways and a dropper in her ear. She finished by putting a last drop on her tongue, coughing softly and licking her teeth. "So. *Watashi wa Nihongo ga hanasemasu.* Your turns."

I took the bottle and refilled the dropper. The honey-colored liquid sparkled in the gray light, and...was it *whispering*? Okay then... A drop in each eye, one in each ear, the last drop on my tongue making me wrinkle my nose as I swallowed. The stuff tasted like *dust*, like endless hours of study and heavy, boring books. I replayed Ozma's words in my head, and laughed. *"I can speak Japanese."* Nice. *"I am a beagle. I can't find my shoes."* It worked as long as I didn't think about it, and I felt infinitely better; at least I'd be able to read the street signs and understand what was being said around me.

After examining our papers and cards, we turned our rings and did the transformation from Magical Girls in Black to Vacationing Girls Who'd Lost Their Luggage (even our glowing magic rings disappeared from view when I didn't focus on them). Flying up from our hiding place beneath the beach cliffs, we found the ocean road that ran above them. The rain had stopped, and we walked along the cliff side of the road for only a few minutes before a little farm truck came up behind us headed for Shibushi.

It slowed politely so as not to spray us, then stopped and backed up, and Jacky and I let Ozma step ahead of us to engage the concerned-looking farmer who got out. A brief conversation later we were all perched on the back of the truck, sitting high and dry on top of a load of produce crates full of beets.

I'd forgotten that one of Ozma's superpowers was overwhelming beauty and perfection; she'd explained to our farmer that our car had broken down past the last crossroad, and that we'd left it with our driver to wait for a tow while we walked. A few smiles and a sincere request for help and the farmer didn't ask why we were walking along dry after the rain, or why we would want to walk five miles into Shibushi, and the only reason Ozma wasn't riding in the cab with him was because it was also full of wet dog. Not that he would have laid a lecherous finger on her—or even thought of it. Although the dog would have wanted to adopt her. Our farmer let us down at his stop at the produce market on the edge of town, Ozma thanking him nicely and Jacky and I just nodding as she assured him we would be fine.

Our stop turned out to be lucky; as we walked away up the street we saw far too many of the little police cars for a quiet morning and watchful, if polite, policemen stood about talking to early morning pedestrians. To get to the square in front of the train station—where the plan was to get tickets and ride the Nishinan Line to Miyazaki (not where we wanted to go, but away from Shibushi)—we would have to walk past three pairs of officers checking IDs and...

I didn't freeze, but found a sudden interest in the display window of a clothing store.

"Who are the capes?" Jacky asked, examining a light yellow summer coat.

"They're *The Eight Excellent Protectors*."

"And they shouldn't be here?"

"No!" I made myself turn and look at them—perfectly safe since virtually everyone on the street except the police were doing the same.

Jacky *smiled*. "Are we going to fight them? With capes that pretty, power and skill has *got* to be their least important qualification. It'll be fun." She shrugged when I glared at her. "What? We're supervillains now." Which of course was complete nonsense, but she said it so straight I almost started to tell her so before I realized she was joking.

The Eight Excellent Protectors *were* pretty; all girls from mid-teens to mid-twenties, they dressed in nearly identical costumes that featured high boots and barely-there pleated skirts. White-on-gray with bright seam and shoulder trim matched equally brightly dyed hair to individualize each Protector. Standing together they made a colorfully rainbow-haired team, looking alert while pleasantly acknowledging the townspeople staring at them (a few younger kids even dared to dart up for autographs).

And they had *no* right to be there.

"Ladies," Ozma said. "I feel like breakfast." Taking our arms, she guided us into a ramen shop two storefronts down.

The cheerfully called greetings by the shop's entire visible staff startled me, and the waitress's repeated bows and Ozma's seated bow kept me distracted while she ordered for herself and her "American cousins." When our waitress brought us our fragrantly steaming bowls (filled with ramen floating in broth and topped with slices of rolled pork and sides of bamboo, seaweed, and two halves of a soft-boiled egg), Ozma did a weird hand-clasping bow over hers chanting "*I humbly receive.*" before lifting her bowl closer to her face and using her chopsticks to pick up pork-slabs and take little bites out of them.

When in Rome... Eyes on the doorway, I fumbled the little prayer before picking up my bowl and chopsticks to imitate her. Jacky followed suit.

The ramen was tasty, warm, and actually calmed me down (it helped that nobody was *looking* at us). Well, a group of young male diners were surreptitiously staring at Ozma and at Jacky, who looked even taller in Japan.

Focusing on Ozma's Japanese-princess perfection kept reminding me that *I* looked no different than anyone around me, too. Nobody would see me and shout "Astra!" Or even "American!" The moment I started to relax was the moment the policeman stepped into the shop. Of course.

He nodded at the called greetings and engaged the nearest waitress in whispered conversation. The table next to them might not have heard him, but even with the cheerful pop music playing on the shop's entertainment system my super-duper hearing picked up "visitors?"

Mentally counting the number of bystanders in the shop, I looked down at my bowl. My last bite lodged in my throat and the ramen I'd eaten wanted to join it. "We take anything outside," I whispered. This was going to be a short adventure, after all.

Two tasteless bites of pork later, the officer stood by our table and gave us a polite "Good morning." Bean-pole thin and barely taller than me, his short-sleeved uniform shirt and checker-brimmed police cap damp from the rain, he didn't look old enough to be wearing his badge and gun.

Ozma matched his minimal bow. "Good morning, sir. It is a wet day."

"It is. I am sorry if it has inconvenienced you. You are passing through Shibushi?"

"I and my American cousins are going to see our uncle."

"Ah. I am sorry for the difficulty, but may I see your identification?"

"There is no difficulty." Ozma reached into her purse and handed him a green-edged plastic card. I could see her picture and information. "I am from Chiba prefecture." The officer accepted the ID card with both hands and read it carefully. I tried very hard to look curious instead of ready to surrender to the authorities.

"And where does your uncle live?"

"In Shibushi, presently," said the man behind him.

Half an hour later, I was looking at a picture of my dad and the rest of the founding Sentinels.

"Why did you choose Shibushi?" our new "uncle" asked.

The man had shown the policeman a gold-bordered ID with a second card, eliciting a deeply respectful bow and apologies. Our imminent arrest averted, he had sat with us while we finished our ramen and then escorted us to his car (parked in the yellow-zone in front of the train station) and drove us out of town to the last place I'd expected to actually visit: Shibushi's Heroes Without Borders East facility and airstrip.

Standing in his office, I'd let my eyes go right to one of the many framed group-pictures on his wall.

"Erica," Ozma said softly—the name on my forged passport—and I started. Right; we were half-caught so she didn't need to play the local and socially superior cousin. Mister Konishi had skipped right to English anyway.

"I'm sorry. Shibushi is isolated and not near anything sensitive. I thought it offered the best chance for arriving unnoticed." I didn't tell him that I'd also picked it because Dad and the rest of the Sentinels had worked from this facility during their time with Heroes Without Borders in China. "What happened?"

He smiled from where he sat. The manager of the facility, he had offered us all chairs and joined us instead of going behind his desk.

"Two things. First, a deep-sea fisherman reported a high-altitude explosion to Defensenet. It was far enough offshore that nothing was likely to come of it, but with recent events being what they are, Defensenet sent The Eight Excellent Protectors here just in case."

"Recent events?"

"Shibushi was the home of one of Japan's largest oil reserve facilities, until three weeks ago. A kaiju attack set it on fire and would have created the biggest environmental oil disaster in history if our country's hydrokinetics and pyrokinetics hadn't been able to contain it. The port was almost destroyed, and the reserve facility will not be rebuilt, costing many local jobs. Defensenet was criticized for not responding quickly enough to the initial sighting report, thus The Excellent Eight Protectors. The police are another matter; a Defensenet boat in the area found debris consistent with a craft's fuselage. Again, not likely anything threatening, but it raised the possibility of unauthorized visitors. And here you are."

I winced. I'd read about the attack in our weekly threat-briefing, but had no idea it had almost been so bad. There were so *many* kaiju attacks.

"Okay," Jacky said. "Here we are. Why are we here, and not under arrest?"

"It is not my duty to supply the deficiencies of the police." He said it like it was supposed to mean something, and sighed when none of us replied.

"Really, do none of you children read your own great literature anymore? What would you say if I told you that you presented me with a three pipe problem?"

"Sherlock Holmes!" I laughed, feeling much easier. His smile turned saturnine.

"Indeed. However, I did not *deduce* your identities. Indeed, I do not know them. The *second* thing that happened this morning is I received a telephone call from an old associate. I have worked for Heroes Without Borders since its inception, and being the sort who often crosses borders, I am a useful man to know. Some years ago I did favors for an associate whose identity is still unknown to me. He would occasionally call and ask me to deliver things. Not harmful things, merely things that would not otherwise be there; things he did not want anyone to know were going there.

"In return, my associate would occasionally pass along a bit of prescient information. A coming disaster, manmade or natural. A humanitarian crisis that would soon require our attention. These early warnings allowed us to prepare and often saved thousands of lives. Do you know my associate?"

Jacky had stiffened as he explained, and I fought to keep my face straight. Mr. Konishi had to be talking about the *Teatime Anarchist*. He'd been part of his network, the same way Jacky had, even if he'd never met him. But since the Anarchist was dead... "I think that I at least know someone who worked for your associate."

"Indeed. We have not traded favors for some years now, but this morning someone representing him called and informed me of your arrival and your need. He assured me that you are no threat to my country. Is this so?"

"Yes." *That* at least I could say with absolute truth.

"Good." His smile softened. "I have a list of things to acquire for you, and I can take you as far as Miyazaki. However, since I do not know when my associate will again be in a position to repay me, I must respectfully ask that you do something for me as well. I am informed that you are 'up to it?'"

"Do we trust him?" Jacky's voice told me she didn't.

Mr. Konishi had shown us to an empty barracks. The Spartan facility had men's and women's sections, rooms with nothing but rows of beds and lockers, showers and baths, and a common social room full of old furniture. We wouldn't be staying, but he thought we'd like to relax while he made arrangements.

Looking around us, I shrugged. "It looks like Shell did. And we don't have a lot of choice."

The job he had for us was simple, really. There was a reported outbreak of a savage strain of flu virus in the Chinese state of Anhui. Few healthy adults would die of it, but there were a lot of unhealthy adults there as well as vulnerable children and seniors. In about an hour, he was taking receipt of a planeload of vaccines and palliatives for the medical stations in the poorer districts; all he had to do was refuel the plane and send it on its way.

But superhumans working for local warlords were hijacking planes in flight, and as the empty rooms showed, he currently had no HWB superhumans in the facility to ride with the plane. He'd get some, in a day or four, but the medicine needed to get to Anhui now; each lost day meant dozens or hundreds more falling ill and increased the risk of the outbreak turning into an epidemic. Mister Konishi was willing to help us evade capture, if we safeguarded the mission.

"Hope is correct—we do not appear to have a choice." Ozma had found a selection of teas in the open kitchen-area, and was preparing a service. That seemed to be one of her main social modes; when you need to talk about anything serious or contentious, you make tea. "And certainly the cause is worthy. Afterwards, you can always bite him and help him forget we were ever here. Or at least suggest that we are better released back into the wild."

I blinked at the surprisingly cynical and workable idea. On the other hand, the facility had its own security and while we'd seen very few employees we had seen some. We were certainly now on enough security footage and in enough memories that it wouldn't help if he decided to turn us in afterwards. And working with superhumans as he did, he probably had ways of dealing with 'suggestions.'

Jacky stretched in the old lounge chair she'd plopped herself down in. "So what is the deal with the Eight Great Pop-Idols? Aren't they a Tokyo group?"

"The Eight Excellent Protectors. And no, they're just based in Tokyo most of the time. They go where Defensenet sends them. All the Japanese teams do."

In the wake of The Event, most countries had either adopted some variant of the American Model—where cities and states hired superhumans as contractors—or outright drafted tactically useful superhumans into military and government service. The second option hadn't worked out too well for most places that tried it, but Japan had created its own third option: mandatory registration and training, but voluntary government service.

It was against the law in Japan to hide a breakthrough from the government, and all children and teens who experienced powerful breakthroughs went to one of the government academies. They were rigorously educated and trained, and continuously tested and ranked; they were also heavily indoctrinated in the duty they owed to their nation. Adults were sent to training facilities for the same treatment over a more intense three to six-month course.

And the only way to be a cape legally in Japan was to join the Japan Superhuman Self-Defense Force. Wear the cape illegally, and you were a *ronin*, a vigilante. All Japanese teams belonged to the JSSDF, were directed by Defensenet, and were costumed and marketed like anime heroes. The Eight Excellent Protectors were Japan's premier all-female team, and the Nine Accomplished Heroes were their male counterparts.

All of them were mega-pop idols, but despite what Jacky had said when she saw them, whatever their individual power levels they all trained within an inch of their lives and had won their positions in brutal competition.

Jacky had gotten pretty good at reading my face. "So, we really don't want to mess with these girls?"

"There will be no messing." I sighed and rubbed my face. "If we have to *fight* a Defensenet team, we fight to break away and disappear. If we can't break away, we surrender. They're the good guys." Which ronin were *not*—whether supervillains or vigilante mystery men of the American variety, most ronin were regarded as antisocial and unpatriotic criminals by most right-thinking Japanese.

"What if—" Jacky stopped when I held up my hand; with my super-duper hearing I could hear an incoming twin-prop plane.

"Our ride is here."

"Time to change, I think." Ozma set the tea service on the table, and I saw she had laid it with seven cups; three for us, three for the incoming flight crew, and one for Mister Konishi. Three ring-twists later, we were again the Magical Girls in Black: tall heavily-armed Jacky, beautiful elegant Ozma, and the little girl with the big sword. Dammit.

"Shit," Jacky said. "We need names."

Chapter Ten

In the West, breakthrough types tend to follow the "superhero" template, with an admixture of science-fiction, supernatural, and religious influences. All of these types also appear in the East, but with the influences reversed; more Eastern breakthroughs are influenced by mythology, religion, and even martial-arts movies than are influenced by superhero and science-fiction stories.

Barlow's Guide to Superhumans

If Mr. Konishi was surprised to see us in costumes and gear we'd had nowhere to hide, he didn't show it. The three men in wrinkled flight suits who entered the common room behind him looked less impressed by our youth and darkly shiny newness.

None of the flight crew were breakthroughs but I knew from Dad that it was traditional for all members of Heroes Without Borders, superhuman and normal, to adopt codenames—it was part of the organization's spirit. Mr. Konishi introduced them as Eight Ball (the pilot, a bald Australian black guy), Cue Ball (copilot, an equally bald French white guy), and Chowder (mustached engineer, Italian?).

There he stopped, lacking our codenames, so Ozma introduced *us* as Hikari, Mamori, and Kimiko; everyday girls' names, even if when I looked them up later the meanings (light, guard, and child-empress) sort of fit. She finished by bowing and saying "We are the Three Remarkable Ronin. It is an honor to meet you." *Not* something we'd agreed upon, and I swallowed a semi-hysterical laugh while Jacky snorted.

While Ozma observed the social niceties, I tried to get a grip. I hadn't been *thinking*, and Jacky's realization that we hadn't even picked *codenames* had shocked me out of a state I hadn't even known I was in.

It was like I'd gone to sleep. Or had been walking around dazed. Sometime after getting the diagnosis that, some night soon, I was going to disappear from the world I knew, I had stopped seriously thinking about What Happens Next. My part of the mission-planning had barely been the flight in, and the only reason we hadn't been tripped up or stuck worse than we were was Ozma and Jacky were picking up my slack without saying a word about it.

What was going on in my *head*?

The necessity of introductions distracted me; following Ozma's lead, we sat down for tea and talked about ourselves—actually Ozma talked and Jacky and I nodded. My sole contribution was when Eight Ball asked what I was; I replied *"Attilus-Typeh,"* carefully adding the extra syllables that Japanese threw into English words. I wasn't much to look at—but the hundred-pound sword slung over my back was proof enough for Eight Ball to accept that at face value.

The crew needed to freshen up and stretch a little before we flew out, so we finished tea and left them to the common room. Mr. Konishi led us out to the hanger, where the facility's ground crew were in the process of checking over and refueling the plane.

Seeing it, I almost felt homesick. It was a modified C-23 Sherpa, the kind of twin-prop cargo plane we'd used to get about in the Mississippi operations just three months ago; with a boxy fuselage and rear-drop cargo ramp, it could seat thirty passengers or take three large cargo pallets, less if outfitted with extra fuel tanks like this one obviously was. This plane wasn't built for heavy delivery—it took low weight but high value cargo to places it needed to go. The name stenciled on its fuselage, the *Draw Shot*, was framed in crossed pool sticks.

The cargo ramp lay open and down, and I stepped up inside. Two fully laden pallets filled the rear of the bay, marked with bold red crosses and strapped down with a drop-gate to keep them from sliding right out if they somehow came loose. That meant I could exit in flight by half-dropping the ramp without worrying about them, a very good thing. The fuselage sported two gunports, empty but built for machinegun mounts—an old but returned military design in a world where flying people could intercept planes.

"This plane and crew normally flies only the Pacific circuit," Mr. Konishi explained when I asked. "It does not have a fighting crew and we do not have time to mount weapons and find gunners."

I nodded. "You said that the Chinese flyers have been avoiding planes that are visibly escorted?"

"Yes. They are bandits, not soldiers."

"And the waiting base?"

"A Heroes Without Borders station attached to a military base, well able to defend itself. They will oversee the delivery of the vaccines to the regional clinics."

I nodded again, decided to ask something that had been bothering me.

"Mister Konichi? Why are none of the flight-crew Japanese? And the pictures on your wall—" I wasn't sure how to finish that sentence without implying *something*.

But he understood and smiled. "Why did you see no Japanese faces on the wall of heroes there? Are there no Japanese heroes in Heroes Without Borders? No. In matter of fact, Japan has many heroes in our band of brothers and sisters—it is a favored calling for ronin who wish to wear the cape but do not wish to serve at the pleasure of the government. You will find my countrymen in Africa, the Middle East, all around the world where we are needed."

His smile left.

"But you will not find many of us serving in East Asia and especially not in the Chinese States. There, and elsewhere where memories are long, they are targets for nationalist action."

"Oh. But we—" I looked down at myself.

"Since you will not be staying, you should not become a target. And—" His smile crept back. "I am certain you will ably represent my country." He performed a deep bow and left us with a deeper apology and declaration of paperwork.

The flight crew was barely half an hour cleaning themselves up and eating, but they came aboard looking bright-eyed and bushy tailed as Mom would say. Before the plane closed up, Mr. Konishi came back with one more passenger—a Chinese man wearing an impeccably tailored business suit and carrying a single overnight bag, who introduced himself as Ren Li-kai.

Chowder looked dubious. "We're taking passengers now? What's going on?"

"Question of the day, that is," Eight Ball agreed, arms folded. "This isn't a milk-run."

Li-Kai put down his bag. "Please forgive me," he said in equally impeccable English. "I understand the risk, I promise you. I come from Kyoto, where I have been advising the Anhui delegation at the conference in my spiritual capacity as a daoshi and priest." He rubbed his head, as bald and shiny as Cue Ball and Eight Ball's. "We have heard of the outbreak and I must return to give my services in my original profession, as a physician."

Eight Ball continued to stare him down, and when the doctor didn't look away he shrugged. Taking medical personnel where they were needed and protecting them while they were there was half of what Heroes Without Borders did.

"Okay then, buckle up. We're nonstop to south Anhui." He turned and squeezed through the hatch into the cockpit where Cue Ball was already running preflight checks. Chowder stayed to make sure we buckled in. Mr. Konishi gave the three of us a final bow and a "Please look after them for me," before trotting back down the ramp.

"What's a daoshi?" Jacky asked our new friend while we watched the ramp close up.

Ren Li-kai smiled. "A daoshi is a Daoist master. My family are the hereditary priests of a temple to *Guanyin Dashi*. As the younger and more rebellious son, I went off and became a doctor before I fell into the study of Daoism and returned to my family's way by something of a back door."

"Daoism?"

"The Way. It would take me ten years to explain, so to sum up using your western masters, Nietzsche said 'To do is to be,' Kant said 'To be is to do,' and Sinatra said 'Do-be-do-be-do.' Sinatra was a Daoist master. What is your Way?"

For some reason he looked directly at me and I blinked, startled into the truth. "I'm Catholic."

"Good. The name to which you pray is irrelevant. If the heart is sincere, God will reveal His power." He said that last like a quote.

Jacky and Ozma buckled up, choosing seats in the single rear-facing row. Ren Li-Kai fumbled with his harness, Chowder making sure he got it done right. After making sure I knew the control panel for the ramp (the flight-crew could open it from the cockpit, but better safe than sorry), I unsheathed my sword and took my own seat, propping the big blade beside me.

"So," Jacky started again once Chowder checked us all and left. "How do Daoists explain the world?"

Daoshi Ren's smile crinkled his eyes. "I assume you mean the modern world? The Post-Event world?" Stopping, he gripped the armrests when the *Draw Shot's* engines banged and spun up. He looked green already, and Ozma began fishing in her box. "Many

Chinese believe that breakthroughs are good or evil *shen*, spirits—what the Japanese call kami. Others believe that breakthroughs are merely possessed by shen. Of course there is more religious and philosophical diversity in China than you find in America or Europe, but a true Daoist rarely asks the question and isn't that interested in the answer."

Ozma opened a colorful tin and offered him a lozenge without speaking.

"Thank you. I traveled here by train and boat, but…" He took it and closed his eyes, his lips moving in silent prayers of his own while he regulated his breathing. I could relate; planes had made me nervous once, too.

Leaning back, I took my own moment.

Shell's absence was an ache, like phantom-limb syndrome; I kept thinking of things I should know and starting to ask before remembering she wasn't there. Like, what kind of sky-pirates were we facing? Mr. Konishi hadn't been able to tell us, and his assurance that the bandits were staying away from escorted flights wasn't *that* reassuring. Ozma had told me she had something for Jacky that would allow her to join me outside, and that she'd added a couple of 'extras' to The Sword back when it had been meant for Grendel. All that helped a bit, but I missed the intel-dumps Shell provided.

Heck, I just missed Shell. Although that was something that might be fixed soon. *Please, let that be fixed soon.* If it wasn't, I had more worries than a cherry tree and sky-pirates.

A large warm hand settled over mine. Daoshi Ren had opened his eyes to watch me, and he gently patted my hand.

"We shall arrive safe and whole. Certainly Guanyin wishes us to attend to her children."

Guanyin. I blinked, breath caught. Used to hearing the westernized version of the name, *Quan Yin*, I'd missed it the first time. "Maria-sama," I said without thinking and this time my Japanese mastery attached the respectful honorific as I crossed myself. He smiled.

The plane's bumping picked up and then vanished as the engines threw the plane forward, pushing us back in our seats, and I reversed our holds to lay my hand on his as he gripped the armrest hard.

We were off on a quest for the second time in two days. Hopefully, this one would go more smoothly.

Flying directly to Anhui meant cutting across the southern edge of Kyushu and then heading out directly over the East China Sea. I waited until Cue Ball announced that we had left Japan's national airspace, then unbuckled and half-lowered the ramp to bail out to fly above the plane.

We had climbed above a low storm front circling south over the sea, and I could only see the occasional fishing boat beneath breaks in the water-heavy clouds. We were headed into the heavy Plum Rains of China's early summer. Behind me, Kyushu faded to a line on the horizon and then disappeared.

"Miss me?" Shell floated beside me wearing an Indiana Jones outfit, complete with fedora and bullwhip.

I could breathe again. "We're not tomb raiding, Shell. Where did you go?"

"Defensenet locked me out," she groaned disgustedly. "I'm beginning to wonder how common quantum-interdiction is going to get."

"Thanks for contacting Mister Konishi."

"I know, right? It was all I could do not to laugh hysterically when I called him up and he told me about the job." She mimicked him. "'Will their leaving Japan for a day or two be a problem?'"

"So, how will we stay in touch when we go back?"

"The old-fashioned way, duh; we're buying new cellphones."

"Yeah, that will work." I should have thought of that. "Tell me about the sky-pirates?"

"Not much to tell. Chinese and League forces don't know much about them. They're active over several of the new states and pick easy targets, and only a few distant sightings reported back give any descriptions. We don't know much more than that the largest group spotted was five flyers, mixed types. They don't leave survivors or take prisoners, even for ransom, but they shouldn't be anything we can't handle—especially with Ozma's power-ups. Speaking of, have you introduced yourself to your sword yet?"

"Intro— Shell, what did Ozma do to it?"

She grinned like an urchin. "Go on. Say hello."

Rolling my eyes, I drew The Sword. It was still the big chunk of European-style claymore I'd seen before. Double edged blade, ridiculously flared towards the crosspiece, hilt long enough for me to easily wrap both hands around. It wasn't glowing or doing any other obviously magical things. Feeling stupid, I cleared my throat.

"Hello?"

"It's about time, girl. Are you done talking to the voices in your head?"

I dropped the sword.

Chapter Eleven

What is a person? Shell is a person, and she's an Artificial Intelligence living in a computer from the future. Detective Fisher is a person, and he's a fictional character. Nix is a person, and she's a magically animated action-figure (so is Nox, although he's not a sane person). So what's the definition of personhood? As far as I'm concerned, it's self-initiative and personality—a person is someone who acts like a person. Everything else is semantics and theology.

From the journal of Hope Corrigan.

I caught the sword before it fell more than a hundred feet.

"You're not filling me with confidence," it informed me. "*Both hands.*"

"How are you *talking*?"

It was the Dust of Life, of course; Ozma had used the Dust of Life on Grendel's sword, the same stuff used to bring homicidal Nox and happy Nix to life. But they were poseable figures who at least had faces and mouths...

Porcelain faces, painted-on mouths. Raising the sword to look closer, I spotted the acid etched figure on the blade. An angel. Sort of. His wings were made of blades, and he wore a poncho and a flat-brimmed cowboy hat. And smoked a cigarette. It was Clint Eastwood as Gabriel.

Well, that explains the rough voice...

"Yeah yeah, I look pretty."

"Um, okay." Why would Ozma animate a *sword*? It didn't make it sharper, did it? "Can you fight by yourself? Can you come back to me?"

"Hardly, girl. But throw me at something, and I guarantee I'll hit it with my sharp end. And once I'm into something I won't let go unless you make me."

"Don't call me girl." And now I was arguing with a sword.

"The word fits. You call me sword."

"Oh!" Shell laughed. "I vote for Mister Slicy. Or Sir Cutsalot."

I sighed. "What's your name?"

"Name? Mmmm. Cutter. That's as good a job description as you could ask for, and I am what I do."

"What you do— You heard Daoshi Ren inside?"

"I'm not deaf, girl. I just don't open my mouth when I have nothing to say."

"If you're done talking with Mister Slicy," Shell interjected before I could tell my sword not to call me *girl* again. "Jacky says she's coming out to join you."

"How are you talking to her? And how can she come out?" Jacky was a "daywalker" now, but she still couldn't use all her powers in the daylight.

"I'm using the plane's satellite uplink, duh. And Ozma's given her a bottle of wind and some 'sunscreen.'"

I opened my mouth to ask what that meant but Jacky arrived in a miniature whirlwind, dropping out of mist so fast it almost looked like she'd teleported. We were several thousand feet over the East China Sea and pushing three hundred miles an hour, and yet she landed lightly on top of the *Draw Shot's* fuselage and stood up. Dropping down to meet her showed me how she could do it; a bubble of gently circling air surrounded her, stirring her hair and making her jacket skirt flap against her legs, but forcing the airstream to break around her.

"Nice view!" she yelled over the wind. "I wanted to move around a bit before we get close to land again! Eight Ball says we're going to pretty much fly up the Yangtze River into south Anhui, and from the coast on in it's all 'interesting territory!' Ready?"

I nodded, openmouthed, and she cross-drew her two shoulder holstered pistols, sighted across them.

"I needed to tell you—these are new Vulcans!" She tapped the one strapped low on her right thigh to show that she meant all four of the long-barreled guns. "Yeah, he named them after himself!"

"And what are Vulcans?" Shell relayed my words to Jacky's earbug.

"Variable-projectile electromagnetic guns, basically mini railguns. The ammo is uncooked Vulcan-stuff that's shaped in the barrel for variable density, frangibility, that kind of thing. I can dial it down to knock an unpowered target on his ass or up to seriously bother anything short of an A Class armored type. So I'll be able to back you against some of the heavies and trust me, I can get close. You all right?"

I'd been nodding stupidly; now I shook my head.

"No! I haven't been involved with *any* of this! I let you guys build this whole plan without— I didn't ask you *anything*, just drove the bus and even messed that up—"

"You got us here alive. For the rest, Shell told us where your head was so we took care of it. You back, now?"

"Yes."

"Good, because it looks like our dates have arrived."

They hadn't even waited until the coast was more than a smudge on the horizon. Four dark shapes, three obviously human and one much bigger and snakier, flying between us and land. They had used the sea of rainclouds to get closer than they would have otherwise.

"Recognize anyone, Shell?" Jacky asked.

"Just the flying lizard. That's Heavenly Dragon, and he's a One-Lander. No idea about the guy on his back or the other three flying escort."

"Heavenly Dragon." I nodded. "Got it. What's his rep?"

"If you take him you'll become a national hero in five Secession States."

"This will be interesting," Cutter said. "How's your grip now, girl?"

"Hope, I'm not sure you can take these guys..."

I heard her, and I should have been scared. I *was* scared, somewhere, but my fear was a small voice behind my anger. This plane contained *life*. Life for thousands of loved children and beloved old grandparents. Since the day of my breakthrough I'd seen far too many small bodies, and the fliers closing the distance on us meant more death.

"Shell? Please ask Eight Ball to maintain course and altitude? And ask Daoshi Ren to pray *really hard*?"

"They're already on it."

"Jacky?"

She checked the settings on her Vulcans. "Havoc rules, right?"

"Oh yeah." *Cry 'Havoc!', and let slip the dogs of war.* No rules, no mercy. Fight to kill until you held the battlefield.

"Shell, talk to them if they have radio. Tell them we're escorting medical supplies and any closer approach will be considered an attack."

"Got it. And yep, they can talk...aaaand nope. The nicest thing the guy riding Heavenly Dragon said was something about you and a turtle."

"Okay then."

So the leader was likely the armored figure on the snaky Chinese dragon's back. If I took the dragon, that would suck in at least one teammate to rescue him from a long fall if he couldn't fly himself. Of the other three, one of them flew the way Jacky stood on the plane's back: upright and ignoring the airstream to stand on an improbably thick and speedy cloudlet. He had to be an aerokinetic, an airmaster of some kind. As for the staff-carrying Kung Fu woman and the winged stone monkey flying beside him…I had no idea but I was pretty sure the stone monkey wasn't from Oz.

"Safe bet they're all conventionally bulletproof," Jacky said as the whining hum of her guns climbed in pitch. "Since they couldn't count on the plane being unarmed."

"They'll have some defense, anyway. How fast can your little wind carry you?"

"As mist? Faster than the plane."

"Then hop on and we'll confuse them." It was one of the sillier-looking moves we had, but we'd change up after the opening bit.

A Vulcan in each fist, Jacky jumped up as I dropped under her, wrapping her legs around my waist and leaning close to hang on hands-free as I took us ahead and *up*. Only her supernatural strength, equal to any Olympian weightlifter's, kept her attached to me as we climbed hard to command the sky above them.

Heavenly Dragon angled up to meet us, swimming through the sky like an eel through water, as beautiful and terrible as a Siberian Tiger, while the others continued onward. I let him climb, pulling for distance from the plane until I hung vertically above dragon and rider and the other three were far behind us and closing on the plane. Shell designated the pair Alpha and the trio Beta, marking them with virtual icons for me and whispering to Jacky through her earbug.

I waited until I could hear the slithering rattle of the dragon's scales over the wind, then rolled at the top of my climb. "Beta one-two-three *go*!" I called out as I turned over to fall into a graceful dive. Jacky let go, fell, and disappeared in a blast of wind. Left alone I fell toward Heavenly Dragon, arms out and hearing the sonic *cracks* of Jacky's first shots far behind me as I closed the distance.

"He breaths *ice*!" Shell yelled as I fell. Of *course* he did; dragon breath was a near-universal weapon whether European or Asian—and while the white-and-silver pattern of his horns, whiskers, and scales was a clue it wouldn't be fire, cold could *burn*. I let myself fall until Heavenly Dragon's climb stuttered as he gathered himself and his mouth opened—then I flew *hard*, breaking down and left. The sky above me split and screamed as the air in my lungs froze, but my burst of speed generated a miss and the fanning razor stream of hyper-frozen water blew harmlessly past.

"Now girl!" Cutter shouted as I swung, two-handed. Heavenly Dragon screamed and silver blood sprayed out as I struck beneath his almost vestigial front legs. The giant snakelike body twisted in air but I hung onto Cutter, stuck into Heavenly Dragon's underside, and pulled myself close beneath his body to grab a spasming leg before wrenching the sword free to hack again.

"The rider can't reach you!" Shell yelled, probably watching from the plane's exterior cams. The leg almost threw me and I clung to Cutter again, used my free hand to punch into the first deep wound to grab onto a glistening rib. Quicksilver blood froze my hand as I freed Cutter to desperately hack deeper.

The screaming head flailed around in an attempt to get at me, but I pulled away and leaped up higher on the long neck, screaming myself as the razor ice washed my feet. *This* time Cutter twitched in my hand as I swung, slicing through the rider's saddle harness before biting into more scale. Silver blood washed my face, choking and blinding me and I spat, unable to feel my tongue. *Hacking is too slow*. "Shell! Show me his spine! His spine!" A virtual red targeting icon bloomed in the black as I pulled Cutter free and *thrust*.

If the barrel of Heavenly Dragon's snakelike body had been thicker, cutting up through the underside I would have failed. If Cutter hadn't been forged by Vulcan to slice through main-tank battle armor, if he hadn't turned himself with living will to lunge between bones, we would have missed. We didn't miss, and Cutter severed Heavenly Dragon's spine, ending his flight. We fell. Curling in to push against the stricken dragon's side, I pulled us free of his deadweight bulk to throw myself outward and follow a Shell-painted icon away.

"They're falling!" She supplied redundantly as I blinked desperately, digging past my shades to wipe at my eyes. If dragon-blood was acidic I was too cold to feel it. "Rude Dude can't fly either!"

Which way which way— "Jacky?"

"Vulcans make *big* holes," Shell reported. "Beta One and Three are out and are going to splash and Kung-Fu Girl is retreating—wow that girl can dance!"

That made it easy. "Tell the rider if he surrenders I'll catch him!"

A heartbeat, two, and the guiding icon spun right and down. "He surrenders! He's shedding his armor!" I saw him, barely and through stinging eyes as I dove. Closing the distance to fly past his flailing hands, I gripped him from behind and below to pull us out of our dive for the sea. Below us Heavenly Dragon continued to fall away, great head twisting as if trying to escape his lifeless body. I watched until he splashed and sank beneath blooming ice, then turned to catch up with Jacky and the *Draw Shot*.

Chapter Twelve

The first of the Three Deeds of Hikari, the small leader of the Three Remarkable Ronin, was slaying Heavenly Dragon while bringing life-saving medicine to the children of Anhui. The day of the First Deed is commemorated in Anhui with a children's festival celebrated with wreaths of flowers cast upon the nearest river. It is considered especially good luck if the day is marked with rain.

A History of the Brief Career of Hikari and the Three Remarkable Ronin.

Ozma put my prisoner to sleep with a single puff of Oz-poppy pollen, and Zhejiang Air Control gave us a fighter-escort in from the coast so I didn't have to return to flying watch outside. Jacky reloaded her Vulcans and then closed her eyes and stopped moving while I sat and stared at the pallets of vaccines, waiting to be warm again.

Heavenly Dragon's blood evaporated like water on a hot sidewalk.

"Hope? You okay?" Shell had ditched the Indiana Jones outfit for her default shorts and t-shirt. She'd also covered the tee with a Rorschach pattern.

I closed my eyes. "Everyone keeps asking me that." If I talked at a whisper, the drone of the twin props and vibration of the hull gave me at least a little privacy. "I'm alright. It's just been an interesting couple of days."

"You sure? 'Cause, you did just cut your way through someone. Which was *sick*, but if you weren't incognito The Harlequin would be having to schedule medal ceremonies. Are you in your happy place? Are you thinking about bunnies?"

"Children. I'm thinking about children."

"Ooookay..." She didn't sound at all sure about that, and I really should have been thinking about the fight.

The fight.

The plane had been visibly escorted but they hadn't stayed away—which was not what Mr. Konishi had suggested would happen. Had they specifically targeted the flight? For the medicine or the passenger? Who knew about Daoshi Ren's addition to the flight? Would he be a valuable prisoner? Could they have targeted us? That made no sense unless Mr. Konishi was playing a *very* twisty game.

And the sky-pirates hadn't acted like a *team*. Shell had only been able to identify Heavenly Dragon, but even if the saddle implied he and the leader had been working together, the other three hadn't been coordinating at all.

I asked Shell to replay the fight in my head, watched Jacky's side of it. Our improvised feint had only worked because they'd *sucked*. Since I'd flown out to meet them with Jacky on board, they'd assumed she couldn't fly herself and her three had ignored us to go for the *Draw Shot*. Yes, she'd popped in on top of them riding Ozma's pet wind and engaged two with close-in shots— starting with their aerokinetic—before they'd known she was there. But if they'd just spread out, or been supporting each other, then their mistake wouldn't have been so immediately fatal; they'd attacked with no method, no science.

So, two from One Land, leading three local bandits with no real team training? It would be a way for the terrorist organization to leverage its remaining numbers after its losses at Whittier Base.

Was Heavenly Dragon dead as Jacky's two? Remembering my Comparative Mythology course, Chinese dragons were elemental creatures. His elements had probably been air and water, an ice-storm personified. So could he drown? If he hadn't, would he heal?

Zhejiang Air Control handed us off over Anhui and I returned to my outside escort station, but we touched down on HWB Anhui South's airstrip without any more attacks. HWBAS shared their strip with a joint League-Anhui military training base, and armored trucks waited with their drivers for us to unload in the warm rain.

The base's military police took away our prisoner, and then taking inventory and dividing up the pallet loads took an hour as the trucks pulled away one by one, headed for the towns and clinics of south Anhui. With each departing truck, my heart lifted a little. Daoshi Ren shook our hands before climbing into the last truck out.

"C'mon, girls." Eight Ball heaved his flight bag over his shoulder. "Let's all get something hot in us."

"Nowhere to go until tomorrow," Chowder seconded. "And the local cuisine is very good."

We fell in behind them to cross the half-drowned runway to the HWB building, and I couldn't help asking, in Japanese-accented English, "Chowder-san?"

"Ma'am?"

"I understand Eight Ball and Cue Ball's names." I tapped my head. "But why are you called 'Chowder?'"

"Because in just about every storm system we fly through, I lose my chowder."

They took our picture, a group shot of all six of us together to go on the HWB building's crowded hero's wall. The base was small and empty now, more a waystation than a base since the major fighting had moved elsewhere. South Anhui hadn't seen much destructive fighting in the past couple of years; according to Eight

Ball its army-stiffened militia system was standing up nicely and its regulars—breakthrough and normal—were forcibly bringing peace to the hill country and rooting the "liberating" bandits out of the mountains. Heroes Without Borders capes hadn't been needed to help protect the civilian population centers for a while, but like the Shibushi base, Anhui South had all the amenities visiting capes might need. The food sent from town in insulated pails was tasty and filling, and the hot showers were even more welcome.

Alone in the shower, I turned up the hot water until I stood in billows of steam. Wrapped in a towel and wringing my hair out, I found a little coffee-and-cream colored cat sitting on my clothes and tongue-bathing itself. I was so tired I didn't recognize it.

I tickled it under the chin. "Hello, furball. Are you the station mascot?"

"As if. You're my human." The cat stretched luxuriously, jumping down to rub against my naked calf.

"*Shell?*"

"In the fur. Ozma thinks we need more than cellphone contact when we go back. Did you know she'd packed the drone in her box? Her witchy majesty is pretty smart for royalty."

I reached down and scratched behind Cat-Shell's ears, making her purr and arch. "And how are you more than a holographic projection?"

"*Oh* that feels good. She did her bibbity-bobbety-boo on the drone after I'd powered it up and linked to it. It's temporary and not like Nox or Nix, but for now I'm an internet-prowling quantum ghost who also *really* wants some fish. More on the ears now."

Sometimes my life is too happily ridiculous for words. I sat on the bench beside my clothes, lifted Shell onto my towel covered lap, and proceeded to give her the kind of allover body scratching Graymalkin got if he was a good kitty. Resting my chin on her head, I let her buzzing purrs vibrate through me until the tight cold knot inside untouched by the shower loosened and fell away.

God made cats for a *reason*.

When I kissed the top of her furry head and set her on the bench she flopped into a boneless purring heap and let me dress without commentary. I picked her up again before opening the bathroom door. Sleep that night found me back on a now-familiar cloudhome, where Mistress Jenia spent the dark hours patiently drilling me on Japanese honorifics, bows, and other modes of politeness.

We didn't return to Shibushi.

Jacky said it first the next morning—flat-out stated it. We weren't returning to the Shibushi base with the *Draw Shot*. And we weren't telling Mr. Konishi in advance.

"But he said he would help us!" I protested.

"Doesn't matter. We don't need his help now except for the plane ride that gets us back into Japan, and he could just as easily have the Eight Excellent Protectors waiting at the runway for us."

"He wouldn't—" I shut up; we didn't *know* that, and like Jacky had said, we didn't need his help now. In an operation requiring secrecy, needless trust was what Blackstone called an unnecessary point of potential failure.

"The thing that worries *me*," Jacky went on, "is that he might be twisty and *smart*. If he is, or whoever he talks to is, then the Eight Excellent Protectors will be waiting for us when we cross into Japanese airspace."

We still needed to get back into Japan, and if I flew us myself we'd never hit the coast without being shot down or intercepted, so we explained our problem to Cue Ball, Eight Ball, and Chowder. Chowder provided a mechanical problem he needed to fix, promising to finish the job too late for us to get back before nightfall. Which gave us time for other things; we needed to rebuild our "tourist bags." Fortunately the military base attached to the station was a miniature town with the shops we needed; we found three sets of rolling luggage and bought more clothes, toiletries, and even cheap cellphones.

Staying beyond breakfast meant we got debriefed by Anhui Military Intelligence after all, but they followed the Heroes without Borders rule of Don't Ask Don't Tell regarding our identities—HWB had "contracted" us and so presumably vetted us, and that was good enough for them. The fact that we were apparently Japanese (with our chosen codenames it was hard to claim otherwise) kind of shook the two captains doing the interview—Mr. Konishi hadn't been lying when he told us that Japanese capes just didn't do East Asia—but they were more than grateful, and now the *Three Remarkable Ronin* (I still winced at the name) had officially come to China.

The mechanical problem "fixed," we flew out with the *Draw Shot* in the late afternoon—timing the flight so that we entered Japanese airspace after nightfall. I flew escort along with a pair of Zhejiang fighters just in case someone was looking for retribution, but nobody popped up to trouble us. Cutter didn't talk to me, hadn't in fact said a word after making sure I cleaned him up. The sword gave new meaning to "laconic"—he could out-silence *Jacky*—and I came inside before reaching Japanese airspace on our pre-approved flight path.

We overflew Kyushu in the dark. Here was where anyone who was going to meet us would say hello, but as I sat in the cockpit with Eight Ball and Cue Ball watching the sky and Chowder manned the radio and radar, nobody rose to meet us or told us to land.

I sighed. "Thank you Eight Ball-san, Cue Ball-san, Chowder-san. Will you thank Konishi-san for us?"

"Sure kid," Eight Ball laughed. "And be safe—we'll see you around the world sometime."

I stepped back into the cargo bay where everyone else waited. Since I was the load-master for this, I'd thought a bit and finally tied our new luggage pieces together, wrapped them in black plastic trash bags, and hung them on two lengths of rope. Jacky could do a free-drop carrying Shell, going to mist to break their speed at the end, which left me Ozma. Her majesty was fine with perching on the luggage bundle with a safety-clip to the rope. Jacky had suggested she play green jar again, but she demurred to save her magic reserves.

Hitting the button, I ignored the flashing red light as the ramp half-lowered and wind filled the bay. I stepped off to fall with Ozma and luggage held snug, turning to watch Jacky perform a very nice swan dive into the night above me before orienting to the ground and watching our horizon. When no one came for us in the air where we were most vulnerable, I released a breath I hadn't known I was holding.

The lights of Kagoshima spread out in a hatch-pattern east of us, irregular outthrusts of neighborhoods and absorbed towns reaching into the dark wooded hills below. Our L-zone was Higashisakurajima, a little village with a big name, west of the city. I'd picked it for the proximity of forested hillside to the train station, and nobody raised an alarm when we dropped silently into the trees. At nine o'clock we boarded the train, and at nine-thirty we checked into a trackside Kagoshima hotel to sleep. The infiltration of Japan, take two.

With Shell curled up and cat-snoring on top of me, I didn't dream of the tree.

Chapter Thirteen

Defensenet Report, Shibushi Alert Development: Asset-in-place at HWB Shibushi Base reports arrival and departure of Active Non-Government Powers, heard to identify themselves as the Three Remarkable Ronin. See subsequent report of HWB Anhui mission. According to the asset, the ANGPs did not return to HWB Shibushi Base; current whereabouts, inside Japan or mainland China, are unknown.

Defensenet Recommendation: Stand down Shibushi alert, issue restricted countrywide watch notice to all observer assets.

DR106-BV [Classified

The next morning we bought an epad and a carry bag big enough for Shell at a local corner store.

Despite being a flesh-and-blood cat, Shell was totally handy with our earbugs and the satellite uplink, and she synced herself with the epad to download our travel directions. Watching a cat work an epad is an interesting experience.

I couldn't imagine how I could have gotten around without Ozma and her Comprehension Drops. I'd been an anxious child, bothered or scared by a lot of things: doctors (with good reason), frogs, loud noises, trees (bad movie experience), and even existential things like unfamiliar places (I'd *hated* sleeping in hotel rooms, and not being able to read directions had given me the willies). I was a long way from that scared little girl and I'd eventually seen a lot of Europe, but at least the signs there had been written in an alphabet I knew—here I wouldn't have even been able to *sound out* what signs said unless they were also in English (and while a lot of them were, you couldn't count on it).

We used a teller-machine at the hotel to stock up on yen, then found a place to eat breakfast that served recognizably American entries (the ramen had been nice, but I think we all wanted a little of the familiar). Cat-Shell insisted on trying the breakfast sausages. Remembering how much Graymalkin liked them—and the inevitable aftermath—I saved some napkins.

Trains run everywhere in Japan, or almost everywhere; the Shinkansen lines, Japan's system of high-speed trains, would get us from Kagoshima to Osaka by way of Fukuoka. From there a train ride and then a taxi would get us to Tenkawa, the little village in the shadow of Mount Omine where we would find the Miyamoto family grave. I paid for our tickets with yen while Ozma used a casually carried mirror to "do something" about the station's security cameras. As usual her explanation didn't make sense, but it boiled down to "Visual review and facial recognition systems won't recognize us."

So *she* was concerned about Mister Konishi's reliability, too—or assumed that our fight over China had been reported by somebody.

And we'd left a group picture on the wall of the HWB base—even with the black shades, enough for facial-recognition software to scan for matches...*and why don't I think of these things?* I needed to kick my own ass.

We took a pair of facing seats at one end of our train car, and Jacky used her vampire mojo to *push* the other passengers until they were uncomfortable enough that our end emptied and we could let Shell out of her bag.

Nobody said "The cat's out of the bag." I was very grateful.

"First the good news," Shell said. "I've piggy-backed on the epad and I've got great news access. The Eight Excellent Protectors are back in Tokyo and none of the other Defensenet teams are making any big moves."

I bit my lip. "Who did you hack for that?"

"I signed up to a dozen fan sites under a dozen dummies. Over here nobody watches capes—*powers*—like their fans do."

"Worse than home? How—" I shook my head; I really needed to stop getting sidetracked. "So it looks like nobody's looking for us?"

"Not in the cape-crowd, anyway, and if anyone was connecting an explosion offshore of Kyushu with the Three Remarkable Ronin that's what you'd expect."

"That's good. So what's the bad news?"

Shell hunkered down, nervously kneading her claws in the seat. "There's an obstacle I didn't know about. I should have."

Jacky folded her arms and I took a moment to smile; with Ozma and me easily able to pass for sweet-sixteen, she looked like the long-suffering college grad babysitting her teenage cousins and pet. "Talk. I can hurt you when you're like this."

"Tenkawa's haunted. Well, the graveyard is and that's where we're going."

A haunted graveyard. Really. Well, it wasn't like I didn't know about ghosts; Jacky had one living in her residence, twenty-four hour coffee shop, and private investigator practice. Acacia treated it (*him*, he was a dead gang kid) like a pet and knew how to keep him happy. Whether ghosts had always been around and were just "stronger" in the Post-Event World, or they were simply breakthroughs who thought they were ghosts and behaved accordingly, they were real enough. And the ghosts in Japan were scarier.

A *lot* scarier. The Japanese love their ghost stories, and their stories give them real teeth. Sometimes literally.

Shelly spelled it out—a bit over four years ago, the little graveyard in Tenkawa became deadly ground and reports were pretty clear about what was there: a *shinigami*, a death-spirit. Stories about shinigami vary—in some they're demons, in others they're *yurei*, evil spirits of the dead fueled by a serious hatred that twists them and won't let them "move on." In life their hatred might be focused on one person, but in death it becomes a hatred for all that lived.

Shinigami can *kill*. This one could apparently kill with a touch: seven victims had been found in the graveyard in the last four years, hearts stopped, faces frozen with horror, guilt, or grief. The last victim had been a supposedly powerful onmiyoji—an imperial sorcerer, servant of the Chrysanthemum Throne. Since then nobody had entered the graveyard even in daylight. Nobody knew why it was there (there hadn't been any deaths and burials corresponding to its appearance), and so nobody knew how to get rid of it. The only reason anyone still lived in Tenkawa was it couldn't leave the graveyard.

Great. Just, great.

"So now we've got to be ghost-busters?" Jacky asked. "Does it attack everybody who enters, or just the randomly unlucky?"

"It used to be just the unlucky, but the onmiyoji ticked it off. Now everyone who enters sees it—and runs *real* fast." Shell was almost hissing, and I wondered if she realized how instinctively her cat-body was reacting.

"Is it stronger at night?" Jacky dug.

"Nobody knows, best guess is no."

"Good. Ozma could level me up so I can mist in the sunlight again, but I'm really still best at night."

Ozma nodded, shook her head. "My magic really does not deal with spirits—I'm afraid there is not much that I can do directly."

Good to know. "Shell? What was the physical cause of death for its victims?"

"Heart failure from extreme pulmonary stress. Why?"

"Um." I thought hard. "Then I might be immune. At least partially. I can take a *lot* of stress and I do heal fast. Even if it takes a shot at me, I should be fine long enough for me to get what we need and get out. Right?"

I didn't know which one looked more horrified, Ozma or Jacky. Shell was even spitting.

That argument carried us through a lot of stops and a few hundred miles. Eventually Shell went back in the bag and Jacky stopped doing her vamp-thing so others could sit near us, and we ate lunch on the train—little bento boxes full of rice and bite-sized things. I won the debate before we got the taxi.

"Well," Jacky observed, "this doesn't look like the start of every horror movie I've ever seen."

I opened my mouth to say something upbeat, and closed it, defeated.

It was absolutely certain that Tenkawa's shinigami only roamed the graveyard, but it was easy to see that its shadow lay across the whole town. Tenkawa had never been big—less than fifteen hundred souls—but it had depended on tourism: pilgrims coming to hike and view Mount Omine. It had a *ryokan*, a small, pseudo-period hostel converted from the largest house in town, and lots of little shops. At least half of them were closed now, and the equally period main street was almost empty. The village shrine looked neglected, paint flaking from its red gate.

I couldn't see another obvious tourist, but nobody looked at us directly or even seemed curious. We collected our bags, and offered our driver good yen to stay until we were ready to leave; he regretfully but firmly refused and bowed apologies before reversing to get around and back down the road as fast as possible. I got the feeling that, if he'd been an American cabby, he'd have been calling us every kind of idiot.

Looking at each other, we pulled our bags behind us down the street. There was absolutely no sense in trying to blend in or look inconspicuous.

The graveyard lay beyond the shrine, a compact stretch of ground carved out of the woods and full of the Shinto-style gravestones—tiered stone blocks sitting on small plots, with a recessed bowl in the stone in front of each for offerings. The plots looked too small to me, especially for family plots, but that was because Japanese practiced cremation; the ashes of the entire family would be in a box-sized chamber under the stone.

"Yeah, not at all like the movies." Shell agreed from her bag on top of my luggage. "The pet always dies. Let's go eat."

The ryokan was still beautiful and kept up, but we were the only guests. Checking us in, Mister Ushida gently inquired as to why we were here. Ozma explained that we were here to look after a family matter, and though he obviously wasn't certain what to make of that, he didn't push. We paid with yen and under names not on our IDs, and took the largest single room (we'd sleep on futons laid out on the tatami-mat floor). The Ushidas treated us like royalty; soon we were wrapped in yukatas after washing and soaking in the ryokan's hot spring, being served with a multi-course meal (even Shell, who the Ushida girls just loved).

Dinner came with sake—rice wine—and I tried a little out of curiosity. Sake tastes very sweet.

No city lights to cut the darkness when night fell, and that worked just fine for us. The Ushida girls had laid out our three futons and wished us goodnight, and we prepared for bed and then bibbity-bobbety-boo'd into our uniforms before slipping quietly out. The sliding walls of our room made it easy and we went over the wall behind the hot spring like stealthy ninja. Not that we couldn't have left by the front, but I had the distinct impression that if we'd tried the family would have done everything in their power to try and keep us safe inside.

Chapter Fourteen

<Baka wa shinanakya naoranai. *Translation: Only death will cure a fool. Meaning: You can't fix stupid, but you can die trying.*>

(Shell's comment after [redacted])

Jacky drifted, unseen mist over Tenkawa's empty streets, and I flew Ozma and Shell. We touched down on the street running by the graveyard, and I could feel the psychic chill. Either that, or my imagination was working overtime, trying to tell me to Be Smart And *Leave*. Because scenes like this always turned out so well, right?

Bright side; if Casper came for me I could always get elevated really fast. No running around tripping over graves for me. Downside, it was a *graveyard*.

"The civic records have the Miyamoto plot almost in the center," Shell whispered. "But it's along the main walk so we'll be able to see you."

"Great. Ozma? Do you have something for me?"

She handed me a tiny silver box and spade. "I won't need much."

"Okay." I took the box and tool in one hand, kept myself from drawing Cutter, and started walking.

Anyone else would have needed a flashlight, but my super-duper vision got enough light from the low-hanging Moon to read the shadowed names carved into the stones. I really hoped that the shinigami decided to give me a pass, because I knew that whatever Jacky had *said* she'd be doing her best to kill something already dead if it tried for me.

In the pale light the shadows were deep under the still trees, and after a few steps I realized I wasn't hearing any of the usual night-noises. No insects, no small animals making their way under the safety of darkness.

Not spooky at all. Nope. Just a young girl alone in a graveyard. What could possibly go wrong?

I kept walking and checking until I thought I'd gone too far, and nearly missed it. The Miyamoto family marker was big, rising above most of the rest, but it was also old, weathered, and almost unreadable. Even if Mr. Miyamoto had left home to build his post-war business in Tokyo, the family had been part of the village for a long time.

Still no killer-ghost. I knelt in front of the plot. Shell had explained that the chamber for the ashes would be under the front, likely beneath the stone the offerings were laid on. Feeling under the lip of the stone, I realized it wasn't mortared to the marker; I could easily lift it aside, and I did. Beneath was a rectangular chamber filled with ash and bits of bone—the generations of the Miyamoto family.

Picking up the spade, I looked around one more time and—

"Hope!" Shell yowled as the spectral hand reached for me and

"What are you looking at?" John asked.

"The doe and her fawn are back." I let the curtain drop and leaned back into his big chest. I loved how we fit, my head over his heart, but I frowned to feel his muscle-molded uniform. He was dressed for work. "Babe?"

He wrapped me tight, holding me against him. "Blackstone says we've got movement on the newest Villains Inc. and that Fisher has the warrants. I hate to leave you here."

"We'd get in the way, you worrying about us and all." I raised up to tilt my head back and kiss his chin, then giggled when his big hands dropped to slide over my stomach. Littlest-A was barely here but John couldn't resist and I was ticklish; if he kept up the habit I'd be giggling my way to motherhood.

He let me go with a final squeeze. "Back soon, promise."

"You'd better."

I watched from the upper deck of our cabin as he flew away, pouring on the speed until he was just a spot of blue and white on blue above the mountains, flying higher than usual so that I could still see him (one of my whims he happily indulged). He thought I was being all hormonal and fanciful, and maybe I was but half the silly things I asked for were just so I could watch him, laughing at how much I loved the man. We were such a cliché.

"That's right," I said to Littlest A, stroking where John had laid his hand. "Your silly daddy's gone to beat up Bad Guys. Mommy will too once you're safe."

That made me frown a bit. Littlest A would probably never be as safe as she was right now, even with Aunt Jacky and Shelly and the Bees to watch her not to mention the entire team (all the teams if I included Rook, Seven, and the rest of the Hollywood Knights and Heroes Without Borders East). Two years in LA with the Knights and then two years in Asia with HWB East before coming back to the Sentinels and finally getting officially engaged, had given me such a big circle of brothers and sisters in arms and we didn't have enough room for all the baby presents.

Bright side, they were making the world safer for her bit by bit, and we had promissory notes for enough babysitter nights that she was going to grow up knowing all of them.

"C'mon," I whispered to my baby. "Let's go watch Bambi and his mom some more."

I could barely move, my whole body clenching to wrap around my empty core with each spasming silent wail. My mouth stayed open in a frozen scream as my lungs rejected air and my heart tried to stop. *No no no nonononononononono—*

It had been *real*, as real as anything I'd lived in the past two years—my future without the California Quake. My perfect future, my castle in the air, where I'd finished my training gone and off to get experience and make my own name while engaging in a long distance romance so hot that by the time we got back together my journal and our texts would never be published. I remembered the wedding and the wedding-night and the discovery of our pregnancy a year later, I remembered it *all*.

Every breath tasted of the dirt I lay in. *You lost that. You lost that and how are you still alive?*

People were counting on me and it didn't matter. I was Catholic with a Catholic's horror of suicide and it didn't matter. I wanted to die and a tiny piece beneath the screaming part of me finally understood how Jacky had felt when the Teatime Anarchist had given her her mind back and she'd understood everything she'd lost and what her *master* had done to her...

It was that tiny piece that made me breathe, broke the convulsions stopping my heart. Jacky lived. I lived. I had to live *now* because Jacky was shooting at something that couldn't be shot and she was *close*.

I pushed myself up, saw the old man. *Old* man, half shadow, half sickly light, a few strings of hair left to fly around his bald head, dressed in a filthy business suit and laughing at Jacky. Ignoring *me*. Why? It didn't matter—he floated towards Jacky as Shell crouched spitting behind her, back arched and tail bottled out, but what drew my eye was *Ozma*, standing at the boundary of the graveyard with her wand-baton held high, shouting nonsense words as the Magic Belt beneath her sash flashed so bright the black fabric might as well have not been covering it.

The flaring silver light turned night to day and even the old man shielded his eyes, cringing back, only to straighten with another laugh when Ozma finished and the light died.

Until I pulled myself to my feet to grab him, wrapping numb and aching fingers around his now very real and solid neck. He screamed with mindless, animal rage, then screeched in pain as Shell landed on his face after leaping so high I thought for a second that Jacky had thrown her at him.

"No don't—" I protested uselessly, reaching to grab the old man's hands before he could touch Shell. Jacky pre-empted me by ripping him out of my weakened grip and throwing him face-down to the dirt to pin him helplessly. I spun at the sound of running footsteps, Ozma dashing up.

"What did you *do*?"

She almost fell on top of Jacky. "A wish to turn an image to flesh! I had no idea it would work!"

My mind skipped right over the impossibility and to the important bit. "How long?"

"Minutes!"

"That's long enough," Jacky growled. And bit him.

The old man screamed again, then went limp as Jacky whispered in his ear. She kept it up, crouched atop him like a wolf over her prey, hissing airless words I barely caught, repetitions of *rest, forget, rest, it's over, rest, you've won, forget, you can rest*...and pushing so hard with her power that *I* sat back down in the dirt and wondered for a moment where my chilling tears had come from. Even *Ozma* relaxed and Jacky wasn't aiming the whole weight of her will at us.

A wracking shudder ran through the horrible old man, and then Jacky wasn't holding anyone. He was gone. No drama, no fading or...just gone and with him the freezing void that had burned every breath I took. I burst into wracking sobs, and when Shell pushed against me I grabbed her up and pulled her in to curl around her warm body. Five choking gasps shook me before I got control and could hear Shell yelling "Hey hey hey! Squishable cat!"

"We will have company presently," Ozma said quietly behind me, hand on my shoulder. Leaving me, she quickly retrieved the silver box and spade, scooping ashes from the family chamber, and then tried to push the stone back into place. Shaking myself, I set Shell down and finished for her.

And just in time, because she was right. However the villagers felt about the idea of coming here after dark, Jacky's shots and then Ozma's light show had pulled at least some of them out of their homes. One of them was Mister Ushida, and the man beside him had a bald head and concerned look that said "priest" to me. The rest stayed behind them at the edge of the graveyard.

There was no way that Mister Ushida wouldn't recognize us, dark shades or not. If we were lucky, he wouldn't tell everyone our assumed civilian names. I helped Jacky and Ozma to their feet (Shell had vanished), sighed, and bowed.

"We are Hikari, Mamori, and Kimiko. Please forgive our intrusion."

Ten minutes later we sat in the priest's home beside the shrine. Outside, every front light was lit and most of Tenkawa's residents seemed to be out in the street, a respectful mob. The priest, Guiji Sohda, served us green tea as we sat around the low table that centered his main room. He'd had to clear it of his shrine accounts and ledgers first.

Jacky looked corpse-pale, like she'd been without blood for weeks, and I was a little worried she was just going to fall over. Ozma watched her and let me lead.

I made appreciative noises and put down my cup. "Thank you. Guji So—"

"Please. Sohda is fine outside the shrine."

"Sohda-san. Thank you for your hospitality. You have questions you wish to ask?"

"Yes, forgive me." He exchanged looks with Mister Ushida—who had turned out to be Tenkawa's mayor. "The shinigami is gone. What did you do here, tonight?"

"We—" I had no idea where to start that didn't end with grave robbing.

"The shinigami could not harm you?" the priest pressed carefully.

"It could. It did, but I'll survive. We broke its power and— We gave it peace." That was one way to describe what Jacky had done; if shinigami were fueled by past grudges and Jacky had made it *forget* why it was angry in the first place… "I don't believe it will return, although we really can't be certain."

The priest's eyes sharpened, focused entirely on me with a frown of concern. Did I look that bad?

When I didn't elaborate, he smiled. "Thank you. So, you came here to rid us of the shinigami? When the government's onmiyoji failed, we thought there would be no more attempts."

"We—" I could hardly claim we'd come questing for a good deed to do. "We are ronin."

"Ah. I see." he nodded—and that was nice, because *I* didn't. "Please, tell us how we may repay you."

"Letting us leave quietly tomorrow will be more than enough, thank you." I mentally crossed every finger; if they had a responsibility to report us to the government…

"There is another matter, Sohda-san, Ushida-san," Ozma spoke up. "I hesitate to mention it."

"Please. Go on."

"We did not come to Tenkawa to rid it of your shinigami, this was merely a happy outcome of our mission." She held up the little water-filled crystal ball I'd seen her take from her box before on the beach, the one occupied by a clownfish. A very confused, frantically darting clownfish now.

"We must find a person, Miyamoto Yoshi, and came to borrow a pinch of his family ashes with which to locate him. But as you can see, we have failed."

What? It took me a moment, staring at the sealed crystal sphere, to realize that somehow Ozma had put a small measure of dust inside with the fish. A fish. *She uses a tracking fish.* I squeezed my eyes shut, opened them. I was really, *really* tired.

"My little fish should now be pointing us in the direction of Miyamoto-san," she explained simply. "He is not, which means we have made a mistake somehow."

I wasn't the only one staring at the frantic little fish, and after a moment Ozma sighed and passed her hand over the orb. When she took her hand away the dust had vanished and the fish was happy again. She put it away.

"I am certain we selected the correct stone. Is there anything you can tell us?"

Guji Sohda sat back, hands folded and obviously rethinking just how *good* we might be. "May I ask why you seek this person?"

And he won't say his name. I held my breath.

Ozma shrugged lightly. "To lift a curse."

Mr. Ushida coughed and started to choke. Guji Sohda frowned again, then began to chuckle, lips turning up until his unwilling smile crinkled his eyes.

"Then you should have spoken to him before you exorcised him."

Episode Three

Chapter Fifteen

Are "counterfactuals" or "alternate histories" real? Yes, for a specific value of "real." The same can be said for alternate futures— futures provably visited by the Teatime Anarchist(s). All of these realities have been proven to exist as extrarealities, viewable or visitable by breakthroughs with appropriate powers. The ultimate question, how real are they outside of the scope created for them by those same breakthrough powers, is unanswerable and ultimately beside the point. They are real enough for interaction, and therefore real enough for real concern.

Department of Superhuman Affairs, Position Paper HS-1721c: Extrarealities and National Security.

"So, what do we do now? Jacky? Do you need a drink?" I was too tired to think. Guji Sohda and Mister Ushida had dispersed everyone with a promise of a village meeting tomorrow, and Jacky, Ozma, and I had been able to slip away and return to our room at the ryokan.

"Yes," she said flatly. "And you're it."

"What? *No.*" Changing and finally getting a look at myself, I knew I looked as bad as Jacky but I bounced back fast.

"Yes. What did it do to you?"

I looked at Ozma for support, but she stayed out of it. "It showed me what I could have had. Without the earthquake. Or Seif-al-Din." Before the Teatime Anarchist's evil twin had cut off that bright potential future.

"Shinigami are believed to show their victims their crimes." Shell had snuck back and over the wall by herself and now she sat on the center futon, nervously kneading her claws in the blanket. "Or horrible memories. It makes them want to kill themselves. That's not what happened to *you*, is it?"

"I *wanted* to die." Remembering the soul-freezing, crushing despair, I wanted to vomit. How could I have lived? "Its other victims died of heart-failure, well, my body almost did what I wanted it to."

Closing my eyes, I tried not to fall into that pit again. I *wouldn't*. The shinigami had somehow amplified my moment of heartsick despair until it was the only thing in my universe, but it wasn't anymore and I'd be me again soon. I would.

Jacky snorted. "And that's why you're donating tonight. We're at a dead end, and we don't have time for you to cope." Her voice made it a fact. She wasn't pushing with her vampy power, just telling me how it was going to be.

Fine. I nodded, giving up. I was so tired. "Okay. Where?"

We had just the one room and the bathroom; Jacky pointed to the center futon and I nodded again. Pulling my hair out of the way I plopped down on it, ignoring Shell and Ozma. I'd changed back, so I was in my nightshirt and ready to go.

I felt the air move as Jacky knelt down behind me. "Now what?" I tried to remember last time. It was a little fuzzy.

"Listen to your heart. Breathe."

I could do that and I did, silently counting, too tired to shiver at the feel of her breath on my neck. *One, two, three, four...*

Relax. It was more an echo than a word. *Let go*. I let my chin drop, my head fall forward. Whimsy made me smile; I couldn't get more relaxed, when was she—

I woke up between them. Jacky had taken the futon on my right, Ozma the one on my left. Shell sat on my chest, the paw she'd used to push on my face still raised. When I started to tell her she was getting way too into the whole cat thing she put the paw to my lips, little head shaking. *What?*

Someone tapped quietly on one of the room's outside panels, gently slid it open a crack. I could hear him breathing. Not fast, not high, not ready to attack or flee. Just waiting. He tapped again, and this time I raised to pull my blankets aside and quietly float over Jacky to the open panel.

"Hikari-san?" It was Mr. Ushida.

"Yes." I slid the panel wider, slipped through the opening and closed it. He had opened the porch panel behind him as well, and now he slipped backward through it and outside. I started to follow, realized I was in my nightshirt, and twisted my ring to summon my uniform. Then I followed him.

"I am sorry," he said as soon as I was outside. I felt Shell move against my ankle, silent as a ghost.

"Ushida-san? Is everything alright?"

"Yes. I will be able to take all of you to the nearest train in the morning. We will wait to inform the authorities of what has happened until you have gone."

"Thank you."

"But, forgive me but I must ask. Have you met Miyamoto Yoshi before seeing his shinigami tonight?"

Shell jumped. "How did you—" She stopped, hissed her frustration. "Well, crap."

Mister Ushida smiled, looking down at her in the light of the lamp he lifted. "What a tale this shall be to tell my grandchildren. Are you a nekokami?"

"Normally she's much taller. Yes, we have met a man before who introduced himself as Miyamoto Yoshi. A younger Yoshi, around twenty-five? When he wasn't a younger girl, or someone else." *Or a fox.*

Unbelievably, upon hearing that Mr. Ushida relaxed.

"Then you have met the kitsune. Good."

The heck?

Mr. Ushida led us into the woods behind the ryokan, Shell grumbling all the way. I didn't care; the proper sounds of the night were back.

"You know this can't end well, right? Mysterious man, two idiot girls, dark woods..."

"Hush." Amazingly I was feeling pretty invulnerable, even cheerful. Jacky had made me forget the actual bite, but the euphoria remained. Had the shinigami-vision been a true one, the real might-have-been? Did it matter? The void was gone, the pain just a soft echo of regret, the way it had been before tonight. Whatever Jacky had done while I was in her power, my heart had said goodbye to John again, tucked his memory safely away where it belonged.

And I *really* understood why Jacky mugged people for their blood and made them forget it instead of selling the fang-high.

"Fine," Shell huffed when I didn't say anything more. "You realize Ja— Mamori's going to want to kill you when we get back, right?"

"Well if Ushida-san has bad intentions towards us, we won't have to worry about Mamori, will we?" The woods were getting thick as the angle of the ground sharpened, and I picked Shell up so she wouldn't have to struggle through the underbrush that tugged at my coat skirts and caught at Cutter's tip. I heard him grumble and stepped more carefully. "So who's being a silly nekokami?"

"I can bite you, you know."

"You can break your teeth."

Ahead of us, Mr. Ushida laughed. "You two act very much like my Aya-chan and her friends."

I laughed back. "Ayaka-san? She must be a great trial to you."

"She is twelve, she is supposed to be. We are here."

Here proved to be a dark cave mouth in the side of the wooded hill. Mister Ushida's lamp only made the shadow behind its mouth deeper.

"And we're going in *there*?" Shell wiggled in my arms. I was beginning to wonder if experiencing the world in a cat's body was affecting her attitude.

"You may stay outside," Mr. Ushida said. "I have something to show your friend."

"As if. She goes, I go."

"Then we go." He lifted the lamp above his head for maximum light and led us in.

The cave narrowed quickly, and he had to bend and then turn sideways at one point. I was careful of Cutter, not wanting another voice to enter the conversation. After a sharp right turn, the cave widened out again although the ceiling stayed low. It wasn't a perfect inverted bowl, more like a half-deflated weather balloon sagging in at one end, about the size of our bedroom at the ryokan. Dirt and stones gave it a decently flat floor.

Mister Ushida hung the lamp from a chain suspended from a rusted iron spike driven into the ceiling.

"The children spread long grass over the floor in the summer." Old and tinder-dry piles of it lay scattered about. "At least, they did. They do not come here now, so close to the graveyard."

"Will they come back?"

He smiled. "They must! So many youngsters to initiate now. There."

In the corner where the cave roof dropped low, someone had set a low, wide stone. And on it... Shell jumped out of my arms to creep up and sniff it. It was a fox. Crudely carved, but recognizable, a fox with lots of tails, twice Shell's size and carved into old, old wood.

"That is Tenkawa's kitsune."

"Oh…" *Oh oh oh.* So much made sense now. I could almost see it, not *all* of it, but… "Who was he?"

Mr. Ushida squatted to reverently dust off the piece of wood with his handkerchief.

"The Miyamoto family and Ushida family are samurai families, two of the oldest families in Tenkawa although never very great. The story says that during the period of war when Tokugawa Ieyasu unified Japan, a son of the family returned to Tenkawa with a bride. She gave him many children but was always strange. One day only a few years after she came to Tenkawa, her mother-in-law caught her turning into a white kitsune in the woods to hunt. She disappeared then, but since that time someone in Tenkawa has always seen the kitsune when the village has been endangered by misfortune."

"And when the shinigami came…"

"I do not know how Miyamoto Yoshi was able to come all the way from the care center where he lived. He was very old and very sick, and when he disappeared nobody admitted to helping him. But I found his body in the cemetery. He had…died after burning an offering at his family grave. And I met the kitsune." Mr. Ushida frowned, remembering. "He looked as Miyamoto-san had looked when I was much younger, and he helped me to bury him."

"Did you ever see the kitsune again?"

"No. He told me that he had a duty to fulfill, and then he hoped Miyamoto-san would sleep peacefully."

"It didn't work." Remembering the first face Kitsune had shown me, I swallowed, eyes prickling. *Rei.* Her name had been Rei and her mother had been Mari, Yoshi's daughter and only surviving child. "He took vengeance for the Miyamoto family, but that was two years ago. Why didn't Yoshi…"

Mr. Ushida was shaking his head.

"Shinigami are born of a hatred, but they are corrupted. *Who* they hated does not matter, then."

My head spun. It was obvious now that when Mister Miyamoto died he had generated a spectral breakthrough, the shinigami. But had he *split*, become both a spirit of vengeance and the family fox-spirit? No, if Kitsune was a part of him, a member of the Miyamoto family, then Ozma's fish wouldn't have been confused. But then who was Kitsune? Someone who had really *loved* the village, had been initiated into the child-cult that met in this cave?

It really didn't matter. "Ushida-san, may I…"

"That is why I brought you." He took a folding knife from his pocket and knelt by the statue. Whispering an apology, he carefully sliced a thin piece of wood from its base, wrapped it in a linen napkin, and presented it to me with a deep formal bow. "Thank you, Hikari-san. This is a small repayment. You, and your friends, have saved Tenkawa."

Chapter Sixteen

Defensenet Report, Tenkawa Incident: The Level 4 (local) spectral threat appears to have been removed. As Defensenet classed the threat as contained and too dangerous to risk further assets for removal, this action must have been undertaken by Active Non-Government Powers. This is confirmed by the testimony of Tenkawa's mayor and shrine priest. The individuals involved could not be identified; however their descriptions match those of the three breakthroughs recently active with Heroes Without Borders, who identified themselves as the Three Remarkable Ronin.

Defensenet Recommendation: Given the displayed power-levels of these three individuals, government assets should immediately be deployed to learn their identities and purposes. Further action would depend upon their cooperation once located.

DR107-BV [Classified]

The sliver of wood worked, probably the only thing that kept Jacky from killing me and burying me in the forest. Looking at the happy clownfish, Ozma speculated that Kitsune might be an *extrareality intrusion*, as she was (or thought she was). If Kitsune had "come from" an extrareality created or made accessible by breakthrough beliefs after The Event, then that would explain a lot. (Of course it was also possible he was more like Fisher, created by a specific obsession.) What mattered was the wood idol was part of his story, so it worked for us.

We got out of town ahead of the authorities, if they came looking for us at all. Mr. Ushida assured us that the notice he sent would be a bare report of the shinigami's defeat by three visitors, and the government might simply assume that it had been done by a local yamabushi mystic. Apparently there were a lot of them in the mountains and a number of them were non-registering breakthroughs, "conscientious objectors." As long as they stayed in the mountains the government left them alone.

When he dropped us off at the train station Mr. Ushida also let us know that, when asked, he would have to faithfully tell the Defensenet agents of the three Magical Girls in Black he met. But he saw no need to tell them about recent guests at his family's ryokan.

I hoped he wouldn't get in any trouble.

The tracking fish (the cutest little bloodhound ever) pointed us in the general direction of Tokyo, which was a good thing; after making such a splash in Tenkawa, Jacky insisted that we needed to dive into a sea of people and run silent until we'd broken our trail. We caught the morning train, Ozma again playing with her mirror.

"A couple of fun facts," Shell said from her bag once we'd settled in our seats. "Including the twenty-three wards and twenty-six incorporated cities that make it up, Tokyo hosts a population of thirty-six *million* with a density of about seven thousand people per square mile. That's more people than all the blossoms on all Tokyo's cherry trees, of which there are a *lot*, cherry blossoms being the city's special flower and all."

Shell looked up all that and more on her epad while we watched fields and towns pass by. The short-lived cherry blossoms were all about the transience of things and hope of renewal, and I wondered if that said something about the city. Tokyo had certainly been renewed a few times, coming back from earthquakes and fires, war, and now kaiju attacks. Coming in on the Shinkansen line we could see a couple of clusters of large scale tower construction. A kaiju hadn't reached the city in two years; the last one that did got blown into dust bunnies by Tokyo's own Verne-built mecha.

All the way in to Tokyo I kept watching for the Eight Excellent Protectors or some other Defensenet team to drop out of the sky on us. I couldn't even enjoy the beautiful view, which was stupid—yes we'd made a big splash last night, but the delay (hopefully) in the story's reaching anybody who could respond meant that we'd likely gotten away. And if their engagement doctrine was anything like ours, if they really *did* come after us they would wait to do it in a place where we could be quickly separated from the bystanders and collateral damage minimized.

Hard to do on a train.

We had decided to get off on the west side of Tokyo, but as the Shinkansen turned north and glided into Shinjuku Station our magic compass-fish surprised Ozma by smoothly but swiftly twisting to point northeast. Her shout had me looking for enemies until she explained, and then we all scrambled for our bags.

Disembarking into the biggest train station I had ever seen in my life, we promptly got lost in the tide of commuters filling the underground labyrinth, and exited through a huge shopping center labeled *Lumen Est* in two-story letters. After talking to a friendly policeman, Ozma led us back through the station to the west side where we caught a taxi to the Keio Plaza Hotel, smack in the middle of a business and shopping district that dwarfed the Chicago Loop.

We didn't even try and pay in yen here; the place smelled like money and was so high class it probably didn't know how to handle the paper stuff—using cash to pay for our rooms would have made us stand out like we were wearing shirts saying *Move along, nothing to see here.*

Ozma got us to our suite, which was good because I was sort of in shock; Tokyo made Chicago look like *Littleton*; it really was a people-sea, and even with a pointing fish *how* were we ever going to find Kitsune in a place this big? Last night's euphoria was definitely gone.

I did manage to remember *not* to try and tip the bellhop—a terrible insult that would have suggested we thought he expected extra for doing his job. It would have totally labeled us *gaijin*, foreigners whatever we looked and sounded like. He made sure to point out the desk number if we needed anything at all, before closing the doors behind him.

Looking out the windows at the distressingly big cityscape, I dropped onto the furthest bed.

It had been four nights. Doctor Cornelius had suggested I had at least two weeks. Okay, *plenty* of time to use a magic fish to find someone who we probably wouldn't recognize; after all, if we walked right past him the fish would flip around, right?

The mental image of us walking around Tokyo following a fish in a crystal globe, like Girl Scouts following a wayward compass, made me snicker in spite of everything. I was still laughing when Ozma came back from checking out the bathroom. Sitting beside me, she patted my knee.

"The speed with which the Compass Fish turned as we approached the station indicates that Kitsune is not far to the east of us, perhaps within five or ten miles. Of course he won't be standing still, and certainly will not be standing on a street corner awaiting our arrival, but unless he too is on a journey then we will find him."

She nodded decisively. "Shell, would you please tell us what we can expect in this quarter of the city?"

Shell looked up from the bed she'd promptly spread herself out on upon climbing out of her bag. "I can tell you it's going to suck."

Probably not the reassuring answer Ozma had been looking for.

Anyone managing to spy on us (nobody was—Ozma looked in her mirrors and guaranteed it) would have laughed till they peed themselves.

We sat around the suite's coffee table, Shell sitting beside the Compass Fish. (It kept darting about inside its globe and catching her instinctive attention.) Ozma produced the tiny silver service from her box and prepared tea; the copper pot was self-heating, of course, and just the fragrance of the tea unwound the knot inside me.

She gracefully poured and passed to Jacky and me, set out a tiny saucer of cream for Shell and gave her ears a light scratch-tug. "I wish you could have some, my dear, but Six-Leaf Clover is a restorative. It will restore natural vitality, but it will also restore imbibers to their natural state and I do not think you want to be a scouting drone again. The cream is the finest refined cream from the Land of Mo."

Shell dropped her head and lapped the cream, purring like a mini-motor, then started and straightened up looking terribly self-conscious. When she licked a drop off her whiskers I had to cover my smile.

Raising my own cup to my lips, I stopped. Weren't we transformed too? Ozma smiled and shook her head.

"Unlike Shell, we have merely changed outward form."

I sighed with relief; the tea smelled so *good*. Sipping it sent a liquid warmth through me, leaving me feeling like I'd been the recipient of a long spa-weekend. The shadow of the shinigami faded a little more.

"Right," Shell said as we sipped our tea. "About what we're looking at. Guys, we're just down the street from City Hall. That's the Tokyo Metropolitan Government Building, and there's just *got* to be lots of government capes and plainclothes powers hanging around protecting the government of the biggest megalopolis in the world. Then there's Defensenet. Defensenet Shinjuku is the national headquarters—home base for the Eight Excellent Protectors and the Nine Accomplished Heroes."

Jacky snorted. "So we've got to be quiet. That's not news."

"No, what's news is if we start something here or across the tracks and they're already looking for us, then we'll probably be counting our disengagement window in *seconds*. After that Defensenet capes are going to be crawling up our—backsides."

I nodded. "Okay, what else?"

"Then there's all the ronin."

"*All?*" Jacky's voice sharpened.

"Not *all*. But you know about the government training and management system; all the Japanese capes work for the Japanese government."

"Okay…"

"But there are some like you who just aren't joiners. They don't register. Then there are breakthroughs who work in private security, or as consultants, or who are members of international non-government organizations like Heroes Without Borders. We're not even talking about the muscle recruited by the yakuza."

I was getting a bad feeling even the Six-Leaf Tea couldn't banish.

"And then of course there's the breakthroughs who were criminals to start with, or whose powers *really* don't have legitimate uses. The yakuza *love* those."

Yakuza. The Japanese Mafia. "Shell," I said carefully. "When you say 'all,' are you implying that a lot of them are *here*? In Shinjuku?"

"East Shinjuku, actually, right where the Compass Fish is pointing. Akihabara is the center of media-driven cape-fandom—they call capes *powers* here, and cape fans are power-otaku—but East Shinjuku has become the center of the *ronin*-otaku subculture. And it looks like the fish might be pointing at Kabukicho, which is even worse."

Ozma lowered her cup. "And how precisely is it worse?"

"Kabukicho?" I hadn't actually known that many Japanese words until Ozma's magic drops, but *kabuki* was one of them. How could *theater* be worse?

"Kabuki-cho." Shell enunciated. "East Shinjuku is one of the big nightlife and entertainment centers of Tokyo—all that money from the business and government district next door—but Kabukicho is the *adult* entertainment center of Tokyo. For the same reason, really; all the suits with money to burn. The district was named after a planned kabuki theater that never got built."

I blinked. "Adult...*oh*. You think he's *there*?"

"It's got a huge yakuza presence. They run all the gambling and drugs and own most of the host and hostess clubs, couples hotels, and soaplands in Kabukicho. So yeah, I'd bet lunch on it. Not my life, but lunch."

"So," Jacky summed up, "to find and get to Kitsune, we might need to go through ronin who may or may not be yakuza members or clients, and with a good chance of Defensenet capes coming down on us if it gets at all public?"

"Uhuh."

She shrugged. "Doesn't sound too hard, unless he sleeps in some yakuza boss's house. We find out where he closes his eyes at night, go in and get him. My only problem is if we have to go into...Kabukicho? Then I'm the only one who looks old enough to be there and wouldn't be *bait*. You two..."

I almost gagged on my tea. Under normal circumstances it might be fun to walk a dangerous neighborhood for a while and cull the free-roaming predator population (Jacky did it all the time in Chicago and New Orleans), but attracting attention *here*...

This was *so* going to suck.

My first suggestion was that Ozma use her magic belt to "age us up" a bit, only to learn that the famed Magic Belt was a *magic capacitor*. She only used it when she didn't have something in her magic box that would do the job and didn't have time to whip up something in her lab. And between changing us the first time, transforming herself into a green crystal jar, catting Shell, and her stunt the previous night in the graveyard, she'd pretty much tapped it out and it needed to recharge.

Not good news.

So we came up with a plan and armed ourselves—which in this situation meant *shopping*. The clothes we'd worn "under" our costumes, and the extra clothes we'd picked up in Anhui, were not nearly upscale enough for where we needed to go in fashion-conscious Tokyo. We needed serious upgrades, and could "age up" a little in our style choices.

Ozma called the lobby and they sent us to Isetan Shinjuku, Isetan's flagship store and multiple floors of clothing, accessory, and even hair and makeup fashion. Armed with Shell's no-limit credit cards, we hit the place for a complete Girl's Day; that meant hitting one of the fanciest hair spas I'd ever been to for deep cleansing oil massages, shampoos, and blowouts along with manicures and face-care, and then the personal attention of a team of style-guides as we shopped till we dropped.

Sending the purchases we weren't wearing to the hotel, we snacked and window-shopped our way up East Shinjuku (avoiding City Hall). That gave Ozma a chance to implement one of my ideas; buying a quality foldable city-map, she used it like a Girl Scout's map and compass with her magic fish, stopping every half hour to check and draw a new red line orienting to Kitsune.

It looked like he was moving around (not all lines intersected at the same point), but the angles suggested he was staying in East Shinjuku. We'd check again from the hotel during the night hours; if he left Shinjuku we'd follow, if not then tomorrow we'd scout the east side.

Returning to Keio Plaza for a four-star dining experience, we went back up to our suite to confer with Shell over a walking-map of East Shinjuku that would let us make more Kitsune-checks without standing out too much.

When night fell Kitsune stayed in Shinjuku.

Dammit.

We set an alarm so one of us would get up every hour to recheck Kitsune's direction, just in case. Jacky expressed a need to hunt (she promised she'd be careful), so Ozma and I took one of the two big beds and left the other for her. The bath was big enough for us to share, but I wasn't going *that* Japanese even if I knew the proper way from Shell's explanation at the ryokan (wash off completely first, *then* soak in the bath).

I left the bathroom to Ozma while Jacky changed to go out, and found myself looking out at the city while waiting my turn.

The suite's lights were low enough that I could see the glowing towers of Shinjuku and my own ghostly reflection in the window. It had been a few days now, and seeing myself still made me feel…unreal. Beautiful (especially after today's pampering care) but not *me*. A shadow behind me turned into Jacky as she stepped up, looking over my shoulder at the Tokyo nightscape.

"What are you thinking about?" She watched my reflection in the window, and I suppressed the urge to bite my new manicure.

"Kitsune."

"Why? Beyond the usual."

"I— " Why? What had changed? "If Kitsune— If he's really a criminal… I don't know." Oddly, I'd been happy to hear Veritas' theory that he'd been working for the Japanese government in the whole Littleton affair. A spy working for his government—that could be right, even honorable. If he was just a criminal who sometimes did government jobs… But thinking that didn't feel right, somehow. And it wasn't just wishful thinking. Why…

"What do you know about him?" Jacky asked quietly, watching my face in reflection.

"Everything you know."

"Not his file. What do you *know* about him?"

For some reason I flashed back to the second time I'd met him—if *he* was the right pronoun. The first time he'd worn the dead banker's face, then Mom's, and then Yoshi's granddaughter's: a slide-show. But the *second* time…then he'd worn Yoshi's younger face. He'd been nice, even sweet, but the *important* thing was that when Nemesis had shot up The Fortress gunning for him, when I still hadn't known who he was, he'd stayed and helped the victims. And in the whole Littleton thing, he'd risked his game (*her* game— she'd been Allison then) to deal us into it. Because Shelly had been there.

And… *Oh*. I knew why putting Kitsune with the yakuza in my head didn't work.

"The tree," I whispered. My eyes were wide in the mirroring glass.

"What about it?"

My eyes met Jacky's in the window. I didn't know *why* I knew this but… "It's *good*. The tree, I mean. The whole place. Doctor Cornelius called it the High Plane of Heaven and—I know it's not *Heaven*, but—but I don't think anything evil can be there." Folding my arms, I hugged my chest. "It's so…when I'm there I feel so—I really wouldn't mind staying. But…"

But everyone I loved was here. My responsibilities were here.

Her reflected mouth twisted. "'Not evil' doesn't mean good, but if there's a moral requirement I understand why you can be there. You're all 'Please let me save everyone I see, ever.' They don't even have to be good—killing Heavenly Dragon hurt you, didn't it?"

When I shrugged her smile thinned. "Yeah. But that fox is a trickster. He's at least as morally flexible as I am. Criminals can be a mix, too."

She sounded impatient, like she shouldn't have to be stating the obvious, and I sighed.

"I know." I looked down at the cross-hatched grid of lighted streets, relatively quiet now. "It still doesn't feel right. I can't put him and the tree and him and the yakuza in the same picture." When she didn't say anything I looked up. She'd stepped back from the window and into shadow.

"Maybe. But don't get stupid now. Trust is something we can't afford until you're safe. Go to bed—I'm going out."

I nodded but stayed by the window until I heard the door of the suite close behind her.

Chapter Seventeen

The Second Deed of Hikari is celebrated in Tenkawa, a small town in the mountains. Each year, during the week when the three days of the deeds are honored, the town fills with celebrants from across Japan and the families of Tenkawa hold a joyful festival. They publicly celebrate the day that Hikari, sent by Tenkawa's own guardian kitsune, survived the death-dealing touch of a powerful shinigami and freed the town of its evil.

A History of the Brief Career of Hikari and the Three Remarkable Ronin.

A light breeze stirred the flowering tree, plucking white cherry blossoms away to fall like snow. No. *The air was still, the waving branches the only sound, a soft rub and rattle of branch against branch as petals drifted to settle on me.*

Why?

"Hello?" I called softly, turning in a slow circle.

I was being watched. Playfully.

"Hello?"

The petals kept falling to kiss my skin with spots of warmth, like the tree had been warmed by a much hotter sun than the one that peeked through the clouds now.

"Hello?"

The tree was blessing me. Laughing at me. Hiding itself from me? The laughter turned into the alarm and I sat up so fast I threw the blankets to the foot of the bed.

"What did you mean?" Ozma asked beside me.

"What?" I blinked, shook my head to clear it as the alarm chimed again.

"You said 'The world is full of weeping. How can I go?'"

"I said that? Exactly?"

She shrugged in her loose nightgown. "I often need to remember things I only read or hear once. What did you mean?"

"I don't *know*." I ran fingers through my mess of hair, trying not to hyperventilate. Jacky wasn't back yet, and the only light in the room was the ambient light of Tokyo and the alarm clock by the bed. Shell's eyes glowed from Jacky's empty bed where she watched me.

My sleep-shirt had gotten twisted about and I straightened it, turned off the alarm and looked for the Compass Fish. First things first.

This is so *not good.*

I used the fish and map, drew the new line with a hand that shook only a little. Kitsune had moved again, but the newest red line still ran east through East Shinjuku. Dropping back down on the bed, I folded my legs up to sit yoga-style.

The world is full of weeping. How can I go? I'd *said* that? Shell leaped across and climbed into my lap. I absently stroked her ears.

"Did I really?"

"Oh yeah," she said.

A memory tickled me and I chased it down, reciting: "'Come away, oh human child! To the waters and the wild with a fairy, hand in hand. For the world's more full of weeping than you can understand.' The Stolen Child, William Butler Yeats."

"So, now you're channeling a dead poet?"

"*No*. I was at the tree again. And I was wide awake this time. In my dream, I mean."

"Well *that's* not good. Is that Stage Two or something? And you heard that there? The whole 'How can I go?'"

"No. And I only thought of Yeats because that's the only place I can remember reading about a 'World full of weeping.'"

The *words* were sort of the same but the sentiment was inverted, wasn't it? Stay versus go. And why had I said it at all? Had the tree said it to me somehow? It sounded incredibly sad, which was the opposite of how I always felt at the tree. Tonight, *tonight* it had been so happy I'd wanted to laugh and cry at the same time.

I gathered up Shell and flopped back, stretching my legs out and dropping her on my stomach. She stretched out, sphinxlike, and dug into my sleep-shirt with a rumbling purr. Beside me Ozma was asleep again. She even snored elegantly. I wasn't sleeping again tonight.

"So," I yawned, scratching Shell's ears. "What's it like? Being a cat?"

"I want to chase sunbeams and lick my butt."

"Ew."

I made myself the Keeper of The Fish for the rest of the night, checking on Kitsune when the alarm went off. Jacky got in just before dawn looking totally refreshed. She'd once explained that since she'd become a daywalker enough blood could substitute for sleep.

And that sparked my question to Ozma; her answer was yes—a stronger infusion of Six-Leaf Tea could substitute for sleep too. She had enough for three nights; after that I'd need to leave Japan, get out from under the quantum-interdiction if I wanted to avoid the tree by "sleeping" in the Warden's cloudhome while the others finished the hunt for Kitsune.

Since I might have moved into what Shell had called *Stage Two* last night, Jacky wanted me to leave *now*. That argument chased me into the shower, and after that we took our Comprehension Drops for the day, ate breakfast ordered from room service, and dressed for the day's hunt into East Shinjuku.

People-watching yesterday using the fashion eye the Bees had given me, I'd noticed that Tokyo women's fashion mostly ran to high skirts and high necklines and focused on legs instead of bust. I didn't know if that was because of a different cultural aesthetic or because Japanese women weren't as endowed as European and American women, but it worked for me; while nature had left me lacking in height and hips and bust, I did have nice legs and a tiny waist (Shell called me *streamlined*). There was just one wrinkle; the style ladies of Isetan Shinjuku warned us to wear what I thought of as "spanky shorts"—short-legged athletic shorts kind of like my sleep shorts—under our skirts to foil the *up-skirt perverts.* Really.

I'd managed not to act like I'd had No Idea; Jacky had just smiled and bought a really nice slacks-and-blazer outfits that did nothing to hide the panther-like way she moved. Ozma went with long flowy skirts and dresses that would foil any perv not shamed away by her aura of royal perfection.

With my waist-hugging skirt and light sweater, plus the fresh new do and expertly applied makeup I'd bought yesterday, I managed to look adult enough that I *hoped* most places wouldn't card me if anyone looked at me at all. (Out of costume I tended to disappear beside Jacky and Ozma, and today I *liked* it that way.) Once again disregarding Jacky's suggestion that I take the train to the opposite coast and then hug water until I hit the Chinese shore, I led us out. We decided to walk back to the station, entering East Shinjuku using the station exit through *Lumen Est*.

The Isetan ladies hadn't warned us about the gropers. They'd probably thought we knew.

In the crush of the station crowd I got the first one because of my short skirt. It wasn't a passing touch either—the groper palmed my butt under my skirt. So shocked I almost levitated, I reflexively pushed back and sent him flying through the crowd behind us. We managed to look as surprised as everyone else (we *were*), and the crush of packed bodies hid my push as easily as his opportunistic grope. Jacky and Ozma moved behind me after that, and we were okay although one guy behind Jacky screamed like a girl when she reached back and crushed his hand.

Ozma had her mirror out by then so at least we were camera-free. In her bag Shell hissed something about *taking a freaking taxi next time* as we exited the station, but I wasn't paying attention.

I'd only caught a glimpse of East Shinjuku yesterday before we'd turned around, but now I got a good look and I was having a hard time not staring at everything we passed. The buildings here weren't skyscrapers, but they were all tall and they weren't like the buildings and towers of the Loop back home. Advertising took over every vertical surface, from walls and rooftops to benches and curbsides, with so many neon, big screen, and backlit signs in Japanese and English that I was willing to bet that at night the dark disappeared. And I couldn't believe how *clean* the streets were; even the side alleys had no graffiti or litter.

Japanese were big believers in pictures, too; pictures of food, pictures of karaoke rooms, pictures of entertainers told us everything we needed to know about what was inside the shops we passed by. Greeters dressed as uniformed powers or more flamboyantly costumed ronin stood outside entertainment shops and restaurants to call people in; everywhere there was something to see.

We took a cab to Shinjuku Park to work our way back from there, west to east across the south edge of Shinjuku, making fish-checks every block or two, and didn't experience any more gropers. But that was probably because the crowds weren't tight enough for anonymity; what we *did* get was players trying to strike up conversations with really repetitive one-liners—the most popular one was sidling up at a corner pretending they knew one of us. "Ah! It's been so long, how are you doing?"

I even got a couple (What the *hell*? I mean really, what the hell?) until Jacky started pushing a bit of her vamp-influence to project a *Go Away* aura. As if that wasn't enough, the Compass Fish kept consistently pointing north-by-something, tilting further east as we went further west. Which made it official; Kitsune was in Kabukicho.

Dammit. What was he *doing* there?

Then, almost back to the station, we hit the intersection behind the Studio Alta building with its huge TV screen and I forgot about all of that. Because we were staring at *us*.

What? Just...what?

"Well that wasn't there last night," Jacky said.

"How is that even— No—" I tried again. "It's only been *three* days."

Shell stretched up for a peek and started *laughing*. Thankfully she was doing it from the bottom of her bag.

Somebody had not only gotten hold of the picture we'd taken with the HWB flight crew, they'd used it to design and produce a convention-sized billboard print of the three of us. We stood in ridiculously dramatic postures, me on one knee (why?) ready to draw Cutter, Jacky standing behind me with gun drawn to cover my right while behind and above her (maybe levitating a bit?) Ozma gestured dramatically to my left.

What. The. Heck?

Shell wouldn't stop snickering, something that sounded truly weird coming from a cat, but hearing her pushed me past my shock. Okay, maybe it actually made a bizarre sort of sense. The billboard art had to come from the picture we'd taken in Anhui. It had been taken with a digital camera; the crew had obviously taken copies with them, and if someone back at Heroes Without Borders in

Shibushi had put it online then...but *three days*? Three days is all it took for *that*?

Shell snuck another look and managed to control herself this time.

"C'mon, Hope. Remember what I told you last night?"

I nodded, still dazed. Shell and I had talked for hours last night, mostly about Japanese pop-culture and capes.

Popular Japanese capes—power-idols—were managed and packaged to a degree that made the marketing stuff the Sentinels did look subtle and understated. Power-idols were not only trained to fight, they were groomed to perform. They had fitness-fashion specialists, acting, voice, and performance coaches, managers and publicists. Japanese capes were media personalities, pop-gods, and in Akihabara you could always find rabid cosplayers dressed in the color-coded skirted outfits of the Eight Excellent Protectors or the equally color-coded and vaguely military uniforms of the Nine Accomplished Heroes. Factory-made to be completely authentic.

And Japan had a counter-culture—sort of like villain-rap culture but without the *villain* emphasis. The popular ronin weren't supervillains, but they were seen as outlaws, rebels, and just like with power-otaku cosplayers, ronin-otaku showed their love by imitation; below the billboard I could see at least twelve coat-clad and shade-wearing Remarkable Ronin comparing costumes and posing for pictures with passersby.

I squinted. The swords and guns couldn't be real, not with Japan's strict weapons laws, but—

"Wait. It wasn't there *last night*?"

The crowd circling the cosplayers beneath the billboard talked costume details while arguing about our *stats* and excitedly sharing the news of the Three Remarkable Ronin with curious passersby not yet in the know. Ozma politely inquired and was happily directed to an internet ronin board that tracked sightings, and with Shell's prompting I managed to find it on our epad.

The sight linked to news sources in China and confirmed our "kills" while crediting us with the successful medical mission, gave our "names," Hikari, Mamori, and Kimiko, and speculated about our powers. The site's writers correctly pegged me as some kind of Atlas-type, but guessed that Jacky was a physically enhanced teleporting martial artist (a master of gunjitsu). They had no idea what Ozma did, pegging her as a "supporting power."

Beyond that it was all pages of comments and vlog and blog-posts, all speculation, *none* of them even hinting we weren't from around here. I could breathe again, and ask Jacky what she had meant about last night.

For *that* conversation we found a coffee and karaoke shop and paid for a small party room. Our server's cheerful greeting and the three cream puppies in latte foam-art that smiled up at me from my heavy mug didn't do a thing for my black thoughts. I bit their cute little heads off and drank my coffee.

Then my brain caught up with me. I set my mug down as Ozma finished thanking our server at the door.

"Ozma? Would you mind taking Shell out for some fish? We've got our cellphones."

She nodded and put her compact surveillance-thwarting mirror on the table. Taking the bag from me and ignoring Shell's "Hey!" she pinched the top of the bag against her attempt to scramble out. I closed the door behind them, listened to her walk down the hall promising tuna and cream.

Jacky watched me from her comfortable chair, leaving her mug with its cream-puppy topping on the table to cool.

"You went into Kabukicho last night," I said, leaning against the door. She would have walked right by the billboard corner.

"It has my kind of prey."

Players. Wannabe Romeos. Inebriated mobile meals that could be cut from the herd, left a few ounces lighter with a false and fuzzy memory of getting lucky. "I know. Is there a reason you didn't tell us this morning?"

"Like…"

I made myself sit down, didn't know what to do with my hands and settled them on my knees (debutante manners—they never leave you). "Did you—did you have to do anything that nobody should know about?"

"And why would you think that?" My friend had gone still, like only vamps could and she still could even if she was a breather now.

"Because you're all about the intel. You'd tell us what you'd learned unless— Did you not want us to know you'd been there?" I swallowed. "It's okay, you know. I know that sometimes you have to do things I can't— It's okay—"

"Stop." Jacky held up a hand in the universal *stop* sign, but she was smiling. It wasn't a nice smile but it was better than her expressionless watching. "You sent Ozma and Shell away because you didn't want them to hear if I admitted to a *crime*? Beyond my usual?"

"…yes?"

"Why?"

"I don't *know*!" And I really didn't; it wasn't as if Shell didn't know all about the things that Jacky sometimes had to do, and Ozma…I'd long since filed her majesty under the category of *Good, Not Always Nice*—she'd be likely to understand.

The sardonic twist to Jacky's grin said *she* understood, which was totally unfair; it was like I'd regressed to high school and the BF's code of silence. "So, why didn't you share this morning? Since it's obviously not a dark and bloody secret."

She actually laughed at me, reaching for her coffee.

"When I came back this morning and until we'd walked across East Shinjuku, I didn't know if we'd really be going into Kabukicho." Her smile turned whimsical. "And being okay with what I do doesn't mean you're comfortable with it."

I blanched. "Jacky—"

"Hope, it really is okay." She held my gaze until she could see I believed her.

I sighed, shoulders slumping. "...okay." It didn't feel right to let it go, like I was letting Jacky down, but what were we fighting *about*? "So, tell me about it?"

"Not much to tell, really. I sipped from an office lady and an American tourist, and then found me a nice yakuza boy." She tapped the base of her neck with two fingers. "They're easy to spot by the tats, at least when they've got their shirts open three buttons down to show off their ink and shiny bling. Him I kept for a long talk."

"What did you learn?"

"A lot and not much." She sipped her coffee and grimaced. It was pretty good stuff, but even I could tell it wasn't quite up to her own coffee-snob standards. "You know the yakuza isn't like the Chicago Mob, right? They're not just wise guys with tattoos. They have *business cards*. A local office listed in the phonebook. A public complaints department."

"You're kidding."

She fished in her pocket and tossed me a card. "Shinjuku-kai's *oyabun*—the local family's boss—is Imada Masu. He's a big believer in civic responsibility."

The card had a black symbol on the shiny orange side that I decided must indicate the organization, and an orange phone number on the matte-black side. "They're *philanthropists*?"

"They think they're civic boosters. They extort money from the local businesses that they don't own and from the semi-legal prostitution the place is known for, and pay the community back with honest-to-God protection from any crime that isn't theirs. To be fair, it sounds like that means keeping their own minions in check, too."

I turned the card back over. A crime family with a *hotline*?

She shrugged. "My *date* liked to brag—they even publicly support local charities and shrines, march in community festivals. He was in the last one, helped pull the family float."

"And their ronin?"

"He boasted that their oyabun is a ronin, but nobody knows his power. For the rest they've got a stable of C and D Class street ronin, mostly Ajax-Types, but it sounds like people who get to see their high-power ronin in action don't talk about it much—if they're seen again at all."

I sighed. Just once I would have liked something to come easy. "Well, we still—" My cellphone chimed a text, and I fished it out.

It read *"Ozma taken."*

"What?" Jacky asked when all the blood left my face.

"Somebody took Ozma." I barely remembered to unlock the door before going through it.

Chapter Eighteen

Know well what leads you forward and what holds you back, and choose the path that leads to wisdom.

Buddha

Everything happens for a reason. Sometimes the reason is you're stupid and make bad decisions.

Astra.

Shell's next text, *Andre's,* was in English instead of kanji and when I showed it to the greeter at the coffeehouse door she directed me to a café just down the street. My heart in my throat, I scanned the packed sidewalk and traffic but didn't see Ozma or anybody moving in a way that screamed *I'm a kidnapper!*

Jacky a silent shadow behind me, I proceeded at a walk that might have looked casual but would have knocked anybody who bumped me down on his ass until I found Andre's—a seafood café with a narrow front and a long serving and eating counter inside. Shell's bag sat right by the door, Shell crouched low inside it.

"Move!" Jacky whispered as she passed me and kept going without looking at me. Barely keeping myself from following her I picked up the bag, nodded to passing pedestrians, and headed in the other direction. Hailing the first free taxi I saw, I texted Jacky my intentions while Shell kept quiet.

Abandoning the taxi two intersections away, I walked through a street-mall and a department store before heading back to West Shinjuku through the insanely crowded station. Hoping the tides of people would keep anyone from following close, I still doubled back on my path twice and exited south of where we'd exited before.

At Keio Plaza I found a two-story French restaurant with private rooms and flashed my credit card for a small dining room overlooking the street in sight of the hotel.

The waiter left me with coffee. Maybe I'd finish this one. "You can come out, Shell." I lifted her out of the bag and into my lap.

She flattened herself out across my legs. "Ozma'd just asked the greeter if she could get a small box of unseasoned tuna. They got out of a van."

I nodded and stroked her back, eyes on the street. "And?"

"They wore headbands with strips of kanji-covered paper hanging from them. They didn't look at anyone but us, and everyone else looked somewhere else. Not like they meant to—just, like they didn't see that the kidnappers were any big deal."

Magic. I groaned but didn't stop stroking Shell.

"When Ozma saw them she slipped her phone and box into the bag with me and left it. She went to meet them."

I closed my eyes, imagining the scene. A packed sidewalk, a bubble of space where people stopped looking. Ozma couldn't reach her wand or the Magic Belt without transforming first, blatantly and publicly. With no room to run, she left the bag and moved forward into their move, pulling their focus away from her priceless box and away from Shell.

Moving Shell to the chair beside me and fumbling in the bag, I found it: Glegg's Box of Mixed Magic. Ozma had folded it up, its gold and gem-studded wire and filigree sides lying flat against each other as compact as a closed epad. Carefully unfolding the box into its six sides and latching the lid's catch, I opened the box by its detachable *hinged* side (a final "trick" to foil thieves who shouldn't be opening it that Ozma had showed me).

Anybody unfolding and opening it the "normal" way would just find it as empty as it looked when you peeked through the wire-mesh patterns of its sides. Opening it the right way showed me its velvet-lined interior and carefully packed contents. Putting fingers to each corner of the opening, I stretched the box like I'd open a rope-closed sack, and by the time Jacky showed up behind the waiter five minutes later I had everything spread out on the table.

"Smart," she said. She didn't say anything else until our waiter bowed himself out and she had poured her own coffee from the pot. "What did she leave us?"

"The Six-Leaf Tea, the Comprehension Drops, the Compass Fish, a pair of Anonymity Specs, a pair of—I think they're her Seeing Specs—and a bunch of little coded boxes and bottles. And I think these are apothecary's tools?"

Jacky looked over the black-lacquered box of golden instruments and ordered paper sleeves. "Could be. Nothing for us to play with."

I spread some chicken paste on a biscuit for Shell, sighing at how this all looked—a bizarre and sad echo of yesterday's tea. At least my hands weren't shaking. "No, not going to open anything I don't recognize—I'd be as stupid as Alice in Wonderland." Putting together our little lunch plates held me together, let me sit on the little girl inside who'd wanted to wail since seeing the street with no Ozma.

"So do we go get her after lunch?" Jacky tried the coffee, found it acceptable, and reached for the little biscuits. "Because I have no plans."

"We don't know—"

"We do." The cup in her hand stayed as steady as if held by a statue carved of white marble, a statue that spit out words like darts. "The yakuza. Somebody identified me from last night. They followed me today, grabbed Ozma when we split up."

"We don't know that."

"If it was Defensenet then they would have been waiting for all of us, cleared the street while we were in the coffeehouse, and picked us up as we came out after her. We'd have been facing the Eight Excellent Cheerleaders or the Nine Fine Boys. You carved your way through a Chinese *dragon* for God's sake, they know we're a hard target." She set down her coffee to select and munch a paste-covered biscuit like she was biting someone's neck, chewed and swallowed. "The local yakuza boys have got her, so we go get her back."

Blackstone once told me that when you're up to your neck in the brown stuff, wallowing in *"It's all my fault!"* is counterproductive—you don't have that many inches left before you freaking drown. (As an ex-Marine, he said it a bit differently.) Which didn't mean I wasn't going to give myself a huge ass-kicking later; with the blinding clarity of hindsight, considering what Kitsune seemed to do for a living our chances of finding him alone and an easy target somewhere had always been horrible to laughably non-existent. We'd smuggled ourselves into Japan, breaking who knew how many laws, pretty much only to get caught. By the yakuza or Defensenet, it didn't matter.

But it *did* matter for what happened next, and unless I had no other choice I couldn't take Jacky's guess as to who had taken Ozma as the basis for our next moves. Especially since, if the yakuza did have Ozma, our next move would be Find Jacky's Date and work our way up the chain. As quietly of possible, violently if necessary. It would probably be necessary.

I'd hoped somebody might have followed us, but nobody visibly suspicious showed up in Kio Plaza in the hours we watched. Which didn't change anything; we weren't returning to the hotel.

Jacky had a few quiet words with our servers and the restaurant's manager (influence-reinforced, I was sure). I didn't ask, but it was a pretty good bet they thought we were Defensenet agents now—great excuse for a stakeout and we were paying them well anyway. While she did that I thought useless thoughts until something sparked, the only decent idea I'd had since everything began.

The Compass Fish.

Back in the village shrine, Ozma had "fed" the family ashes to the fish without any kind of magic words or ritual. How had she done it? Could I do it?

Carefully sorting through the box of paper sleeves turned up a sleeve with a twist of long golden hair, braided into a short string and tied into a ring-sized circle. The sleeve had a fancy "O" scribbled on it; Ozma's hair? It *looked* the right shade.

I held the sleeve in my fingers, tried to tell myself I wasn't being stupid.

Shell watched from where she sat working her epad. "Remember what you said about Alice?"

"You're not helping." *It's not like I'm going to eat it...*

Squeezing my eyes closed and holding my breath (like *that* would help anything), I tipped the hair ring into my palm.

And opened an eye. I was still me, remembered being me, and was still here. *Okay.* I'd only seen it out of the corner of my eye at the shrine, but it seemed that Ozma had...

"Now that's interesting," Shell said.

When I tapped the hair ring to the crystal sphere that was Mister Fishy's home, it had darted up, seemed to *sniff* the ring, and then grabbed it in its mouth to pull it right through the crystal and into its watery home like sucking food off the surface of a pond. Then it pushed the piece of Kitsune-wood lying on the bottom of the sphere out to drop into my hand. *Of course, must keep things neat.* I put Mister Fishy down and slipped the wood sliver into an empty paper sleeve, wrote Kitsune Wood on it in pen, and filed it in the box before I started giggling.

And now the fish was circling, darting between the hair ring and the side of the sphere where it tap-tap-tapped, pointing us at Kabukicho.

Jacky was right. But we weren't going to need to work the chain.

"It's going to go to shit. You know that, right?"

I didn't take my eyes off the block of little buildings we stood above. They had the numbers, they knew the ground, and we had no backup. We *might* have surprise. "I know."

"And?"

I kept my eyes on the buildings. "We've got a good shot at getting Ozma back ourselves, and if we don't we've got a better chance of bringing enough Defensenet attention down on us that they won't be able to spirit Ozma away to somewhere else. So we all get caught and taken into custody by the Japanese government. I can live with that."

I didn't say that even if the local cavalry arrived Jacky had a good chance of breaking contact and getting herself away. She knew that too.

We weren't waiting for nightfall. Jacky still had Ozma's sunscreen potion and bottled wind so she was good to go, and they probably *expected* us to arrive after dark, when the visitors filled up the place looking for variety and entertainment. But we were still capes; we wanted the opposite.

Jacky had put on Ozma's Anonymity Specs and taken the Compass Fish for a taxi ride around Shinjuku (something we should have done *first*). Doing the Girl Scout survey with the map, she'd pinpointed Ozma in northeast Kabukicho. Narrowing it down told us they'd taken her to a weird little neighborhood called Golden Gai.

Golden Gai. It sounded like a fancy resort but it was the exact opposite. The place was a warren of narrow alleys and tiny two-story eateries and bars barely wider than their front doors. There were more than two hundred of them, all crammed into a small quarter of Kabukicho that had once been a post-WWII black market. Then it had been a red light district until the Japanese government had made prostitution illegal. It had survived the development around it mostly because the bar owners had banded together to keep arsonists working for developers out of the neighborhood—a neighborhood watch with *teeth*.

According to what I'd read about the place, Golden Gai was a time capsule, a window into what a lot of Tokyo had looked like before the massive firebombings of the war's final year had resulted in almost total urban renewal. Now we stood on the roof of a neighboring business building, transformed and ready, looking down into the maze—a historic site if you wanted to call a modern-day hive of crime and villainy "historic."

"Sound check," Shell whispered in my ear. Shell and I had shopped while Jacky scouted and now we wore earbugs better than the ones the Sentinels used, with matching sets of reality-plus shades (able to project the tactical imagery overlay that Virtual-Shell usually did for me through our link) styled to match our ronin costumes. Japan was the country on the cutting edge of new electronics. Shell was far too breakable to directly participate in what was about to go down, so she had chosen an amazingly clean alley three streets over to use as a "base" from which she could act as our Dispatch wingman.

"I hear you fine," I confirmed.

"R-plus check." A red triangle appeared in my vision, the shades painting a marker on Ozma's triangulated location in one of the establishments. A tag, *Aloha!*, floated over it and I wondered if the place's name said anything about the menu.

Jacky—*Mamori*—checked her guns. "Ready to tell us what we might be facing?"

"Not until I've seen them. I've got a catalogue of probables, but I'm not going to prep you for stuff that may not be there."

While we'd shopped Shell had linked to Japan's dark net, found a ronin site that seemed to be a collection of data-files culled from police and intelligence sources. It was mostly public stuff accessible legally, brought together and sorted along with documents (sources unknown) to show patterns and make guesses, but it gave her a chance of identifying our opposition.

"Just—" she added. *"If I tell you to run...run. Okay?"*

Jacky snorted. "Something you want to tell us about?"

"There's something in Golden Gai. Not yakuza, but... I don't know, the place has a reputation. I think the yakuza use it for safe-houses because they really aren't worried about having to fight there. People vanish. Breakthroughs and normals. Nothing in common except they might have been troublemakers."

Just what we needed—we were going to make noise in a place that liked to keep things quiet and might do something to keep it that way. I sighed. "Okay... Are all your camera drones in position?" We'd bought seven for Shell to pilot to strategic locations above the place.

"Ready. I'm holding three to send after you, try for some good look-down on your trail of destruction."

I winced. But her teasing aside, we knew this wasn't going to be neat and pretty. "You're good with the plan?" I asked them one more time.

Jacky gave her holsters a last tug to settle everything. "I clear, you break things, we don't stop moving until we have Ozma and are out. I'm good with that."

Shell didn't say anything; she *wasn't* happy, but it was what it was. We'd renewed our Comprehension Drops in case it went bad (of course it would) and we separated. I had Ozma's box folded up and tucked in a pocket in my sash. With our improvised Dispatch network we were as ready as we were going to be.

I controlled my breathing, building calm. "Do you think she's alright?"

"She's a hundred year old fugitive monarch." Jacky stepped up to the building's edge. "I think she's fine."

"Right." Another breath. Cutter practically vibrated on my back, silent and ready as I adjusted his sheath harness. "Let's go happen to someone."

Chapter Nineteen

On difficult ground, move quickly. On encircling ground, seek opportunity. On desperate ground, fight!

Sun Tzu, *The Art of War.*

You can't always pick the place, the time, or even how much bang you bring. If you've still got to fight, you fight to freaking win.

Atlas

Jacky swapped her shades for Ozma's Anonymity Specs and disappeared into mist, reappeared below in the Golden Gai alley. Shell relayed the view from the camera in Jacky's shades—compensating for the sideways view from where she had tucked them into the front of her costume coat.

   Only a couple of people were using the alley, as expected since it wasn't night yet, and nobody noticed the sudden appearance of a tall figure in a black swirling coat with holstered guns carrying a fish in a crystal sphere. (Really—that was the power of Anonymity Specs; I'd seen them work for Grendel in the middle of a Chicago restaurant, people bumping off of him and not noticing anything except how big he was.)

The view moved as Jacky headed up the alley, following the pointing fish. Halfway up, she stopped in front of the Hawaii-themed café and pushed through a tiki-torch framed door.

The tiny café consisted of a long bar with stools, shelves of bottles behind the scarred old bar. Hawaiian décor covering the walls—mostly posters, carved wood masks and woven mats and (of *course*) little jiggling grass-skirted figures of topless Hawaiian dancers. It was that kind of place.

"The fish is pointing upstairs. I'm going up." Jacky hadn't needed to whisper; the one employee behind the bar didn't even look up. At the end of the long narrow room, stairs on the public side of the bar led up. The only other exit was the door into the kitchen behind the stairs.

I could feel my palms sweating. "Shell, this is a bad idea."

"Got any less bad?"

"...no."

Jacky didn't draw her guns; the bar-guy watching her go up the stairs would ignore her as someone who belonged there—unless she did something overtly threatening; magic had limits.

She stopped at the top of the stairs. *"Shell? Map?"*

"Right." Shell worked her own magic, a dance of data bases and video files. Everyone took pictures everywhere these days, and it was all in the cloud-realm of the internet. Shell sorted thousands of images of Golden Gai, hundreds of Aloha!'s alleyway, and dozens of Aloha!, and built a map of the tiny establishment; the room on the other side of the door had no public images, but it couldn't be more than fifteen by twenty feet and Shell painted it in based on rooms from neighboring bars. Longer than wide, high ceiling.

Down the stairs, the bar-guy finished wiping the counter and went back into the kitchen. The image in my vision shifted as Jacky put away the specs and slipped on her shades, stuck a micro-camera on the wall beside the doorway, uncorked her bottle of wind, drew her guns, and went to mist.

Normally Jacky would have entered the room by flowing under the door. The "little wind" that danced with her now blew her right through it. *"Go go go!"* Shell crowed in my ear. Ozma sat in a chair in the center of the room, unharmed, the door blowing past her and into one of her six guards as Jacky shot through the room in a cloud and reformed opposite the doorway. I launched.

Shell cut the camera feed so I could see where I was going as I arced off the roof and down to punch feet first through the triangle-marked ceiling of our target. She shifted the triangle so that, aiming for it, I came down in the corner of the room in a rain of plaster and wood.

Drawing Cutter, I stepped towards Ozma as Jacky held her guns on the stunned guards and—

The world changed.

The room got a *lot* bigger.

The air filled with the smell of still water.

The walls turned unreal, the shadows of hills behind them.

And the guards weren't stunned at all.

"Oh, shit!"

At least wherever we were, Shell was still with us.

In my months of training from Ajax, he had pounded one rule into me: forget about the movies, because in anything close to an equal fight the one who gets the first solid hit in *wins*. It doesn't matter if the first hit is to the head, body, or limbs, because the shock of the hit breaks the target's focus long enough for the one who scores the hit to get in the *next* hit, and then the next and so on.

And that's just one-on-one; many-on-one makes the first hit equation so much worse. Why? Because if you're one against many you can't hit *all* of them first. You *will* get hit, and if they can take you, they will. So how do you win against multiple opponents?

Winning was relative; in that situation Ajax defined winning as living to fight another day, and his preferred tactic was to *run like hell*.

The yakuza knew what we had done over China. They still thought they could take us. And wherever we were, running didn't look like an option.

Ajax' second choice was *tactical movement*: Move fast, keep moving, put your targets in vectors that blocked each other and only let them close with you singly.

I was moving before Shell finished swearing.

The natural move would be vertical, get above them, but I didn't know what kind of shooters they had and so I just aimed for the biggest target—a massive man in a suit.

He moved too—faster than a normal man that big could—stepping aside to let Cutter slice air an inch from his shoulder but his move put him between me and the rest of them. Bringing Cutter up to the guard position I used with Malleus, I kept the point towards Mr. Big. He didn't attack into my move—instead he *grew*.

Not like Grendel's smooth all-over change; instead he burst his suit one sleeve at a time as his arms expanded and his shoulders widened. His head stayed the same size so that it looked cartoonishly small on his inflating body and he teetered while his legs caught up—I lunged without thinking when I saw the off-balance wobble.

He brushed Cutter aside and touched my shoulder as I passed. *Touched*, not hit, a feather-light contact I barely felt through the shoulder of my coat. The bones in my shoulder tried to explode.

"Hope!" I barely heard Shell through my scream. "*He's a ki-user! Don't let him touch you!*"

"Really?" Chi, ki, qi, focused life force however you spelled it, the go-to breakthrough power for eastern martial artist types.

I flew backward. Behind my ki-monster I could see Jacky flashing point-to-point, dancing in and out of mist to fire at her own targets—a dark-suited yakuza boy who split into multiple sword-wielding attackers, an equally sharp-dressed girl with knee length black hair who *flickered* in and out of sight in short jerking jumps as she tried to come to grips with Jacky...

...and a man-shaped *weasel made of lightning? The hell?*

"Left!" Shell yelled and I ducked left. The air beside me rippled and only my super-duper infrared vision told me what was there—someone flashing by me with wings that sliced the sleeve of my coat in passing. My vision started changing as Shell threw icons up on my shades: the flickering girl was Onryo (*RED*—don't let her touch you), the humanoid lightning-weasel was Raiju (*RED*—don't let him hit you), the near-invisible flyer was Ten (*RED*—don't let her cut you). She labeled Mr. Big *DON'T*, dubbed the multiplying swordsman "Ninja Dude!" and gave the final guard, the older man standing beside Ozma, a question mark.

"Real helpful, Shell!"

"*Sorry! My sources suck!*"

I could practically hear Ajax yelling *Move! Move! Move!* in my head or maybe it was Shell as my world narrowed to Mr. Big. He smiled wide, ran a finger over the column of crossing scars marching down his exposed chest and tapped a smooth spot just above his navel. His kills and my waiting spot, obviously. Knowing that I knew, he went into defensive stance, arms raised to give me the universal *Come and Get It* wave. I *moved*.

I was a spear and Cutter the tip.

Mr. Big brushed Cutter aside again but the block didn't slow me as I let Cutter spin away from my hand and turned my lunge into a punch—fist up to strike with the base of my palm—into his normal-sized head. He went down in an explosion of bone and blood that painted my fist and arm up to my elbow.

That was going to be nightmare-fuel. Recovering Cutter from where he'd stuck in the floor, I spun to try and find Ten.

"Dammit girl, what was that?" Cutter vibrated angrily in my sticky hand.

"Sacrifice move."

"Okay then, but keep it intentional. You don't drop your tools."

"Sorry!" I was arguing with a *sword*—which was better than coming apart over what I'd just done since turning about wasn't showing me *Ten*. Even with my super-duper vision she was nearly invisible unless she was right on top of me. *Move!*

I flew sideways through the center of things, ignoring the hard-faced older guard standing beside Ozma—if he could do something he'd already have joined in. Grabbing her up from where she still sat I placed her behind me as I skidded to a stop across the room. Cutter raised, I pulled her box from my sash and reached back to push it into her hands.

"Thank you."

But I didn't hear the familiar clicking of the box unfolding, didn't hear her move behind me. *Wait—* Her transforming ring was still on her finger, invisible to anyone who didn't know to look for it—so, why? Why hadn't she changed when we'd arrived, brought out her wand and the Magic Belt?

"Ozma—"

And the world flared. *Not* Ozma—Raiju—his dance with Jacky ending where he took a wrong step and her shot caught him between leaping blasts of lightning-form. He fell to the half-real floor of the not-there room we fought in, the lightning that was part of him raging and growing to blinding incandescence—

"Hold!" *Now* the final guard moved, shouting at an empty corner of the room. "Onmiyoji!"

The other yakuza and even Jacky and I froze as the empty corner became occupied by a tall and skeletally thin man in a black kimono—*their* sorcerer—holding an origami paper fan, and *Ozma*, sitting bound in glowing paper strips beside him. The man waved the kanji-covered fan, and the ball of burning plasma Raiju had become went as transparent and ghostly as the walls before disappearing completely. Back into Golden Gai?

"Do not agree with the oyabun." In the sudden silence, the still moment before anybody could think to move, the soft voice in my ear was utterly familiar and I spun to stare at Kitsune.

He—she—wore the face I'd seen once in an elevator; Rei Pascarella, Yoshi's dead granddaughter. But in a touch of whimsy she had added thicker brows and a pencil-thin mustache with a brush of beard underlining her narrow jaw, all blond-white as her hair to show the pale fox peeking through the human face.

And the guard? "The—"

Kitsune nodded. The final, older guard who had stood and watched as I'd "freed" Ozma, was the yakuza clan's *boss*—the oyabun.

I held out my hand for Ozma's box, and she returned it with a wide smirk. Her "Do not," was the ghost of a whisper, only for me.

Do not what? Do not agree with what? And why hadn't the fight recommenced? Jacky stood, guns trained on creepily flickering Onryo, inside a wide circle of ninja swordsmen (not half as many as had started the fight). And nobody moved. *I* hadn't moved except to turn around. I took a step to prove that I could.

The oyabun smiled. "There is no need to fight."

"No, there's not," Jacky growled. Then she *relaxed*. It was like flipping a switch.

She'd agreed. I sucked in a breath as she lowered her guns, schooled my face to Boardroom Polite when the man looked back at me.

"And you, Hikari? Don't you agree that enough blood has been shed?"

It took everything I had to keep from nodding, but I bit my tongue until I tasted blood. How had he overwhelmed *Jacky*? She was a *vampire*—contests of will were her *specialty*...

She hadn't relaxed until she'd *agreed*. Could agreement—even unintentional agreement, be a force-multiplier? Her body-language told me she wasn't even *thinking* about fighting anymore and that was so not-Jacky that it totally freaked me out.

"It's just you and Ozma," Shell whispered through my earbug, and I swallowed, nodding. If the yakuza oyabun had overcome *her* will then she wouldn't be restrained.

"Good." The man smiled and I blinked. What—*oh*. He'd mistaken my nod for agreement with *him*. I made myself straighten up, lower Cutter.

"We do need to talk." *My* intention, not his.

"Yes, we do. Join me?" He grandly waved to the now-empty chair beside him. I stepped forward—not towards him, towards Ozma who happened to be in the opposite corner.

"Shell?" I swallowed again and subvocalized, keeping my lips as still as I could. "The sorcerer with Ozma? His fan?"

"If we're in a magic version of the Littleton Pocket, the fan may be its anchor. Or it could just control a doorway."

Okay. Flip a mental coin? If I guessed wrong would we be any worse off?

Probably not, and as soon as the boss realizes he doesn't have you he can threaten you with Ozma and Jacky. I flexed my fingers on Cutter's hilt, felt him twitch. "The fan, Cutter." My words were a breath and he hummed in answer.

Five more steps and the oyabun frowned—I wasn't *that* great an actor. "Stop—"

I threw Cutter, spinning him end over end and heart-stoppingly close to a calmly watching Ozma, and lunged for the oyabun. "No—" he got out before my hands closed on his tie and I lifted him off his feet. Spinning him in my grasp I kicked the light aluminum chair at spooky, flickering Onryo, and missed.

Cutter didn't miss; a whirling blade, he visibly jinxed in air to both slice the paper wrapping Ozma and neatly bisect the paper fan in the Japanese sorcerer's hand without drawing a drop of blood. The man standing over Ozma staggered back with a strangled cry as the destroyed fan fluttered to the floor in two equal pieces.

Keeping my grip on the oyabun, I tossed Ozma her folded box as she *finally* transformed into a magical-girl in black. Lowering him to the ground, I kept one hand on the tie knot and tugged the narrow end to tighten it against his Adam's-apple.

"I am going to let you talk now." My voice shook—cold and calm as Jacky would have been nice, but barely-under-control was a good threat too. "If you do anything but tell my friend she is free to fight, I will make sure you don't breathe until I feel safe again. If you understand, tap my arm."

The man went deathly pale, and it took me a moment to realize he wasn't looking at me. When I turned to look over my shoulder the golden koi floating beside my head practically touched my nose.

You do not need to fear.

Chapter Twenty

Omega Class: *definition; beyond Ultra Class. Omega Class breakthroughs shatter the accepted scale of powers. Omega Class breakthroughs are ultimate manifestations of their powers, beyond standard means of measurement and equally beyond the power of D, C, B, A, and even Ultra Class breakthroughs to effectively oppose. Omega Class breakthroughs are so rare that encounters with them are largely anecdotal, and most Omega Class breakthroughs appear to no longer be human.*

Barlow's Guide to Superhumans.

I didn't even hear it in my *head*—I just knew it had somehow spoken and what it had said.

You do not need to fear. The golden koi floating by the oyabun's head didn't speak the same words either, but it did. There was no influence in the words, no oppressive weight like the yakuza boss's power, only friendly reassurance, but its little fins idly churned the air and when the tip of its tailfin brushed his cheek he flinched as if burned.

And Jacky stood wound tight and ready again, staring at her own fish. Everyone had one, even my dead ki-pusher.

I let the oyabun go.

He tugged his collar open, loosened his tie. "She has broken your law, Kami-sama! She has killed here!"

And should I / punish her for not taking off her shoes when / she did not know she / had entered my / house? Who brought / her here?

It was a rhetorical question, but as the fish passed their unspoken sentence among them like a ball tossed back and forth, the onmiyoji standing beside Ozma shook so hard I wondered if he was going to collapse. He stared at his own fish like a mouse mesmerized by a snake.

"Shell?" I whispered.

"I think we know what's in Golden Gai now."

"Really? Do you think?" I was going to skin me a cat.

But not everyone / is here / who is here.

Shell dropped into my arms, yowling and spitting. Cutter's weight settled into the harness on my back.

And things / should be neat.

The last shadow of the walls blew away and we stood in the middle of a valley between low purple hills, under a starry sky. The *ground* we were standing on was a frozen pond. More schools of golden koi swam through the air, and silver koi swam beneath the surface of the ice that wasn't ice—it wasn't cold or slick, more like glass pretending to be ice because that's what solid water was.

The silver koi weren't the only things beneath the ice; each burning silver koi swam beside a sunken sleeper. Not corpses—they were alive; I could see them breathing as they slept in their weedy beds.

Bright side, making things neat meant my right arm wasn't bloody up to the elbow anymore and dead ki-guy was gone.

Nor is / deception necessary.

And Kitsune changed from a lightly bearded lady to a gloriously white seven-tailed fox, a glowing ball of white fox-fire floating beside him to match the koi at his other shoulder. Ozma and Jacky were themselves again and a quick tug and peek at my own hair confirmed I was too.

At least Shell was still a cat; we would have looked pretty silly otherwise.

Such interesting / guests. Won't / you introduce yourselves?

I am talking to a fish. If I'd fallen asleep and was dreaming, would I even *know*? Of course I would, because then I'd be talking to a *tree*. Only the thought that laughing at something that scared a sorcerer capable of restraining Ozma might be a Bad Idea kept the giggles in, but the simple request gave me something to focus on. I ignored my incredulous and unhelpful inside-voice, bowing as correctly as I could while holding Shell. "I'm Astra. My companions are Artemis and Ozma. I apologize for our intrusion, please believe that it was not intentional."

It was / intended. Another / brought you and / hid you from / me. He / abuses my offer of / passage.

The onmiyoji pissed himself. I could smell it, the sudden sour reek. I could smell other things too, with my super-duper nose. The pond was the source of the smell of still water from earlier. *Kitsune* had a smell, an aromatic musky scent, stronger now but one I realized I'd smelled before when he'd been Yoshi and Allison. In the middle of the weirdness it made me smile to realize I'd be able to smell him from now on, no matter his form. Or her form.

Focus, Hope. The pretty fish had just made a criminal sorcerer wet himself with terror. "Do my friends and I have safe passage?"

My fish abandoned its float to swim in excited circles.

Perhaps. / So many! You / can win the use of / my doors. A / game. A game / to see what I shall do / with you and with / them!

I blinked, holding Shell tighter. I had not seen that coming, and my eyes darted to Jacky and Ozma. Jacky looked like she wanted to start shooting fish, but her guns pointed nowhere near them. Ozma...

Ozma slowly reached up to lightly tickle her fish's belly. "A game sounds lovely." Her face was a study in pleasant interest. "But we should be allowed to hear the rules before we agree to it, don't you think?"

Her fish wiggled happily.

Of course! / Yes, a / contest to replace such / vulgar fighting. / A trade of things, the / best of each trade winning / the point. The winning / side goes free, the other / to stay with me / and be taught proper / manners.

I barely kept from looking down at the sleepers below us. Not all of them slept soundly. Some of them wore ancient clothing, robes and pantaloons and yukatas, and a couple of them wore samurai armor. How long had *they* stayed?

Ozma smiled at her fish. "Yes, that is very exciting. And who trades? What would the trades be?"

I was perfectly happy to let her take over negotiations—if you could call it that. It sounded more like diplomatic flattery while waiting to hear a victor's terms. Certainly our silent and pasty-faced mob boss didn't seem inclined to jump in.

A trade / of blows! A trade / of power! A trade / of oaths! Yes! I shall / choose which for / each of you. You / shall choose your own / opponents from those / who may match / you! They shall go / first! I will judge! / It will be / splendid fun!

"I see." Ozma's smile remained bright while her gaze touched on me and Jacky in turn. "And the winner gains the privilege of using your doors while the loser remains here to enjoy your company?"

Yes! Some to / go, some / to stay! The terms / and stakes are / agreeable?

What was the alternative? Fight? With no idea what the fish could *do*, all I knew was that they were literally scaring the piss out of people who thought they could handle *us*. With no other cues to go on, I took my lead from Kitsune. He had stayed as silently attentive as his oyabun, but he'd warned me twice already; whatever his game was, it wasn't the same as his boss's.

I nodded. So did Jacky. Shell kept quiet; I hadn't named her and if the fish were happy to treat her as my pet rather than a teammate to involve in the contest, I was okay with that.

"Very well," Ozma approved. "We agree, but we must be clear on the conditions of each contest before choosing our opponents."

Wonderful! / Wonderful! / Wonderful! Every one of our fishes spun about in tail-churning ecstasy. All her hair standing up, Shell hissed at ours. She wasn't talking and I wasn't asking, but whatever this breakthrough we faced was I had to assume she rated it an Omega-Class power. Limited omnipotence? At least inside its own extrareality pocket? The oyabun had called it Kami-sama, *god*; on a scale of one to ten its power might rank at Why Are You Even Asking?

Ozma's fish swam circles around her head. *First! A trade / of power! A / gift! Since only / two can trade / power here your / choice is made / already!* It seemed quite delighted in its cleverness.

Maybe it thought it had tricked her, but Ozma gave it a smile and an acknowledging bow. On the other hand, the onmiyoji looked less like he was going to faint. While Ozma had been negotiating, the yakuza group had gathered around their boss. Giving myself a moment to focus on something other than our god-fish, I gave the oyabun a glance and could tell he'd recovered. He waited, stone-faced and eyes moving between the fish and us.

He probably thought his chances of making it out of here had just gone from zero to fifty-fifty.

Ozma turned to the onmiyoji and gave him a bow as well. "We have not been introduced?"

"Ah." He started, returned the bow. "I am Fourth Wind, Ozma-san."

He had no trouble with her name although he gave it the extra Japanese syllable, *Ozuma-san*. We were Sentinels so everyone at home knew us, but did Japanese sorcerers keep track of powerful gaijin?

"Fourth Wind-san." Ozma bowed again. "It is a pleasure. I believe the first gift is yours?"

"Yes." He stood still, brow furrowed. Ozma might have had no choice, but he had a worse problem. If he knew even a little about Ozma he knew that most of her power was in her charms and enchantments. She carried them with her or shared them with others, and as I'd demonstrated they could be used by anybody who figured out how. So she had a *lot* of things she could gift, from trivial to not-so-trivial, and he didn't dare underestimate her. On the other hand, if *they* won he would have to leave at least one of his tools here. Maybe an irreplaceable one.

Finally he sighed, reaching into his kimono to pull out a small white figurine. An ivory netsuke? It looked like a tightly coiled and sleeping snake.

Holding it in both hands, he breathed on it. And it woke up. "Fly," he whispered, and it did. A tiny white Asian dragon, all scales and furry whiskers, it darted out to swim through the air almost like the golden fish it cheerfully played with before returning to sit upon Fourth Wind's shoulder and wait for instructions.

"Little Dragon can find anyone he has smelled before," the sorcerer told Ozma. "He can smell the approach of magic no matter how disguised, and he is how we found you today. He is incomparably stealthy, and you will be able to see what he sees, hear what he hears. He is also a matchless guardian except when he must sleep."

He stroked the little dragon's furry head. "Go to your new mistress." The beautiful thing rubbed his cheek with its own like a friendly cat, and then launched itself again to fly to Ozma. It circled her twice, hissing at her fish, then settled on her open palm to turn back into a little ivory figurine.

Ozma smiled at it, stroking the ivory. "Thank you. Little Dragon will be cherished." Tucking it into her coat, she unfolded her box and opened it. Placing it in the air in front of her to float like a magician's trick, she widened it and sorted its contents to pull out the little wooden teabox. My stomach sank as she plucked out two of the last three paper packets of Six-Leaf Tea.

She held out her hand, and he accepted them. "A dose of this tea will break any evil enchantment, of any power, laid upon the drinker. It will restore the fundamentally transformed to their natural state. It will restore the weakened to strength and even the deathly ill to vibrant health. It is the master of all natural and magical poisons, all curses, and all death-dealing enchantments."

I sucked in a breath. And she had planned to use the last of her stash just to keep me awake? That was just *wrong*.

"Thank you." The onmiyoji weighed the packets in his hand, looked at his fish. Finally bowing, he smiled ruefully. "Your generosity has defeated me."

Excellent! / Excellent! All our fish practically wiggled with delight.

The insane impulse to do a jumping *Go team Ronin!* cheer was me trying not to think about my turn. A trade of blows? I didn't think anyone here could *survive* a real punch from me. Could I punch—*kill*—someone who just stood and took it? *No.* And a trade of oaths? What exactly was *that*?

And should it bother me that *Kitsune* seemed utterly unconcerned about our side getting the first point? Not that I could read a fox very well—would a nervous one whine like a dog?

Astra! It is / time for your / trade. The trade of / oaths!

I completely froze, not a thought in my head, but Ozma stepped up beside me.

She bowed, somehow exuding apologetic embarrassment. "I am sorry, Kami-sama, we will need some clarification and conditions."

Explain! / Explain! Our fish spun in agitation.

"First, I will assume that the winner is the one who accepts the greater oath?"

Yes! / Yes!

"Then I propose two conditions, in interest of fairness. First, the demanded oath must be performable. Neither party may be required to do something beyond their physical or moral capability. An oath to bring the requester the Moon, for example. Or to kill someone."

Yes! An / unperformable oath is / a forfeit! A performable / oath, unaccepted, is / a forfeit!

"Thank you. Secondly, both we, and presumably whomever Astra chooses to trade oaths with, are bound by our current obligations. Therefore I suggest that any accepted oaths need not be performed here and now—indeed the fulfillment of one oath may have to wait some time if you keep one of them here. So long as they are accepted with the honest intention of fulfilling them once proper conditions are met, that should be sufficient."

All our golden fish froze, fins waving to hold them still beside us. Deep thought? Their stillness lasted only a moment.

Yes! Oaths will / be performed once / conditions are / correct. Once one / is required to fulfill / their oath, the other must / fulfill theirs! / Fair! / Choose!

That was an absolute no-brainer. While I didn't know Kitsune's game, I was hardly going to choose a complete unknown like the oyabun; he could easily pick something I found doable and moral but repugnant. Or... Not knowing me except by reputation, might he accidentally forfeit?

But what, exactly, was the strategy here? My opponent, trying for a win, would go for a requested oath so trivial that my countering request couldn't possibly out-trivialize it. On the other hand, if I chose someone who either wouldn't mind spending some quality time with Kami-sama or who thought he could escape, they might go right for a huge oath and accept the loss. I could be seeing them again next week or in a few years...

Crap. Kitsune probably could escape—he was a kami himself, after all. For that matter I wanted him to so he could help *me*, so the smart move would be one of the others.

A mob boss, a ninja, a bird-girl, or a...whatever she was exactly.

Who could mess you up worst? Huh, smart girl? I had no idea. *Who do you trust most?*

Crap.

"I choose Kitsune."

The white fox *grinned*, its seven tails curling around to wrap its feet. "Marry me."

I dropped Shell. *"What?"*

Chapter Twenty One

Defensenet Report, Kabukicho Alert: As of two minutes ago, the individual who identifies herself as Hikari was observed making a hard-entry into Golden Gai. Given the high level of power and ability displayed by the Three Remarkable Ronin, a Hazardous Situation Alert has been issued in Golden Gai and all available resources have been mobilized.

Defensenet Recommendation: Secure the safety of civilians in the Hazardous Situation zone, secure the Three Remarkable Ronin using any level of force not contra-indicated by the first objective.

DR107-MK [Classified]

Just how many freaking fairy tales am I starring in?

I didn't even think about Shell until she sat in a disgusted heap on my foot and started cleaning herself. She looked up. "Hey, I'm a cat."

I puffed a startled laugh, remembered to breathe.

Ozma stepped close. "You can always forfeit. Artemis can take the last point."

With a trade of blows. I shook my head. I still had no idea what that would mean, and didn't like it. She'd take the blow first. She could lose. She could *die*.

But Kitsune had made the win *easy*. All I had to do was accept his required oath and give him a trivial one. Ask for a single chrysanthemum—even an open ended one-time favor—and then wait for him to get out of here and come looking for me to make good on my promise. He could be stuck here for a hundred years and unless I got myself killed I'd *still* be around waiting for him; Beauty and the Beast, a promised marriage for a rose.

Nope, still not breathing well.

Kitsune wouldn't stop grinning. I couldn't look away.

What could I do?

If I accepted, would he hold me to it? He was an old-fashioned *Japanese* fox; of course he would.

"It's *his* forfeit." Jacky had walked up to my other side without my realizing it, and I nearly jumped out of my skin. "There are laws against that kind of thing." She looked ready to skin herself a fox.

I shook my head again. "Against marrying a kami? I don't think so. It's not like he's an animal—he's a person. Probably a breakthrough who completely identified with the Miyamoto family legend."

"*He*? The first story about 'him' was as a samurai's fox-wife!"

"That's—" I closed my mouth, sighed. "Since he's whatever gender he wants to be it doesn't matter."

"*Dammit*, Hope—" Her fangs were actually growing, making her oddly resemble Grendel at that moment, and her hands twitched like she wanted to pull her guns and start hunting.

But we don't get to choose, whatever we might want. "I—" I closed my mouth. *And things we don't want to do...*

What didn't *Kitsune* want to do?

I didn't know.

What wouldn't a wild spirit like a kitsune want to do? Be unwillingly bound.

"I—" My voice shook but it worked. "I accept. Serve my family."

Ozma actually gasped. Kitsune stopped smiling. Jacky started to snicker as our fish darted about in ecstatic circles, having the time of their weird little lives.

Yes! / Yes! / Yes! / Yes! / Yes!

I held my breath and watched the fox. *Storm-gray eyes*, I realized, blinking. Eyes that narrowed in consideration but not concern. My heart rose into my throat. Would he—

He straightened proudly. "I accept. Well played."

I was pretty sure I was going to faint, or vomit, but our fish were so excited I thought they might explode into raw sushi. Then they froze mid-shimmy, quivering with thought. I started counting heartbeats. Mine, Jacky's, Ozma's... Ozma was calmest.

They finally resumed swimming.

A draw! / A tie! / Splendid! / Splendid! Oh / perfect!

What did that mean? If Jacky lost— I sucked in a hard breath. If Jacky lost then nobody won. One win, one tie, one loss, tied game and nobody went home.

"My turn," Jacky said to her fish.

This was going to kill me, and Jacky didn't seem to care at all.

"My turn, right?" Her fish darted about her head and she didn't bother following it with her eyes. "Pick one, they take their best shot and then it's my turn? Bare hands? Weapons? Can I shoot him?"

You may not use / your firearms, there / is no honor in / them! Swords! / You may borrow!

"Works for me. I pick—"

"One moment," Ozma interjected politely. "To be clear, the one receiving the blow may not attempt to evade or resist it, correct? And may anyone, on either side, assist them after they receive the blow?"

Yes! / Yes! / Yes! / Correct! The shining fish-chorus circled excitedly.

Jacky shrugged. "Are we okay, then?" When Ozma nodded she pointed. "I pick him. The boss-man. Let's see him take his best shot." She didn't bother to bow.

The oyabun glared, but did not object. To be honest, I'd completely forgotten about him; he'd used the grace period of the first two contests to collect himself, and if it wasn't for his racing heartbeat he'd have fooled me into thinking he was cool, calm, and even angry at Jacky's rudeness.

His heartbeat told a different story, but then so did mine; as he took off his tailored silk coat, rolled up his sleeves, and accepted the sword held out by his tame ninja, I tried to convince myself that Jacky wasn't about to die.

Because she could—maybe not *die* die, but something worse for her.

Jacky was a vampire—she had died once already and risen as an undead creature of the night, and she'd told me once that something that died and rose was very hard to kill permanently. She'd even told me about one time in New Orleans when another vamp had *cut her head off* and she'd reawakened once it had been put back on her shoulders and the wound was given a few minutes to "heal."

But could she do that now? "Jacky..." I whispered.

Her hearing wasn't quite as sharp as mine but it was still preternatural and she heard me. A headshake was all she gave me, and my heart lodged in my throat; she knew my concern. Just three weeks ago, after a night-fight that had gotten unexpectedly desperate, she'd let me see her greatest fear.

Jacky's years of being on a purely liquid diet had made her as much a beer snob as a coffee snob, so that night I'd followed her to her rooms and sat and matched her drink for drink while she downed glass after glass of Porter's double chocolate stout, Kona coffee stout, and DuClaw's Sweet Baby Jesus (a peanut butter chocolate stout that tasted like a Reese's Peanut Butter Cup and was so thick and creamy you could almost chew it). With my superhuman recuperative ability it took lots of hammering shots of hard liquor to get me drunk (and even then it wore off fast), but beer couldn't even give me a buzz so I'd still been completely sober when she'd loosened up enough to relax and actually *share*.

And I'd learned that my stone-cold and relentless BF's greatest fear was dying *again*.

Back when we'd fought Villains Inc., we'd been present when Doctor Cornelius had used his Word of Healing—a Word supposedly given to him by The Source, a word more metaphysically real than reality and which he couldn't use again because it was gone from his head. The Word had not only brought Orb back from being freshly dead, it had brought Jacky back from being *un*dead to fully alive; after years of "living" with a liquid diet and a severe allergy to direct sunlight she'd become a *daywalker*, able to experience all the joys of living again.

Jacky was fully alive, now, but if she died again, without that Word could she come all the way back on her own? Or would she rise as an undead fiend of the night again? No pulse, no heartbeat, no breath except to speak, cold as the grave when not full of stolen blood. Forever.

She didn't think she'd be able to live with that. Not again.

But Jacky had obviously watched at least one Japanese historical drama somewhere, and knew what the situation called for. While the oyabun prepared and I silently freaked out for her, she gathered up her hair to let it fall forward over her face and leave her neck bare, then opened and pulled down her high coat collar. When the yakuza boss stepped forward on her right side she knelt, resting on her toes and balancing forward over her widely spaced knees, hands laid on her thighs.

It was the image of the ancient *seppuku* ceremony, honorable ritual suicide—here going straight to decapitation without the first step of voluntary self-disembowelment.

Ozma grabbed my elbow before I realized I was moving, and my own shock stopped me.

"Trust her. And trust me."

And the oyabun actually hesitated. I couldn't imagine what was going through his head. He was about to strike a fellow superhuman, and he didn't know the full extent of her powers. Since she was *letting* him, she had to be insane or insanely confident she'd get her turn. Was that *smart*?

I started praying.

He stepped up behind Jacky's shoulder. "Are you ready?"

She shrugged. "Don't mess up my hair."

For a breath-catching moment I thought he wasn't going to do it—then he raised the blade high over his head, planted his feet, and struck with a shout.

Jacky's head fell to the pond surface in a spray of red and Shell stopped cleaning herself. "Now that's just every kind of wrong."

The air left my lungs without a sound, but I was already moving. So was Ozma. If the oyabun hadn't moved he'd have been flung to the ground as I flew forward, and as Jacky's headless body slumped I reached around her and grabbed her head. Reaching us, Ozma grabbed Jacky's shoulders and pulled her back and down to lie on the surface of the pond.

"Wait," she said before I could hold Jacky's head to her blood-leaking neck. She'd folded and put away the magic box, but reaching into her sash she pulled out the last paper packet of Six-Leaf Tea. Neatly ripping it open, she sprinkled the fine-crushed leaves over every inch of the gory stump with impressive speed and precision. "Now."

I pushed Jacky's severed ends together, holding her by the sides of her head and trying not to feel the rough shock of her neatly bisected vertebrae rubbing against each other. Ozma felt around her neck with steady hands and corrected my position a fraction of an inch while I closed my eyes and listened for a heartbeat while counting seconds.

Nobody moved. Not the oyabun, not Shell, not Kitsune. Even the fish were still. The human brain can survive without oxygen for only minutes. Did Jacky's vampiric state add to that at all? I didn't know, tried not to think of anything but holding still. One minute, two, and my cheeks were wet.

Please, please come back alive. Please. If you don't then you'll hate me and I'll hate me, and it's not going to be any fun.

Jacky's first strangled gasp lifted her chest and pulled her head from my grip. She reached back to claw for my reaching hands, grabbing them in a crushing hold as she choked, coughed, and filled her lungs again and I heard the first powerful beat of her heart. She kicked against the pond surface beneath us, bowing her back and spasming repeatedly before slumping, head on my knees, to just breathe.

"Sh-shit." She choked and spat. "That was worse than the last time. Hurts more when you're alive."

"Serves you right—you're not the Green Freaking Knight! You scared the *crap* out of me." It was all I could do not to pull her up into a front-to-back hug and never let her go. I could listen to her heart forever.

She barked a laugh—probably shocked by my near-obscenity—and coughed and spat again, lips red with her own bright blood. Our hands were tacky with it. Her own fish darted down to lightly touch her red-stained neck.

Things should be / neat. And suddenly she was, nothing but a thin red line on her pale skin to show where she'd come in two. My hands were just as clean, my cheeks were dry, and I couldn't smell the onmiyoji's little accident or my own rancid fear-sweat either. The ice shown spotless where Jacky's blood had pooled. Total reality control, and the fish used it to keep their little world clean and tidy.

I started laughing, couldn't stop.

"Can I get up now?" Jacky asked from my lap. When I let go of her hands she pulled herself up before I could help, turned her head side to side. "*That's* never going to get old."

I stopped laughing. "Don't you *dare*—" Biting off the rest, I took a breath. "Twice is a career limit. *Promise* me."

My fish rubbed my cheek and I jumped, spun to look at the little golden koi. It ignored me to watch the oyabun. All of the fish were. When Jacky stood I did too, staying close behind her, and when she looked back at me her smile was evil and her fangs were out.

"Let me borrow your little knife?"

"Are you going to kill him?"

"If he's stupid enough to get on his knees." She hefted Cutter. Her preternatural strength wasn't close to mine but I'd seen her pick up a three hundred pound man and dangle him by his throat; she could do the job of swinging Cutter's hundred pounds for at least one good executioner's blow. "Stopping me?"

"No." The skin of my face felt like ice, and she stopped balancing Cutter to search my eyes.

I understood. I *did*. He'd *cut her head off*. She could have died and not come back, or worse for her come back halfway. And it was the deal—a blow for a blow. How could I tell her that, as much as holding her severed head in my hands was going to contribute to today's nightmare fuel, seeing her kill a man in cold blood was going to be so much worse?

Whatever she saw in my face, she nodded. "Okay." Resting Cutter on her shoulder she turned to the others. The mob boss stood talking to his pet onmiyoji.

Then / we are ready! The / final trade!

The oyabun nodded agreement, stone-faced. The sorcerer stepped up beside his boss, one of the Six Leaf Tea packets in his hand. I wanted to laugh hysterically. They'd watched that horrible scene, the oyabun had felt Jacky's head come off under his borrowed blade, and they'd *lost*; even if his man could do for him what Ozma had done for Jacky, the best they could hope for was a draw—which still meant a win for us. So, *why*?

He's hoping Jacky can't do it. My trapped laugh became a strangled choke. *Or that I'll stop her.*

His gamble was breathtaking—hoping that we weren't as ruthless as he was, that we'd forfeit. Sure we'd killed two of his men, but that had been in a *fight*; we were killers, could we be murderers?

The man bowed to Jacky, with a smirk as he showed her how it was done, and knelt. Adjusting his position, he nodded to her. My palms ached where my nails bit into them.

"One moment." Ozma held up her hand, actually managing to look apologetic.

Yes? / Yes? / Yes?

"I feel that I should inform my colleague—" She bowed to the onmiyoji. "The tea treatment may not be so effective for your employer. Our friend has supernatural healing powers which, on their own, have saved her before. The tea may have sped the process considerably, but for your employer…"

"It may not be enough." The rail-thin man studied the packet in his hand, returned Ozma's bow. "Thank you for your warning. The choice remains my oyabun's."

The mob boss grunted without looking up. "Get on with it." But his shoulders relaxed minutely and I choked down my unthinking protest. He'd taken Ozma's warning as a ploy to shake him, which meant he really didn't think Jacky could do it.

But Jacky wouldn't risk a forfeit. Maybe for herself, but not for Ozma and me. She wouldn't risk it.

She was going to do it.

And I was going to watch, because she deserved that from me.

I stopped breathing, opened my hands. I wasn't going to hurl. I wasn't going to move again until it was over. Then… I'd keep it together until we were out of here, until everyone was safe. And I'd find someplace I could be alone to deal with it without putting it on Jacky.

Jacky's mouth moved, and I could have heard her but I wasn't listening to anything but the rush of my blood. And she swung.

Blood sprayed, the oyabun's head rolled as his body slumped—and then it didn't. I blinked, gasping, and for one moment thought he'd pulled a Detective Fisher *reset*. No. No, my memory told me what had happened; I'd anticipated the awful moment so strongly that I'd virtually hallucinated it but there was no severed and rolling head and slumping corpse. Jacky had drawn in, sliding on her back foot as she'd swing to shorten the reach of her swing, and Cutter had kissed the yakuza boss's neck with only the barest flick of blood to leave a long red cut right over the spot where Jacky would normally make her bite.

It barely bled, a thin red line to show where she had made her mark instead of a kill.

Done! / Done! / Done! / Done! / Done! / Done! / Done! / Done! / Done! / Done! The fish danced an ecstatic gavotte.

My hands shook. I shook. Jacky had *forfeited*? Why?

You / have / won! Our three fish gleefully announced. Ozma burst out in a beautiful, musical laugh.

She shook her head, laughing at Jacky and an increasingly red-faced oyabun.

"That is not possible!" All of his stone-faced stoicism had vanished. "I delivered the greatest blow! This gaijin could not do it! She barely even scratched me!" He swiped at his neck.

The fish were hardly insulted, and didn't stop dancing. *Yes! / Yes! / Yes! / All trades / same!*

Ozma's laugh tapered off, but only because she considered excessive laughter improper. I had to look as confused as Jacky and the rest. Even Shell wasn't talking.

She knows! / She knows! / She knows!

Jacky handed me Cutter, reached out with supernatural speed to grab her fish. *Everybody* froze.

"No more games," she told it. "Or I'm going to see if you taste like tuna."

Her fish laughed at her.

The gifts! / The oaths! / The blows! / The victor in / each the more / generous / giver!

Wait, what— Oh. *I* started laughing. It wasn't fair to Jacky—I could see in her face that she'd risked everything to draw a tie, both of them surviving their traded blows, and she had *no* idea.

"Ja—Artemis, the *sorcerer* said it."

"Said *what*?"

"He said 'Your *generosity* has defeated me.'" Ozma had given most generously. Kitsune had required an oath he could wait forever to ask me to keep and I'd done the same. The oyabun had tried to take Jacky's life and she had generously spared his.

Yes! / Yes! / Yes! And so / you are / free! The others / and I have / much to do! / Goodbye!

"What—wait!" But all of our companion fish flared, blinding. I blinked desperately. "Wait! We need—"

We stood in a smoking crater surrounded by the steel and concrete towers of Kabukicho.

We were our magical-girl in black Japanese selves again.

We didn't have Kitsune.

"YOU ARE ALL UNDER ARREST!"

And we were surrounded.

Chapter Twenty Two

I've been arrested a couple of times. Neither time involved my "resisting arrest" even though one of those times had been a dangerous mistake. Why not? Because when you're a breakthrough capable of doing significant collateral damage—forget about potentially fatal harm to the proper authorities attempting to arrest you—then you resist the authorities only if it looks like they're trying to kill you and have a good chance of doing it.

Astra, *21st Annual Metrocon, Police Relations Presentation.*

It was *nighttime*, and I'd deal with that later; I couldn't see all of them behind the spotlights, but the uniforms I could see told me we were looking at capes from the Eight Excellent Protectors and their male counterparts, the Nine Accomplished Heroes. Overkill, much?

But I'd been ready for this all day. "Kimiko, can you manage one transformation?" Ozma nodded. "Break away, now."

"DO NOT MOVE!"

Ozma vanished as Jacky scooped Shell up, and I saw a flash of emerald-green appear around her furry neck before Jacky disappeared into mist with her, whisking them all away in a rush of unbottled wind.

"DO NOT MOVE!"

"Cutter? How hard can you grip something?"

"Let me bite, girl, and I won't let go."

"Good. Stay *here*." I drew and thrust him into the exposed rock at the bottom of the blast crater in one smooth motion, driving him in to just below his hilt. The two-handed move brought me to my knees and I stayed there, clasping my hands behind my head.

I hoped they'd appreciate my showing initiative.

Blacklock sells its line of heavy-duty superhuman restraints in Japan, too, and two obvious heavy lifters dropped out of the night and the spotlight glare to do me up with a very familiar rig before anybody else got close. I knew I should watch their moves, guestimate what they could do in case I had a chance to actually fight them later, but I didn't much care. They'd be too professional for that, and I was just done.

Why fight? Whatever cell they put me in, I was going to exit through a metaphysical trapdoor soon enough anyway, leaving nothing but a mystery behind.

How do you restrain someone who can punch a hole in a tank? Material strength is only half the secret; Blacklock wrist-cuffs are narrow titanium bands connected by even stronger cables, they're not padded *anywhere*, and the shackles have an inside edge on them. Cuffing my wrists behind my back, the two securing me ran a narrow cable from the cuffs up and around my neck, and then attached ankle-cuffs of the same design with their short cable connected to my wrist-cuffs.

That locked me into a kneeling position, hands behind my back, and if I tried to straighten my arms or legs I'd garrote myself on the neck cable before I broke the shackles. If I tried to break the cables joining my wrists I'd dislocate or disarticulate them before the cables broke. What was to keep me from flying away? After they secured the shackles they lifted me out of the crater and onto a heavy truck with an iron box on a concrete bed, attaching my ankle and neck cables to its locking clamp; sure I could lift the truck—but by my neck? I'd crush my windpipe. More narrow neck-cables locking me to the frame of the box ensured that pulling side-to-side would have pretty much the same result.

(Yes that left me inhumanely immobilized, but with superhumans you had to make allowances. I'd been on the other side of this drill before.)

After locking me in tight, they removed my earbugs and shades, ran security wands over me to find any other gadgets, and closed me up in the dark. *Let the psychological warfare begin.* The heavy truck lurched smoothly into motion and I laughed, hoping I confused or scared whoever was listening.

Because I'd lost. Kitsune was trapped in whatever weird little extrareality pocket we'd just played our games in, and now we didn't even have a chance of going back to ask the game-playing fish if we could borrow the sneaky fox for a moment—or even play a second game for him. So sooner or later, I was going to go to sleep and fall down the rabbit hole.

Would I ever make it home?

But that wasn't my problem now; *now* my problem was making sure that Defensenet didn't figure out who I was, because if I could just hold out until I pulled my disappearing act then none of this would blow back on Jacky or Ozma. They'd be able to get themselves home, and our little adventure wouldn't wreck their careers. They'd be able to tell Mom and Dad what had happened to me.

And Japan could just suck it.

I took the opportunity of the quiet (the box was soundproofed) to review what I knew about my situation. It was illegal for Japanese citizens to not register breakthrough powers with their government, and since I wasn't registered they could detain me indefinitely until they were sure I wasn't a threat. Normally this meant testing and registering me *involuntarily* if they had to—but since they'd almost certainly checked our faces against their citizen database and *we didn't exist*, they had to already know they couldn't even do that. I was Hikari, mystery-girl.

So they'd have to interrogate me until I gave them what they wanted. Japan was a civilized country, so "interrogate" didn't mean "torture," but there were lots of ways of breaking me down that didn't involve extreme physical or mental trauma if they were patient and had the time.

I giggled in the dark. They didn't.

Who knew the prospect of falling asleep and getting sucked into an extrareality realm would become the light at the end of my tunnel?

The truck eventually stopped for good, and then I felt the whole box lurch. Dismountable? I pictured them sliding my box into a wall of them. Another lurch and an echoing bang, shaking me hard as they locked the box in, confirmed my guess.

And then it was quiet again. I wondered when they'd come and talk. They'd secured me facing away from the openable wall of my box so I wouldn't be able to see them until they moved around in front—but that would be hard for them to do with the small space and all the cables attached to me. Did the wall in front of me open too? How long would they give me to sit in the dark and work myself up before they began? If this was the movies, they'd start with blinding lights and disembodied voices. Something to look forward to, but if they decided to take it slow I might go to sleep before they started at all.

I was *so* going to hug that tree.

I was wondering why it was *nighttime* outside (did time go slower in the fish's little extrareality pocket?) when I felt the tickle in my mind and almost garroted myself.

Crap crap crap crap crap! They weren't waiting to try and debrief or interrogate me, they'd brought in a freaking *telepath*! I started hyperventilating, forced slower breaths, counted them—a good start to build on. *Fight time.* I began singing in my head. *No backing down, no giving in—I pick my fights but I fight to win. Though the Reaper draws near me I cry, CONQUER OR DIE!*

I love the classics.

Mindreading isn't a common Psi-Type power—it's seldom survival oriented and wannabe-breakthroughs pushing for psi powers usually wind up with telekinetic gifts or at best mental manipulation—but after last month's Littleton adventure we'd all been deemed to know enough government secrets that the Department of Superhuman Affairs had sent experts to give us the counter-psi training course. That was on top of the exercises for detecting mental manipulation that Chakra had already taught me.

It had really seemed a government exercise in paranoia at the time, but I was desperately grateful for it now—because while mind-reading was illegal in most situations (a criminal invasion of privacy *at least*), it *was* legal if circumstances warranted. Very, very narrow circumstances, usually involving national security.

And apparently they thought I was a threat to national security.

But it's not like on TV—a mind-reader can't just rifle through your memories like a computer file index. What they really do is piggyback their mind's-eye to yours (thus the "tickle" as the space in your head gets a little bigger). It's like planting cameras in a room and then watching remotely as the room's occupants put on a show; so the trick is to let them see and hear only what you want them to.

You can even fight back.

In training I'd chosen *Conquer or Die* by Have No Fear as my mental soundtrack of choice and karaoke'd to it until I could sing it in my dreams. The half-shouted lyrics, with the full throated scream on *CONQUER OR DIE!*, could give any mindreader a migraine if he listened too long, and I could keep it up for hours. If my mind started to drift, I could just keep replaying the awesome music video in my head.

And I could give my viewer more fun stuff to deal with; now was as good a time as any to take care of my own mental hygiene.

Because I'd killed a man today. I'd *had* to. Just like with Ripper and Volt in the Dark Anarchist's "supervillain's lair," I'd been faced with someone too fragile to take a real hit from me—but who could have taken *me* given the least chance. My shoulder still throbbed and ached where Ki-Guy had brushed it, and I was willing to bet that if Doctor Beth took x-rays right now he'd find hundreds of tiny microfractures all through it.

Ki-Guy had seen me flying and swinging Cutter like a toothpick, he'd seen me survive one of his own ki-pushing attacks that probably would have exploded a normal person's shoulder into bits of bone and red mist, and he'd *still* taunted me to come at him. Now I focused on that, replaying the scene in my head and hoping that the scarification art he'd flaunted had really meant what I'd thought it had; that he'd killed before and wanted me for another "notch on his gun."

Because if he hadn't…

Doctor Mendell had taught me the technique—replaying potentially traumatic memories while performing breathing exercises and calmly de-stressing them, deconstructing them and putting them into perspective. If I did the exercise soon enough after a bad situation, it helped detoxify it in my brain and lowered the chance of it becoming new nightmare-fuel.

And tonight for an added bonus, it couldn't be fun for my "watcher" either.

The tickling went away before I'd cycled through three singing playbacks and detoxifying episodes, and I started giggling again. You wouldn't think it was so bad for the poor baby, but "listening quietly" meant he had to suppress his own thoughts and focus solely on mine. He had to ride them with me, helpless passenger on my thrill-ride rollercoaster, and the only thing he'd learned was I'd killed somebody and knew an American hero-pop song.

With him gone, I finally gave in to the luxury of trying to figure out what the hell had happened in Golden Gai. Not with the fish—that was just a bucket of crazy—but with our attack and ambush.

They'd known we were coming, or had a pretty good idea that we would. Which meant that they'd been confident that we could track them somehow, or at least track Ozma. But they'd also been confident they could handle us, and we'd taken two of them even before I'd broken the onmiyoji's fan. I'd captured the yakuza *boss*. And Kitsune might have been working with them, but he'd warned me of the boss's power. If the fish hadn't shown up, that by itself might have turned the ambush into a win.

When the moves don't make sense, someone is playing a game you don't understand. So, whose moves stood out? Kitsune's. The yakuza boss would have been insane to set all that up, and make himself part of it, if he hadn't been totally confident that they could handle us. But the Three Remarkable Ronin had only been in one public fight so far, so we had to have been almost complete mysteries to them—unless someone *recognized* us. That would have been Kitsune.

But if Kitsune's goal had just been for us to win and escape, he could have warned us before Ozma got snatched. Heck, he could have simply told his boss we were too tough to safely mess with and to leave us alone.

So he'd *wanted* the fight. Why?

If I hadn't destroyed the fan, if the crazy fish had never known we were *there*, we might have won. We'd been *winning*. With the boss in my hands, we'd have made them take us back to Golden Gai...and we'd have taken Kitsune with us.

Could he be *that* sneaky? And if he was, then *why*?

It hardly mattered now, but my spinning thoughts kept me busy and I lost all track of time in the silent dark. When the wall in front of me dropped into the floor I jumped, tightening my neck cables painfully as the floor of my box slid out into a new room.

It was a cell, and the shackles at my wrists and ankles unclamped as I blinked against the dim light. A moment's exploration showed me that the primary neck cable had unclamped from the floor as well, and with hands free it took me less than a minute to free myself completely. It took me another minute to stop shaking and uncramp enough to climb to my feet.

The frame I'd been attached to slid back into the wall when I stood. Closed up, it left me in a completely featureless cube. I didn't get much time to get used to it before a soft female voice made me nearly jump to the ceiling. "When you have cleaned and changed, food will be provided. Place your clothing in the box." The *box* slid out of the bare room's wall, open at the top like a cabinet drawer. Looking in, I found underwear and a red jumpsuit.

The voice repeated. "When you have cleaned and changed, food will be provided. Place your clothing in the box."

Looking around I couldn't see any place to *clean*.

"Place your clothing in the box."

Right. Was humiliation part of their technique? I pulled out the clothes they'd provided for me and set them on the floor, and then stripped. Everything went in the box: black coat, pants, sash and sword-harness, boots, underwear; everything but Ozma's "invisible" magical-girl transforming ring. Finishing, I stepped back and held my breath. Would they "see" the ring? Demand it too?

The box pulled back into the wall, and two more niches opened up, one revealing a showerhead and the other containing soap, bath brushes, and towels. A drain opened in the floor. *Okay.*

I covered the underwear and jumpsuit with the towels, and showered. Finishing as fast as I could, I dried myself and dressed, then dried the floor. The now-empty box slid back out and I fed it the wet towel. Everything closed up again, and a niche in the opposite wall opened to reveal a tray of food and a bottle of water.

"Eat, and return the bottle and tray."

Since the room didn't provide a table or chair, I took the tray and bottle and sat on the floor. Rice, spicy beef balls, sliced cucumbers and an apple. Disposable wood chopsticks. I ate slowly, drank all the water, and put the bottle and tray back. They disappeared.

"Do you need to use the toilet?"

"Yes, please." I hoped they couldn't see my blush. They probably could. The niche I'd expected opened to present a prison-style metal toilet and sink combination. At least they provided paper, soap, and a hand towel. I finished fast, washed thoroughly, and stepped away to let it close up.

"Prepare your bed. The light will turn out in five minutes."

A low niche next to the meal niche popped open, and I found a futon and pillow inside. No blanket. Well, the temperature in the cube was comfortable enough even for someone who wasn't me. I laid out the futon and pillow, lay down to look at the ceiling, and let my mind drift until the lights went out. I took their word that it had been five minutes.

To sleep, perchance to dream...

But I didn't dream.

Episode Four

Chapter Twenty Three

Superhuman containment is almost always a major effort, especially for the higher classes. Some superhumans can be contained with merely reinforced rooms; others require non-physical measures. Ironically, superhuman security—both containment measures and intrusion countermeasures—is one of the major fields of both Verne-Type science and invention and Merlin-Type enchantments.

DSA Security Brief: Superhuman Capture and Containment.

The spike of pain woke me, a flare of agony from my shoulder when I rolled onto my side. Pushing myself up, I yelped and pulled my left arm away from the floor to hold it against my stomach. Hunching around it, I clamped my jaws to hiss out a long breath instead of a scream.

Ki-Guy had hurt me more than I thought; it felt like *serious* soft-tissue damage, and hurt worse than it had last night. Something was wrong—this wasn't the way my body healed.

And though I couldn't see a thing in the pitch black, the futon under me and the closed air around me made it obvious that I was I was still in my cube. Painful breaths turned into panicked ones. Why was I still here? I'd been *ready*.

You're in a cage for superhumans, duh.

I tried to bury that thought, but it wouldn't die; I was being held by *Defensenet*—they dealt with monsters of strength, transformers, teleporters, ki-users, telepaths, and *spirits*. I was so obviously in a super-security cell that I was willing to bet that, behind the reinforced walls, my cube sat inside a Verne-Type's version of a Faraday Cage. Of *course* it was proof against any kind of external influences or intrusion—material, spiritual, psychic, or metaphysical. Impenetrability worked *both* ways and the tree hadn't been able to find me here. Probably even *Ozma* couldn't find me here.

Indefinite detention. I wasn't escaping this, even into another world.

When I could breathe again I realized I'd flown myself into a corner, curled up tight in the dark. Forcing myself to straighten my legs, I focused on my shoulder and Chakra's breathing exercises.

Okay, how bad was this? They couldn't just keep me in this room forever; they had to *process* me. Open a file. Classify me. Level criminal charges if it came to that. Or did they? They could just be holding me while they tried to catch up with Jacky and Ozma. They wouldn't—Ozma had her magic box full of toys and if they hadn't found us before they wouldn't find them now. But—

Oh. Oh, God. Sometime today the Comprehension Drops were going to wear off and they were going to learn at least one thing about me; I couldn't really speak Japanese.

And they weren't *stupid*; knowing that I'd been "enhanced" by magic in one way, they'd look for other ways. How long would it take for their sorcerers, onmiyoji, whatever, to test me and figure out Ozma's little race-bending bibbity-bobbity-boo? Reverse it?

I wouldn't be able to keep any secrets at all.

I had no idea how long I sat there, the chain of horrible sequences in my head crushing any coherent thought. The lights coming on broke my mental paralysis.

"Food will be provided when you put away your bed."

"I am injured." I had to force the words out. The voice didn't repeat and I counted breaths.

"Turn around and place your hands and feet in the indicated spaces." Another low section of wall slid up to show four slots ringed in yellow-and-black banded paint. They were spaced so that I could kneel and move back to push my hands and feet into them behind me and be clamped to the wall.

"Turn around and place your hands and feet in the indicated spaces."

I stared at brightly marked holes, realized I was breathing too fast again. I *couldn't*. I'd let them shackle me last night, but I couldn't— I *couldn't* do it for them. I'd be helpless again, locked into metal and concrete and now I didn't know when it would end.

My arms and legs felt numb, like I'd shatter into a million pieces if I tried to move.

"Turn around and place your hands and feet in the indicated spaces."

"I can't."

"You will not receive treatment until you have secured yourself."

"I can't."

...

"Turn around and place your hands and feet in the—"

"No!"

"Turn around—"

"No! No! No!"

If I stopped talking, if I stopped responding, they wouldn't know when I stopped being able to understand commands. But I couldn't focus forever, couldn't keep their mindreader away from my secrets indefinitely. They didn't have to play games—they just had to be patient and there was no move I could make that would turn this into a win. I'd lost.

Slapping the tears from my cheeks, I pulled myself further into the corner, ignoring my screaming shoulder to scrub my face again when the waterworks wouldn't stop, and locked my jaw like I was biting air. They weren't going to hear a thing—no more words, no protests, no whining or crying. Whatever they took, I wasn't going to just *give* it to them.

I half-expected them to turn the lights off again, but they didn't. They didn't do anything, and after silent minutes I rubbed my eyes and studied the walls, looking for anything that might indicate weak points. They'd let me loose in here knowing pretty much what I could do, so the cube had to be strong enough to hold me. They'd certainly have some way of stopping me before I could get more than a few hits in anywhere—but if I didn't *try*, they'd win.

They'd win anyway, but not until I let them. *So let's see what countermeasures you've got.* It sounded weak even in my head, the defiant hiss and spit of a kitten, but I came out of the corner and hit my picked spot.

Pain flashed through my fist and through my opposite injured shoulder just from the jarring, but the reinforced concrete cracked and caved. My second hit pushed in as something in the wall broke. My third hit— I screamed against the fire that poured through my bones, sucked air, screamed again, and got in one more hit before the world went away.

This time I woke up with the lights on. My fist hurt, my shoulder throbbed, and every nerve ached with the residual memory of pain. *Some kind of neural attack.* A hit right to my central nervous system? It had to be built into the room; I'd seen no visions of the tree in the darkness in my head, there'd been no slipping away into another awareness like when the bratva supervillain had kicked me in the head. That meant they hadn't had to turn off the Faraday Cage for it; I had to think that if the room had been "unsealed" when I'd lost consciousness—

I giggled painfully; if the room *hadn't* been sealed then I might have vanished like a popped soap-bubble, become a totally freakish escape from their super-security cube the instant I passed out. Vomited and passed out; I was covered with it.

At least it wasn't breakfast.

Forcing myself to sit up, I clapped a hand over my mouth as nausea spun my head, dropped back to the floor.

"Turn around and place your hands and feet in the indicated spaces."

"No."

Lying with my good arm over my face I cycled through my catalogue of memorized songs. Not for the mindreader but to stop thinking. I also tried not to smell myself; I reeked.

And my shoulder was getting more sensitive to the least movement. Was it still morning? I supposed the voice would let me know; if I didn't understand the next command, it would be sometime in the afternoon.

"Good morning, Hikari-san." It was a new voice, a male voice. "I will be visiting with you shortly. Before I do, would you like to clean yourself up and eat?"

I uncovered my eyes. "Yes. Thank you."

"Splendid. Please do not linger."

The niche for the futon opened and I folded it quickly as I could one-handed. The clothing drawer and shower niches appeared, and I pulled the fresh clothes before painfully stripping and shoving the filthy jumpsuit in to be taken away. I didn't linger with the shower, but got all of my dinner off my skin and washed away the panic-sweat. Painfully climbing into the fresh red jumpsuit boosted my morale one hundred percent—a boost that wouldn't last but made me smile anyway.

Breakfast was *exactly* the same ramen bowl I'd had for breakfast that first morning in Shibushi—ramen noodles in broth, pork, bamboo, seaweed, and the soft-boiled egg. I was able to hold the bowl on my knee with my left hand (my left shoulder had *no* strength in it at all) while I used the chopsticks on the bigger bits and slurped the noodles.

Finishing the bowl and putting it away, I didn't have to wait long; a section of wall opposite the side I'd come in through last night slid aside to expose a shallow niche filled with a door sized flat-screen. The man on the screen, a nondescript Japanese man in a black business suit you might see in any office, sat *seiza*-style, kneeling behind a low table. A single file sat on the table in front of him.

I blinked. Was he being polite? He wouldn't want to stand for a long conversation, and if he'd sat at a regular table either he'd loom or the view screen angle would make our face-to-face rather odd. Sitting as he did put us at eye level when I folded my legs under me and rested my throbbing shoulder back against the wall.

"Good morning, Hikari-san," he said again. "Do your injuries require immediate treatment?"

"I—I think they might."

"Then when our business is finished here I shall see that you get it, regardless of what is said. Will you object to donning a somnolence cap if necessary so that they can safely examine and treat you?"

They. Distancing himself from my keepers? Or was he being correct and not part of this installation? He waited for me to say something.

"No. A cap will be fine. I could use more sleep." It was stupid—there was no difference between immobilizing myself with their wall-shackles and putting myself out with a cap, but looking at him I could actually breathe and agree to the option.

He nodded. "That is good to hear, and I will try not to take too long. I am Agent Inoue, and I have had the task of understanding and capturing you from the moment we learned of your fight with Heavenly Dragon. We have followed your steps back to your first arrival in Japan."

I managed not to wince; I'd really known that looking at my breakfast—it had been an easy message to read. Since he seemed to expect something I tried a polite question of my own. "I hope nobody is in trouble? And may I ask what your power is?"

"A certain Heroes Without Borders base supervisor has been warned that his operations will be watched more closely. And I am a clever little monkey."

I smiled. I couldn't help it, he reminded me of Veritas. "So you're not the telepath who intruded earlier?"

"No. He went to bed last night with a severe headache."

"Well, better luck next time." I was lying my ass off; I'd won last night, but I wasn't confident and focused anymore and one slip would blow it.

"I do not think so." If Agent Inoue saw how much I didn't want that, he ignored it, opening the file in front of him. "There was not complete agreement concerning his employment in your case, and I do not think he will be used again. Shall I call you anything other than Hikari?"

"No." I shook my head, carefully, trying to remember the sessions I'd had on interrogation techniques. *And now he suggests he knows more than he does.*

"Very well, then. Hikari-san, you remain a complete mystery and one I do not have the time to solve."

"I—I'm sorry?" That so wasn't the program.

"I know that you, and your partners, are tactically powerful superhumans. Your companion, Mamori, is superhumanly strong and able to transform herself into a gaseous form. These are two powers that do not normally appear in the same configuration, leading me to suspect that she is something much more than that, but that is idle speculation. Your other companion, Kimiko, appears to be a sorceress and yet she does not apparently match any

Japanese magic tradition. You yourself appear to fit the American superhero paradigm, specifically the Atlas-Type, but that tells me nothing since pop-culture penetration means that such types have also appeared in Japan."

He smiled briefly. "But you seem to have acquired a rather interesting cat. That, at least, is somewhat traditional."

He gave me a chance to interject, went on when I didn't comment to confirm or deny anything.

"You are also trained to a level only generally observed in elite government and military superhumans. This strongly suggests that despite your apparent youth you are government operatives. And yet you are operating openly on Japanese soil in contravention of many Japanese and international laws. I cannot imagine why any foreign power would authorize such a mission and yet you have behaved like 'superheroes,' publicly fighting and doing good deeds here and in China."

"Here?"

He cleared his throat. "Forgive me. I should have said that we know of your activities in Tenkawa. We do not know precisely how you exorcised the shinigami there, since spiritualistic magic does not appear to match your displayed skill sets. Your actions in Golden Gai have not been similarly beneficial, however."

"Did anybody die?" Despite my resolve to stay cool the question came out in a trembling whisper. I'd been careful not to think about that since seeing the crater.

He regarded me thoughtfully, ventured a thin smile. "No, Hikari-san. Assets in Golden Gai reported your rather aggressive entry and Defensenet triggered an immediate civilian evacuation of the neighborhood. This station was already watching Golden Gai and I ordered the mobilization of the Eight and the Nine. We found the gate through which you departed, and when Raiju came back through the gate and died quite explosively, the surrounding establishments had been emptied."

He clinically measured my relief. "However, your fight has destroyed much of Golden Gai, nearly one hundred small drinking and eating establishments in a historic quarter of the city."

"I am sorry."

"This is one of the reasons we do not tolerate adventurous and powerful ronin." He closed the slim file, folded his hands. "Now, are you going to tell me where you are from and why you are here?"

"No. I am sorry."

"I see. Can you at least confirm my belief that it has something to do with the Miyamoto family kitsune?"

"I—excuse me?"

"I sincerely hope that it does, and that you will be able to help us."

He let me sit and stare at him. Not that I had a lot of choice, about the sitting or the staring. How did he *know*? And why wasn't he following the script?

I licked my lips, focused on my breathing, tried to slow my racing heart. Nothing had changed. Not really.

When I didn't break and start asking questions or explaining myself, he smiled. A tight, humorless smile—respect that I wasn't falling into the silence-trap?

"So, Hikari-san. You have been trained to fight, to resist mental intrusion, and apparently to recognize conversational interrogation techniques. A most comprehensive package. I appreciate this. If you know the steps, you will know when I do not dance. Will you listen to what I have to say?"

Chapter Twenty Four

"'The enemy of mine enemy is my friend.' The earliest known expression of this basic strategic concept is found in a 4th Century BC treatise written in Sanskrit. The unspoken follow-up is also important: 'Until we have dealt with our enemy.' Atlas, who has never read much history, has his own take on it: 'We take care of these guys first, and then we talk.'"

Professor Charles Gibbons, *Modern Experience and Superhuman Policing.*

You remain a complete mystery and one I do not have the time to solve. If he'd really been our personal Inspector Javert since we'd gotten here, what did *that* mean? And why was he even here now if he wasn't the one who'd caught me? Defensenet had been watching Golden Gai?

None of this made any sense, but I realized Agent Inoue was still waiting and quickly nodded. Settling himself, he folded his hands.

"Much like yourself, the Miyamoto kitsune is a mystery. We do not know his origin, and are certain only that he, or she, identifies himself with the fox-spirit of Miyamoto family legend. As a seven-tailed kitsune, he believes himself to be centuries old, a sort of family guardian, and he is very, very powerful.

"His known abilities are total physical transformation, at least into any living creature larger than a field mouse and smaller than a tiger. He also possesses some gift with illusions, and we believe he may be able to travel to extrareality kami realms although none appear to be his home. When he is human, which is most of the time, his preferred faces are those of past Miyamoto family members."

It was time to cooperate a little. I nodded again and the agent's smile grew more natural.

"Then you have met and recognized him. More than once?"

"I've seen two Miyamoto faces. He introduced himself by the family name the second time we spoke."

"Interesting. Do you consider him an ally?"

I actually laughed. "More of a mystery and nuisance, really."

"Good." The agent nodded agreement. "He is not evil or amoral, and like many breakthroughs who self-identify as kami, he has a kami's personality traits. He cannot lie, directly, and he will obsessively fulfill any debts, formally accepted or perceived. This includes collecting on debts for wrongs done to him or others he likes. He is not— He is honorable but not tame, if you understand my meaning." He gave me a moment to think about that.

"Why does he work for you?"

Agent Inoue's eyes sharpened. So did his smile.

"He can sometimes be convinced to work for the Japanese government, when the good of Japan means the good of Tenkawa."

I shook my head. Maybe the pain was making it hard to think, but... "But the last members of the family are dead. There are no more Tenkawa Miyamotos."

"True enough, but I have no doubt that, human passions being what they are, there are a few unknown family members still around. Likely in Tenkawa. In any case, he seems to consider the family and the village to be much the same thing."

"Yes, he—" No, I wasn't going to tell him about the secret shrine kept by Tenkawa's children.

Agent Inoue waited for me to finish my thought, went on when I didn't.

"Three weeks ago, he disappeared. That in itself isn't unusual—indeed it is unusual for us to know where he is—but he disappeared in the middle of a mission vital to our security. He was attempting to infiltrate certain nationalist and criminal underworld groups to determine the whereabouts of a very dangerous Verne-Type breakthrough, a Chinese nationalist who we believe has been brought into Japan to carry out a terrorist attack for Beijing."

"But— Japan isn't militarily involved in China."

"No. But we have been *materially* involved since the beginning of China's current troubles. We have donated staggering amounts of humanitarian aid to the breakaway states, sent them tools and machines for rebuilding their own industries, sent them military arms to defend themselves. We leave the boots on the ground to America and the rest of the League, but we have done everything possible to help them develop. Even if not all of our leaders think it wise, it is a debt."

"And Heroes Without Borders."

"Yes, Hikari-san. And that. Although you are the first 'Japanese nationals' to perform a mission there." His smile widened and his eyes even twinkled a little, like he was aware of the irony. "In any case, he believed he was close to learning his target's location and how he was getting his materials. His last call was made from Kabukicho."

My breath hitched, flashing pain into my shoulder. "The gates."

"Yes. We saw one gate yesterday. And you came out of it. Our kitsune is not *now* in Kabukicho, but since you went from Tenkawa to Kabukicho I can only hope that you yourself came here seeking him. Can you tell us where he is?"

I was sure my heart actually skipped a beat before it started racing. *This* was it, the reason for our friendly talk, and my breath stuttered. Did I actually have *leverage* here?

"You can't use the gate?" I asked weakly.

"It appears to be closed. It may have even moved."

Maybe. Doors, plural, the crazy fish had said. What else had they said? I really hadn't thought through the whole bizarre experience yet; there was too much I wanted to forget about it. *Jacky's head, rolling on the ground*. I blinked the memory away.

Your secret agent is trapped in the weird home of a mad little god. Would it help at all for me to tell him that?

At least now I understood—maybe—why Kitsune had played his game; he'd wanted us to *extract* him. For some reason he'd been stuck with the yakuza group he'd infiltrated. Because of the boss's power? He couldn't get away to complete his mission, so he'd sucked us into a fight that had had a chance of breaking him loose. And we'd failed.

But, what had the fish said? We could win the use of its doors? I swallowed, mouth suddenly dry. Agent Inoue had just told me that kami couldn't lie, at least directly. We'd certainly won the game, and the "use of its doors" implied a lot more than just permission to leave.

Defensenet couldn't get in—they didn't have *permission*—but I was trying to breathe again.

Ozma and Jacky couldn't find me here, and last night I'd been imagining them getting out of Japan, going home and trying to use whatever leverage Blackstone could bring to bear to spring me—if the Japanese ever admitted they had me.

But that wouldn't be their first priority, would it?

They'd still want to get to Kitsune, to solve my little problem. Maybe they'd even try and enlist him to find and help spring me if he wound up seriously owing them. Would Ozma and Jacky remember what the fish had said—that we had won the right to use those "doors?" If they thought of it would they try and go back on their own?

Not just yes, but hell yes.

Stupid, stupid, stupid. And of course they'd thought of it. Maybe not Jacky, but Ozma? She'd been the head of state of the land of trick questions and she'd negotiated like a pro yesterday; there was *no way* she'd miss it.

They weren't just going to go home. They were going to go back after Kitsune and I couldn't do a thing to stop them.

I'd closed my eyes to think and when I opened them Agent Inoue was still there, watching me with mildly curiosity. I swallowed again, licked my lips. "I—we—may be able to take you to—to Kitsune."

He nodded. "That is very good, Hikari-san. We are trying to keep somebody very dangerous and very angry from turning Tokyo into an ashtray. And what do you require in return?"

Clamping down on the hysterical giggle that tried to climb out of my throat, I managed to answer with a voice that was only shook a little. "I've got a list?"

My immediate release was non-negotiable, along with a full amnesty for all of us. Defensenet would return my communications gear, but before I'd use it they had to provide assurances that they would let the mystery of the Three Remarkable Ronin go and not seek to prosecute us for any of our activities since arriving in Japan.

I expected Agent Inoue to tell me he couldn't do that, or at least to say he needed to talk to his superiors, but he agreed immediately and without conditions. Either he was a lot higher up Defensenet's command-chain than I'd imagined, or they were in an even more desperate hurry than I was.

They never even brought the somnolence cap; at the conclusion of our conversation the screen blanked and recessed further into the wall, sliding open to become a door. Two armored guards waited for me in the hall, but they didn't bring shackles—instead they just escorted me to an elevator that took us to an infirmary level. There the medical staff (all dressed like something out of sci-fi anime) stripped me out of my jumpsuit to give me a full medical exam while x-raying and scanning my shoulder. Doctor Arai, a no-nonsense lady nearly as petite as I was, helped me get dressed before showing me the results.

"Your injury matches that of four victims we have in our superhuman-crimes data base, Hikari-san." She showed me images of my shoulder. "Each of the victims experienced crushing damage to bone and muscle, with no apparent source of the trauma. The lethal force appears to have erupted from inside their bodies."

I watched the cycling images in queasy fascination. I'd been right about the micro-fracturing and the soft-tissue damage; the black areas in the colored scans showed where tissue in my left deltoid and trapezius muscles had simply burst on a cellular level, shredded by exploding ki-force. Part of me was *dead*.

"Ki-use," she continued, "*chi*-use in China, is a fairly standard breakthrough power for martial artists although this level of force is unusual. Ki attacks carry their own individual and unique signatures, and since yours matches the others in signature if not degree, we are now able to close four superhuman murder cases."

"Um, you're welcome?"

She smiled where someone else might have laughed. "The investigators may thank you later, Hikari-san. Since you are the first known surviving victim, you are my concern now."

That didn't sound too good. "What do we need to do?"

Her look pinned me to the examination table. "We need to operate. Immediately. The necrotic tissue must be excised thoroughly, before it poisons your system. It is already damaging tissue surrounding it."

"But I heal—"

"Do you wish us to immobilize your shoulder and test whether or not your body can fight off systemic infection while it purges the necrotic tissue? The muscles in your shoulder are dying, Hikari-san. Perhaps too fast for even you to heal." She looked abstracted for a moment, shook her head. "It would be good for science, but not for you."

I nodded weakly, *really* wishing I could introduce her to Dr. Beth. "I need to make a phone call."

"And I will prep a surgical team."

Agent Inoue had promised the return of all of my things, and he delivered before Doctor Arai was ready for me. The bundle included my earbug and I wiggled it into place and turned it on, trying to hide my relief. "How's my little magic kitty?"

"Ho—Hikari! Where are you?"

"I'm in Defensenet's Shinjuku base, and I've cut us a deal. I'm— I'm about to go into surgery for my shoulder. I'll be fine, but I needed to know if Kimiko-san could deliver some drops?"

"...got it. We'll send a courier." I closed my eyes and waited. One long beat and... *"Are you okay?"*

The concern in her voice almost broke me down. "I will be, promise. They need a friend of ours more than they want us, and we're going to help them. Tell—tell everyone to sit tight? Please?"

"...got it. Be safe? Be here soon?"

I nodded, scrubbed my eyes and held back a sniff. Spend one night in the local lock-up and I was losing it. Jacky would laugh. "Okay. Bye now."

Steps one and two accomplished: Jacky and Ozma weren't going to be stupid without me there to be stupid with them, and I wasn't going to suddenly revert to English.

I still kept my mouth shut and waited for a sudden lapse into incomprehension until the drops arrived—with flowers and a funny *Get Well* card. Dr. Arai raised an eyebrow at the tiny plastic drop squeezer Ozma had put my doses in, but didn't say anything other than to ask if it was magic as I applied it to my eyes, ears, and tongue. No drugs before surgery.

Instead of putting me out, Dr. Arai and her team worked some techno-magic of their own to just shut off the nerves across the upper left side of my body. A screen prevented me from watching, which I decided was definitely a good thing; the paralyzing numbness took in my whole left arm as well, and I doubted I could handle watching them cut into what looked and acted like lifeless tissue.

Once they began I thought about *anything* else; two years a cape—a job that for me had meant more encounters with medicine and therapy than soldiers and football players usually saw—and I still had to fight my old phobias. Somewhere inside was the little girl who'd kept a stiff-but-quivering upper lip for chemo-therapy and the constant exams and then cried her way through nightmares.

Life doesn't make you tougher. It just teaches you that you'll live.

I'd thought that they'd employ a psychic surgeon—and they did, a man who introduced himself as Dr. Nakadad—but from the back-and-forth it sounded like Dr. Arai was using some kind of scanner and robotic super-scalpel, relying on him only for instant sealing along the incisions as she cut out my dead bits.

She kept stopping to request *muscle-clips* and *vascular tubes*.

"The micro-fractures in your scapula and clavicle already present remodeling," she informed me conversationally, carefully guiding her probes. "There is some tendon and ligament damage, but not enough to compromise the joint. You are a very tough young miss."

"Thank you?"

"I will thank you when we are through. We are learning a great deal."

Dr. Nakada smiled beside her. Would they go out for drinks later? Would I be an excuse to "talk shop?"

That first dry reassurance marked an end to the intense preoccupation with which she had begun the surgery, when every word had been terse instructions for her team. Now she kept up a stream of reassurances as she finished and closed me up. She needn't have—I was finding speculating about her and Dr. Nakada far more interesting.

"Want to see?"

I blinked. "Really? Can I?"

"Have you received ocular damage you did not tell us about? No? All done." An assistant removed the screen and she put a hand on my chest where I could feel it. "Turn your head, don't try to move it yet."

Carefully turning, I let out a breath, eyes prickling with relief. I'd expected to see angry red lines covered in multiple staples, maybe purpling flesh, but my shoulder looked pale and smooth, only a network of light red lines to show where she'd cut into me.

"That looks—that looks good. Right?"

"Very good. Given your gifts, the incision lines should be gone in a few days. We're going to restore feeling, now."

That was all the warning I got; I choked, hissed to keep from screaming when every nerve in my shoulder lit on fire. It felt like someone had drawn a dull saw across every last one of them and I gasped again, squeezed my eyes closed against the ambushing pain and felt tears spill down into my hair. Dr. Arai's hand didn't move.

"Shhh, shhh, breathe and count."

I choked a laugh—like I didn't know *that* drill already. But counting helped and my nerves sorted themselves out, decided what was still hurting and what wasn't there anymore. The torturing rasp became a throbbing ache and then just a feeling of tightness and heat.

"Now?"

I sighed. "Better. Mostly gone."

She removed her hand. "That may be a poor choice of words, little miss. Sit up. Carefully." When I did she guided my left arm through a sequence of rotations. No sudden flashes of pain, no seizing, but it didn't feel *right*. Not at all.

"I had to remove significant sections of tissue from both muscles." She probed lightly with her fingers. "Thanks to Doctor Nakada, the surviving tissues have been joined and are now nearly as strong as if they had always been together, but you will find significant weakness remains—you simply have less muscle there now than you did. I do not know enough about your particular breakthrough to predict future healing. Do you regenerate?"

"N—no." I tried to feel the differences, shook my head. "I heal fast, but I don't think if I lost a finger or arm I'd regrow it."

"Then you may not recover complete strength in this shoulder, and that will affect your arm. You might be able to strengthen the remaining muscle-tissue sufficiently to compensate, but that is for a physical therapist to help you with. I look forward to seeing what you do with it."

I swallowed, forcing myself to be optimistic. "Thank you." *Muscle mass has nothing to do with what we are.* Atlas had once told me that, but it wasn't *quite* true; my physical muscles still shaped the expression of my superhuman strength somehow—one of those mysteries Dr. Beth was forever going on about. I could feel the difference, even without trying to push my limits. "Do I need to be careful for now?"

"We do not need to immobilize or support your shoulder, no. But go lightly, Hikari-san. I know enough about fighting to say that it will throw your movements off, fool your physical reflexes until you relearn the balance of your body's strength." She finally gave me a full smile. "I have practiced superhuman medicine for seven years, so I won't tell you not to fight. But yes, be careful."

I could do that. At least, I could confidently say that I had no intention of trying to go out and arm-wrestle an insane godfish.

Chapter Twenty Five

"Japanese society applies tremendous pressure on its people to 'conform and perform.' Social harmony is vital, for families, for organizations, and for the nation. This creates powerful social cohesion and strength, but at the cost of enormous psychological strain. It is, therefore, no wonder that Japan has the highest breakthrough-to-population ratio of any developed nation. It is also no wonder that a disproportionate number of these breakthroughs are 'dark breakthroughs,' destructive manifestations of complete psychotic breaks."

Dr. Mendel, *Cultural Stressors and Breakthrough Phenomena.*

Agent Inoue's solution to the issue of our legality, which he explained as we made our way from the infirmary level to his office, was laughably simple; Defensenet had registered us as "attached consultants." It was exactly the designation given to foreign capes who came to Japan legally to work with Defensenet in some vital capacity. Mostly it was for training, but sometimes to provide a unique power or skill set.

So after all that, the magical disguises, the stealth entry and re-entry, the sneaking and the hiding, we were *legal*. All they did was check a box for the *unknown but provisionally trusted mystery man* category. They had a *box* for it. Easy? You bet—it was just that we were the first "hypothetically Japanese citizens" the category had ever been applied to. It was insane; we were criminal trespassers, they knew it, but they needed us and so we weren't because if we were they couldn't work with us. And when it came to superhumans, Defensenet was the Law and the Government.

It made my head hurt.

None of it meant I was suddenly popular; Agent Inoue was obviously keeping what he thought he knew about us compartmentalized, which meant to everyone else in Defensenet Shinjuku I was still a *ronin*. Back in costume, the most tatted-up yakuza thug, carrying holstered autopistols and spitting on the carpet, couldn't have stood out more than I did in my magical-girl-in-black coat and shades. Outside of the guards and medical staff, base workers visibly shrank away from me. *Me*, little miss pixie.

I wondered what they'd think of Riptide.

I knew what he'd think of them—he'd have loved to go three rounds with Kaminari, the looming leader of the Eight Excellent Protectors, except that the Latino ex gangbanger had been raised not to hit girls. The first words out of her mouth when she met us in Agent Inoue's office were "We speak of duty as Americans speak of liberty. It is the great virtue of our people."

That was her response to my polite "It is an honor to meet you." I honestly didn't know what to say to that, but Agent Inoue went on with introductions as if Kaminari hadn't just verbally spat in my face.

"Hikari-san and her friends have agreed to assist us in recovering our lost asset, Kaminari-san," he explained calmly. "In return we have agreed to treat them as colleagues until our business is concluded, and to refrain from holding past crimes against them so long as they refrain from future unsanctioned activities."

On our way up to his office he had informed me that the Three Remarkable Ronin were teaming up with the Eight. Why not the Nine? Or a mission-mix of both? No idea, but then I still didn't understand why Japan's two biggest and most iconic national teams were *girls'* and *boys'* teams.

Now Kaminari measured me from head to toe with obvious disbelief. "And they can help us?"

The knife-sharp pleats in her skirt and creases in her uniform jacket had told me something about her before she'd opened her mouth, and she'd stepped close enough that having to look up at her made my head hurt worse. I'd already had enough from Miss Tall and Angry.

I shrugged. "No we cannot, Kaminari-san. I am a liar grasping at straws and promising anything I can think of to win my freedom. If you want to take shots at me, then shut up and fight like a girl."

You arrogant sailor-suited crapweasel.

The vein in her forehead stood out like it was about to explode but Agent Inoue just smiled, obviously amused. "Do you question my intelligence, Kaminari-san?"

She smoothed her face, but didn't back down. "Perhaps I question your desperation, sir."

Good answer. Maybe her disgust was personal? They'd missed us in Shibushi—we'd walked right by them that first morning in Japan, and that had to sting. I sighed and dialed it back; who knew that my inner bitch sounded a lot like Megan?

"I apologize, Kaminari-san." I even gave her a bow. "In honesty, if we can assist you at all then it is through recent circumstance and by nothing special that we ourselves can do."

Agent Inoue smiled and shook his head. "You are too modest, Hikari-san. The Three Remarkable Ronin sought and found our asset where we could not. Together, I am sure that we can find him again." His gaze nailed Kaminari and she looked like she was sucking on something sour, but she nodded.

"Then our first move?" she asked me directly.

"Go pick up a sword and look for a door? Bring your team's onmiyoji."

Meeting us in the garage, the Eight Excellent Protector's onmiyoji turned out to be a stereotype—a wisp of a woman with less to her than I had going for me but stretched out with more height. She wore thick bifocal glasses, carried a big magic book everywhere, and looked like a stiff wind would blow her away if she let go of the book.

Which was kind of appropriate since her superhero codename was *Kochi*.

"*The names of the Eight Excellent Protectors,*" Shell whispered in my earbug, "*are Kaminari, Kochi, Seifu, Kitakaze, Minamikaze, Raitoningu, Taifu, and Arashi. They mean thunder, the east, west, north, and south winds, lightning, typhoon, and storm. Someone has obviously been stretching for atmospheric symbolism, and none of their names have anything to do with their powers.*"

We exchanged greeting bows. "What kind of gun do you use, Kochi-san?"

"I'm sorry?" She blinked at me from behind her thick lenses. Which I noticed were secured to her head by an athlete's strap.

"I can smell the gunpowder." I tapped my nose, sniffed lightly to demonstrate. "Either you shoot one every day or stand beside someone who does."

Kaminari scowled behind her, but Kochi actually laughed. Then she opened her thick doorstopper of a book and showed that the last couple of inches of "pages" hid a holster pocket. I didn't recognize the make of the sleek black pistol inside, but the intricately carved symbols that covered it shouted that its purpose was shooting *interesting* targets.

"For when there is no time for writing spells." She let me lean over and properly admire it.

I had to ask. "Charmed bullets?"

"Of course. And jade or silver rounds, blessed." She was a regular pistol-packing ghost hunter and her smile was a boast of its own. "You did a very good job in Tenkawa."

"*Jacky and Ozma are going to love her,*" Shell whispered, and I had to agree.

Kochi flew (riding her *book*) but Kaminari rode with Agent Inoue and me in Defensenet's own variation of an aircar. I didn't recognize the ultra-light material, but the quadcopter design with its four containing rings was something we were seeing more of back home. Our ride returned us to Golden Gai in minutes.

It was a ride I'd have rather not taken; Kaminari's frozen disapproval was bad enough that I'd have flown myself if she hadn't made it clear I was riding in the quadcopter with them—but the view of Golden Gai was worse. It wasn't there anymore.

"No one was killed?" I asked, looking down as we circled in to land beside the crater. I'd been told the answer already, but seeing the damage in the light of day made it impossible to believe. The pocket-neighborhood of tiny buildings and narrow alleys had been devastated; Raiju's transcendently explosive death really had flattened half the place. It should have set the rest of it on fire.

When Kaminari didn't answer Agent Inoue cleared his throat. "Defensenet monitors on the area saw you go in hard. It's standard procedure to evacuate an area when a fight between unknown superhumans begins. Also, when an obviously self-destructing Raiju emerged from the gate, Kaminari ordered the teams' force-manipulators to erect containment walls. Most of the force of the explosion was channeled down and up."

That explained the deepness of the crater and the mostly intact buildings beginning at its rim. If they hadn't been there... Fighting the sudden urge to vomit for the second time in one morning made me dizzy.

Raiju had been dying because we'd killed him, because *we* had gone in after Ozma without knowing what we would be facing. We'd gone into a hot situation, against breakthroughs of unknown power, in the middle of an unsecured zone full of innocent bystanders.

If Defensenet hadn't done *our* job, dozens could have died. Atlas would have been ashamed of me. *I* was ashamed of me. Blackstone would be when he heard—they'd taught me better than that.

Shell didn't say anything. She didn't need to.

We landed by the crater rim, the four foils kicking up a cloud of concrete dust from the shattered foundations. Wind and rain hadn't had enough time to cleanse the site, and crews already worked in the dust to tear down the broken but still standing structures that ringed the crater. A unit of looming three heavy mecha and ten tinman suits who reminded me of Littleton's Cerberus unit guarded the crater perimeter. Were the tinmen Ajax-Type breakthroughs, or was the armor fully powered? The tinman with the fanciest shoulder flashes stepped away from the shade provided by one of the heavy mecha and saluted us—Kaminari, really—as we got out.

"The perimeter is secure, ma'am," he informed us through his suit speakers. "We have not seen the ronin Base informed us would be arriving."

"They weren't watching hard enough," Jacky stepped out of the same shadow, Ozma behind her. The officer's face was hidden by his helmet, but his whole body twitched and a cluster of red targeting laser points spotted my friend's black-clad forms.

"Hey—" Before I could finish my protest the red dots were gone.

"*Great fireteam discipline,*" Shell whispered. They could probably give the Scoobies in Camp Necessity a good fight.

Kaminari ignored Jacky. "Has anything happened in the crater?"

"No ma'am. Crews stopped trying to remove the sword before dawn, and the gate has remained quiet."

I blinked. I hadn't expected there to be any danger, but if they'd posted three heavy mecha here to watch it then they were treating the gate like it was the potential beachhead of an invading army. But then again, maybe they had reason to.

Post-Event Japan had been through a rough time. Being just across the sea from China didn't help things (although that really was getting better); but the Japanese Islands were still basically under siege from the Kaiju Plague—the *Godzilla* Plague until different types started showing up. Tokyo Bay was now protected behind massive sea walls and weapon emplacements, but the nation had responded to the threat by also drafting every known Japanese Verne-Type breakthrough into national service to build the "mechanized forces." Mecha, from the powered armor teams to the fifteen-foot tall Street Mecha, were designed to fight kaiju—but they also came in handy against unique and sometimes horrific breakthrough manifestations.

They'd had more than one awful experience with "gate intrusions," too, and being the first line around a site like this was as much part of their job as backing up Defensenet capes.

I cleared my throat. "I'll go recover my sword, then. Kimiko-san?" I turned to Ozma. "If you could speak with Kochi-san about our experiences on the other side, they want our help recovering someone we are both interested in."

Ozma stepped into my vacated spot, giving Kochi a bow. Standing together, if I ignored the military schoolgirl uniform and black coat and shades then they looked like a prim librarian and respectful student. If the student had close to a century of life on the librarian...

Kaminari and Jacky followed me, none of us speaking as we stepped and slid down the cracked and dusty slope of the crater. We could have flown, but I was totally conscious of a now-invisible gate somewhere over our heads where the shop's second-floor room had been. Cutter had stayed right where I'd left him, but the rock around him had been fractured even more—evidence of where superhumans and machines had sought leverage trying to unsheathe him from the earth. I pulled him from the ground in one smooth draw, using the motion to swing him through a series of one and two-handed arcs to test my shoulder.

He didn't say anything, but he hummed in my hands and when I reached back to put him away he twitched and positioned himself for a snug slide into the sheath. He made me look much better at handling him than I was, and I hid my smile even as I flexed my tight and weakened muscles.

"Who *are* you?" Kaminari hissed, wiping my smile away. She looked furious and I really didn't understand it; it wasn't as if we were the only ronin in Japan, or the worst. We'd *fought* the worst.

I straightened, let my arm drop as Jacky stepped up behind my back. "Nobody. We're nobody. And after we're done here you'll never see us again."

She looked like she really wanted to spit. "Then you abandon your duty? As strong as you are?"

Oh. *Oh.* I opened my mouth and had nothing to say. They hadn't traced us back further than our obviously fake "civilian" covers, so whatever Agent Inoue might think he knew, *Kaminari* thought we were all Japanese citizens—at least one and possibly three tactically powerful superhumans, refusing to use our powers in the service and protection of our nation. As far as she was concerned, we were utterly without honor.

"We follow our duty," was all I could say. Her eyes hardened but I refused to back down and she finally shrugged angrily. A low humming sound made me look up, and she followed my gaze so that we both saw the high-flying drone circling above us.

"News drone." Her mouth had gone back to a sour twist. "Japan is watching."

"I could shoot it," Jacky offered.

I just winced. After all my hours spent with The Harlequin practicing "public face," learning safe media responses, and making quick-and-dirty judgments of how any particular scene might go over with the public, I could see how this looked.

Cordoned off disaster area, check. Wrecked neighborhood, check. Defensenet heroes standing around with new and mysterious ronin... I could see the same calculations going through Kaminari's head.

"Wanna fight?" The offer popped out of my mouth before I had time to think it through.

"*Hey!*" Shell sputtered.

Jacky's objection was a laughing breath beside my ear. "It's not like you're really Hikari, Mistress of The Sword."

But Kaminari's eyes lit up. "I accept." Whispering instructions into her own earbug, she nodded to Agent Inoue up on the rim. Then she dojo-bowed to me. "Touch only, and if you fly then stay under five meters," she instructed and shifted her weight onto her back foot.

Jacky sighed and backed up as I made my own hasty bow. "Okay, what—"

She held out her open right hand and her weapon sprang into existence, one moment not there and in a blink appearing and growing from a charm-sized trinket to a full sized and totally lethal looking spear. One with a long and straight single-edged blade on the end. It glowed. Of *course* it glowed.

"She uses a naginata!" Shell supplied. "*It's like a sword, a spear, and a staff!*"

"So she pokes, slices, and bashes?" Wonderful, and she had the reach on me even though foot-to-tip it wasn't *that* much longer than Cutter. "Is she tough enough that I don't need to worry?"

"*She's not fragile—A-Class or close to it and* you should worry about *her!*"

"Good enough." Drawing Cutter, I slid my own foot back, holding him point forward and hilt high by my shoulder in the standard two-handed opening form I at least knew from watching Sifu's martial arts students. It mirrored Kaminari's stance, point forward and angled down.

And we waited. Still waited. *Any day now...*

Cutter vibrated and turned in my hands before I saw Kaminari's move and I instinctually put muscle behind the downward swing Cutter dropped into. He batted her low-lunging blade aside and my own reflexes sent me into a high backward leap as the naginata hilt came around in a back-swing off the force of our parry. Kaminari followed with a series of stamping advances—lunges and swings blurring into each other until I stopped falling back and stepped inside her last swing to give her a solid check-push with my whole body—

—which didn't connect with her own spinning sideways-slide, settling us into our original opening stances.

She studied my stance. "You don't use your point?"

I shrugged.

"And your shoulder?"

"It's fine." Cutter hugely outweighed her weapon but his weight was a negligible issue for me, and her swings weren't bringing as much force as mine could even if she was *fast*.

"Good." Kaminari showed no inclination to renew her attack, waiting with sword-spear ready until I realized it was obviously my turn to move first. I opened with a flying horizontal leap, her point came up, and I *spun* with Cutter extended so that his counterweight put the center of our spin between us. We orbited each other as we came down—Cutter batting her extended blade away as I rotated into her with all my spinning weight. She fell hard but gracefully, rolling away without letting go of the naginata and returning a low sweep that brushed my toes as I jumped over it—which gave her time to roll to her feet and come back into guard position.

Neither of us were breathing hard.

She straightened up, looked up to the rim to check on our pair of experts. Their heads bent together in conference, they completely ignored our little show.

"Again?"

I realized I was grinning. "As long as the experts are conferring, we've got nothing but time."

Kaminari *could* fight like a girl; by the time Ozma and Kochi called us up out of the crater we were both covered in dust and she'd "touched" me three times. I'd made it hard enough that I hadn't looked stupid, but I wasn't sure she was using her full speed. Plus-side, we'd given viewers enough fight footage to satisfy any fan's wish for hero vs. ronin action. Minus-side, my shoulder throbbed hotly again, and even though we'd been fighting for touches and I hadn't been going all-out either I could feel the weakness there. Dr. Beth would tell me I'd pushed it too early and Jacky wasn't happy; she could tell something wasn't right.

Kochi looked the three of us over and pulled a stiff paper card from her book, blowing every trace of our sparring match away with a muttered incantation. Nice.

"We think we understand what we're facing, boss." *Bos-u*; she used the English word with the extra syllable, and waited. Kaminari made her naginata vanish.

"Are you going to tell us today?"

"Yes." She folded her arms. "Kimiko-chan and I are in agreement; we are facing an immortal, an Omega Class breakthrough."

"Well hell," Jacky said. I wanted to use stronger words; it sucked to know I'd been right.

In theory, breakthroughs had no physical limits. The difference between manifesting a D Class breakthrough and an A or even Ultra Class *or higher* breakthrough was all in the mind; the stronger the personality or the trauma-induced mental spike, the stronger the breakthrough, no limits. That was the *theory*—but in reality A Class breakthroughs were a small minority and Ultra Class breakthroughs were rare enough that each newly discovered one was an event in itself. *Omega* Class breakthroughs, with powers that could only really be described as *godlike*, just didn't manifest in the real world.

Someone like Doctor Cornelius would simply argue that Omega Class powers were too *real* for what we thought of as the real world and he called the orange peel of reality. And certainly that seemed to explain what actually happened—confirmed Omega Class breakthroughs had only ever been encountered *elsewhere*, somewhere out in the pockets and planes of extrareality. They were gods, elemental forces, omnipotent within their domains.

Like the "frozen" pond and the godfish.

Jacky shrugged. "So it's going to be a sneak and creep."

Chapter Twenty Six

The key to winning is controlling the game. If the only moves open to your opponent are moves you have allowed him, then you will know how to respond whichever way he turns. When you do not control the game, you will not be able to respond to all moves your opponent may make. When you do not know the game, any move your opponent makes is likely to be a catastrophic surprise.

Ozma, Empress-in Exile of Oz.

My life had officially gone mythic. Fairy tales? Who needed them; I'd moved on from all that to the story of Orpheus in The Freaking Underworld.

One of my first-year courses at the University of Chicago had been Comparative Religion—a hot Post-Event topic since religious and folk beliefs shaped breakthroughs as much as popular culture—so I knew a *little* of what Kochi was talking about. "Shinto," the name of Japan's native religion, meant *Way of The Kami*. Under all the folk-magic and religious festivals it was mostly about keeping good relations between us and the spirits—kami—that shared our world. Which meant that Shinto wasn't very afterlife-oriented; instead it left a lot of that to Buddhism (because sure, why not?).

Newer Shinto beliefs stressed apotheosis, which fit with Japanese Zen Buddhism. But older Shinto stories talked of a land of the dead, Yomi, that sounded a lot like the ancient Greek myths about Hades. The place even included stern judges.

Which was what Kochi thought we were looking at.

Going from "insane godfish" to "fishy judge of the underworld" sounded like a huge leap to me, but I wasn't the onmiyoji and from what I understood onmiyoji were as much priests or shamans as they were sorcerers. Kind of like exorcists, maybe? Her inferential evidence for the godfish's localized omnipotence came from its total control of its environment and the yakuza onmiyoji's reaction to its appearance.

And Ozma totally backed Kochi's assessment; she even hinted that if her Magic Belt was fully charged she still wouldn't consider a contest of power. Basically, if all of the Eight and the Nine tried to storm the godfish's weird kami realm, chances were that Defensenet would need to recruit abroad to replenish its high-powered ranks.

But, and they agreed on this too, the godfish wasn't *omniscient*. The yakuza onmiyoji had been using the gates without the fish's knowledge. Kochi had identified the elaborately caligraphied paper fan as a *deception*, a charm that had made a little pocket of the godfish's realm invisible to it. We would have been able to finish our fight there in peace and quiet—the yakuza boss's likely plan—if I hadn't destroyed the fan.

So yeah, nobody was saying it but the whole subsequent contest and trapping Kitsune in the underworld was sort of my fault. Pretty much all my fault.

Bright side, after explaining what we were up against Kochi pulled a sheet of stiff white origami paper from her big book (which I was beginning to think was a lot like Ozma's magic box) and folded a new fan to Ozma's specifications—she'd had a lot of time to watch the yakuza onmiyoji while waiting for us. After Ozma confirmed the shape, Kochi worked over the fan leaves with ink and a writing brush, covering it in symbols. Finishing, she fanned it to dry the ink and then carefully examined her work. Satisfied, she whispered something to it, drew a circle in the dust, stepped inside the circle and opened the fan, and disappeared.

Shell regressed to a fifteen-year old—*"That is so cool!"*—and I burst into startled laughter. Kochi reappeared inside the circle, fan folded.

"The yakuza onmiyoji would have drawn a wider *kekkai* to define the borders of his charm. You described an enlarged room?" When Ozma nodded, she waved at the crater beside us. "We can fix the kekkai to the rim. That will give us a lot of room to move around the fan when we enter the gate."

"And who do you think should go?" I'd almost forgotten about Agent Inoue, he'd been absolutely silent.

"Kochi-san?" I avoided looking at Jacky. "Can anyone use the fan?"

She nodded. "I need to draw the kekkai, but that is all."

"Then I'll go. Just me."

Jacky's simple "Like hell," wasn't the strongest statement; Kaminari and Kochi had a huge problem with it. Agent Inoue went back to silence, and Ozma just looked more serenely inscrutable than usual.

"Numbers will not be effective," she said once the volume had died. "Neither will power. Hikari knows how to be cautious even if she doesn't always display that virtue."

"Look, I can scout." I tried to keep my voice reasonable. "If there is a way to retrieve Kitsune quietly, I can do it. If I can't then I can come back and tell everyone what I learn. If something happens...better just one of us over there than all of us."

"I agree," Ozma seconded. "Kaminari-san, Hikari has a relationship with the one we seek which may prove decisive."

I could see Kaminari choking on it; she was the leader of the Eight, and her breakthrough made her a fight-monster like me—it was her *job* to go through the door or into the breach first, soak up whatever hit was there to take. She led from the front, so how could she trust a ronin to do her job?

She lost her staring match with Agent Inoue, finally nodding, but if her eyes shot lasers I'd be dead.

"No freaking *way*," was all the warning I got before Jacky grabbed my good arm. "Excuse us a moment," I said to everyone as she pulled me away.

I let her pull me a few yards before "digging in" and stopping us. She glared down at me and I glared back; we *really* didn't have time for this.

"Can you *shoot* it, Mamori?" I barely remembered to keep it low and use her new codename. "It's a *god*, at least in its own little pond."

"It's a *crazy* god!" she shot right back. She didn't try to push me with her vampy powers—if she did I'd...well, I'd *know*, and then we'd see what happened.

"We don't know that. And I'm not going after it; I'm going around it. And two of us can't be sneakier than one."

"Dammit—" The cold logic stopped her; two couldn't do anything one couldn't do, and if only one of us were going there was no way I'd let it be anyone but me.

Then she smirked. "What if he's asleep?"

"Asleep—" I sucked in air.

"Asleep. Under the ice. You think fishy's going to leave him wandering free-range? And if we find him asleep, how are you going to wake him up? Love's first freaking kiss?"

Her nasty jab caught me so off-balance I actually squeaked like an infuriated mouse before I could find the words. "Oh, now that's just not—"

"*Girls*," Shell drawled in our earbugs. "*We have an audience. And Jacky's right, she's going. You've got the karmic connection, she's got the mojo.*"

Et tu, Shell? I couldn't make my mouth work. "Ja— I— No! I watched him *cut your head off*!"

"The view wasn't great from my angle, either. We're doing this."

And she had me; everything I'd learned about tactics said you took what you needed, or even thought you might need, and then you took everything you didn't think you needed but wouldn't compromise your mission. *You're not prepared until you're over-prepared.*

If it was still just about me I'd tell both my BFs to bite themselves (Shell was a cat now, she could do it), but after my interview with Agent Inoue my personal problem wasn't even in the picture anymore.

When you wear the cape, you do the job. That thought would always come with an easy Texas drawl behind it, and I sighed. "Okay. We're going."

But whatever happened, Jacky was coming *back*.

The Littleton Pocket had been created with Verne-Type superscience, and we'd had to use a big "translation" machine to get us in. If the *godfish's* extrareality had been created by ritual magic, then it would have probably required circles, incantations, or at least some kind of pre-keyed charm to get us in. Which we didn't have. But Kochi explained that kami governed their creations pretty much by pure will; if we had "permission" to use the godfish's gates then we'd be able to just by wishing it.

Kochi drew the kekkai circle, first, and then to be on the safe side she opened and waved the fan herself rather than trying to teach us the words, handing it off to Jacky and trudging out of the crater to where the world had gone blurry and indistinct—a good sign that the charm was working.

One last step. "Shell?"

"Ready on my end."

"No, you're not. You've got to promise me something. If the fish finds us, you *immediately* unplug us from your end—don't ask, don't argue, don't hang around to see what it has to say to us. Last time it was able to pull you in just through your open channel to my earbug, so you *promise* or Jacky and I are leaving our earbugs here when we go."

I got a minute of sulky silence. "*...fine. I promise. Now* let's go."

I was pretty sure that Orpheus hadn't taken a living vampire and a quantum-ghost on his trip down into the underworld. *And that story turned out* so *well.*

Everything depended on the gate staying where it had been, even with all the destroyed real estate around it. Getting up to the gate would take a gantry or platform. Or me.

Jacky turned around and, saying a silent prayer, I lifted her in a front-back hold while she held the open fan before her. And there is was; we could "see" the gate above us as we rose. Permission to enter gave us permission to *see*, I supposed—or not "see" so much as just somehow know it was there. I surprised myself with a giggle.

"You going to tell me?" I couldn't see Jacky's face but her tone meant an eyebrow was raised behind her shades.

"If we're entering the *under*world, shouldn't we be, I don't know, *going down*?"

And then we were in.

Chapter Twenty Seven

"I've been to a few extrareality worlds in my years of wearing the cape: the odd but pretty mundane Littleton Pocket, the [redacted], the cinematically superheroic Universe Alpha, Oz. The weirdest place I have ever been was the [redacted]. Learning what it really was didn't make it less weird."

Hope Corrigan, aka Astra *(An excerpt from heavily redacted files available in the Sentinels Historical Library.)*

The underworld is a pretty quiet place when nobody's taking their fight there—which might have been the point. We found ourselves standing on the "frozen" pond again, the purple hills mostly invisible behind the ghost-shapes of the crater and the still-standing buildings of Golden Gai. The stars were beautiful, something I hadn't had a chance to appreciate before.

With no sign of nosy golden koi anywhere.

"Okay, well?" The fan was rock-steady in Jacky's hand, but her other hand was full of one of her Vulcan-made superscience pistols. It hummed softly, reminding me of Cutter.

I turned in a full circle. Nope, no fish. "Now we find Kitsune."

Kochi had told us that in this kind of extrareality realm the topography, landscape, even directions and distances tended to be purely metaphorical things. Listening to our description, she'd posited that the pond above the ice represented a kind of "lobby" or central access. The sleepers below the ice, each with their accompanying silver koi, could be actual sleepers or could just as easily be representations of guests the godfish had placed into their own little pocket realms. Even through the "fog" that was the projection of the crater floor, we could see dozens of them drifting in the slow currents.

How long had they been here?

I shook my head and tried to clear my thoughts. According to Kochi, trying to use Ozma's magic compass in here was one risk too many—but she believed that I might be able to locate Kitsune through my "special link." It was worth a shot.

"Well?"

I couldn't help the smile. "I'm concentrating..." So, which Kitsune to focus on? The white seven-tailed fox? The one I had always met at the tree? I tried for only a moment, gave that up and settled on a young Yoshi Miyamoto. That was how he'd introduced himself to me that night in The Fortress, when he'd charmed me with romantic poetry and then stuck around after the shooting to help injured club patrons.

It seemed ridiculous that after everything I'd still think of Kitsune as Yoshi, but there it was.

And... I pointed. "Look down." We hadn't visibly moved, but looking straight down beneath our feet we could see a sleeping Kitsune. He wasn't the white fox-spirit, but he wasn't exactly Yoshi either; androgynously beautiful, he (she?) looked enough like Yoshi to be a brother or sister. Fine white hair drifting in the sub-surface currents, seeming to caress his own hypnotically focused silver godfish.

Jacky rested her gun on her shoulder. "So much for finding him alone."

"Maybe. But Kochi said everything here is likely metaphorical—maybe the godfish with each sleeper just means that it's aware of them and linked to their dreamworlds? The shoal of gold koi we talked to last time might have been just a metaphor for the kami's attention."

"*Hold on,*" Shell murmured. "*I'm sending these images to everyone. FYI, the difference in time-rates is really annoying—you guys are taking* forever. *And they agree. Took ten minutes of arguing, but Ozma says that this place is like the fairy realms. It should respond to sufficiently strong will.*"

"Well that makes it easier." Jacky holstered her gun and knelt, putting her free hand on the "ice." Which wasn't ice, it was a *metaphorical barrier*. I had one second to realize what she was doing and grab her shoulder before the ice gently softened and we sank into the pond—which turned out to be air. Air that supported us like water but was just fine to breathe.

A vampire's will is a weapon of its own.

The silver koi didn't so much as twitch as we sank down beside Kitsune, but I still held my breath when I almost brushed it. What would happen if I poked a metaphor? I had the sudden and insane urge to put my hand between Kitsune and his watcher-fish. What would happen?

I crushed the urge. When you have no idea what will happen if you do something, and you don't have to do it, *don't*.

"He's kind of cute this way," Jacky observed. Kitsune's black yakuza business suit waved around him in the current, his narrow tie floating almost vertical above his chest, moving with each sleeping breath. "I say we just grab him and go."

"Works for me." I carefully took his hand, eyes on the godfish. Still nothing.

Jacky held up the fan. "You first—I don't want to accidentally leave you without this."

I nodded, closed my eyes and took a calming breath. Ozma had said—and Kochi agreed—that leaving would be as easy as entering;

I could click my heels three times and think "There's no place like home." Well not in those *words*, just focus hard on returning to the crater.

I *really* wished for that crater, opened my eyes. No crater.

So much for the easy way.

Kitsune was *stuck*.

At least that was the professional opinion of our experts. Anchored was probably a better word, but it was their considered opinion that he was stuck in a dreaming sub-pocket realm of his own and so not in the "lobby" where we could slip him out the door.

Meanwhile every move we made was making me *twitch*; I felt like Indiana Jones, staring at a golden idol sitting on a booby-trapped pedestal and wondering if tomb raiding was really a good career choice. Because any second now we were going to do something stupid and get squashed by a huge rolling boulder.

Think of Tokyo. Ashtrays. If it wasn't for what Agent Inoue had said, I'd walk away and take my chances with a tree—which, just from the feels, I was pretty sure loved me. Thirty-two million people I'd never met said I couldn't. Jacky was right—I wanted to save everybody, ever.

Neither of us said anything as we waited while Ozma and Kochi conferred some more—even Shell was keeping communication to a minimum just in case. Opposite me, the "water" around us made Jacky's longer hair float like jet-black seaweed in the warm current, giving her the look of an angel of death as she floated over our sleeping and beautifully kissable Prince Charming.

And whoa—where did all that *come from?* Obviously from remembering that I was kinda-sorta *engaged* to this…this…*arrghh*. This was so *not* helping.

"There's Plan *V*," Jacky said quietly and I jumped. "There's always Plan V—if I can't shoot them I vamp them."

"That's—" I swallowed my automatic denial. It was risky as hell, but it was why Jacky had come. And it might work. Maybe. If Jacky forced Kitsune awake, then that would bring him to "our side" of this pocket and we could drop out of this weird place with him. If we moved fast. Really, *really* fast. Maybe.

I gave everyone on the other side of Shell's relayed link a chance to weigh in with objections or better ideas.

"They've got nothing." I could hear the very real fear in my BF's voice.

Sometimes when you have no idea what will happen if you do something, you have to do it anyway.

"Do it." Realizing I was still holding Kitsune's hand, I let go.

And looked away. To watch the fish, really. But my super-duper hearing worked just fine here, and I heard Jacky move, heard her take off her shades and loosen his collar. And bite. And somehow I was holding Kitsune's hand again. Watching Jacky, who had just become totally fascinating. I could…

I let go again, pulled back and thought about *anything* else. The fish. The nearest drifting sleepers, beautiful in silk court robes. The question of how we could *breathe* this stuff that was thick enough to float in—*anything* but the pull of Jacky's mind. Seconds crawled by like minutes and—the pull snapped and was gone.

And Kitsune's eyes were still closed.

Now I hissed. "Jacky! What the hell *was* that?" When she looked up I flinched and looked away.

"What was what?" She only sounded frustrated—she had no idea.

"I could *feel* you! You know, like when you've bitten me. You were in my head!"

"When I—" Her eyes went wide. "I couldn't pull him out of it—it was like trying to wake up a drunk halfway to a coma. You felt it?"

I nodded, almost choked on the stuff we shouldn't be able to breathe. "Wait—" It could *work*. "What if you vamp *me*?"

"What?"

"What if you vamp *me* instead? Send me into his dream? I've obviously got this—" I searched for a word "—*thing* with him. He's been in my mind, or at least in my dreams. Which is where we just connected, right? In *his* mind? We need him, now!"

Jacky's eyes turned dark, hooded. She wasn't buying it.

"If we can't do this—" I chose my words carefully. "If we can't get him out of this, things are going to get real bad for people. If we can't do this, then Plan B is to talk to the fish. Close the fan, say hello, and hope we can make a deal. Because we can't leave without Kitsune."

"I can always vamp you and send you home and talk to fishy myself."

"I'd come back." Absurdly, I was grinning back at her black scowl. "You know I would. And look, you won't even need to bite me—it's only been a few days, I should still be plenty susceptible to your vampy powers."

"And if I can get you in but can't bring you out?"

"Then you can talk to the godfish."

Still no move from the silver fish watching Kitsune—I was beginning to think the individual fish really *were* purely representational—physical markers of the godfishes' awareness, and the awareness of the silver koi was only of their sleepers. If I went in, would it be aware of me?

Did it matter? If we couldn't sneak me in, we were talking to it anyway. "Should I be touching him? Will that help?"

Jacky sighed and gave up. "A Sleeping Beauty kiss might be appropriate. Yes, just—stretch out where I can see both of you at once. Try and picture a mental scene of your own. Something natural, with both of you in it."

Okay. I could do that. Moving in and carefully stretching out along Kitsune's side, I tried to imagine a more natural scene than this. The tree? Nope, *not* a good idea. *We're in Burnham Park, watching the boats on the lake.* I could see it; we'd just eaten lunch and had stretched out in the shade to drowse in the summer heat and think about nothing at all. A warm wind pushed my hair in my face and I tucked it away, shifting to rest my head on his shoulder.

I forgot about Jacky and just dozed. The day was too beautiful to do anything else, and—

"What are you doing here?"

I stopped running and stared up at the astonishingly beautiful—and frowning—lady. "Shinji ran this way. I think he's hiding in the cave."

"Do you?" The lady laughed and sat on a fallen tree, arranging her fine yukata—made of embroidered silk and fancier than anyone in the village had ever seen—and watching the woods around us. "And who's Shinji?"

That was silly. "Shinji is— Shinji is—" I didn't know.

The lady nodded. "And who are you?"

"I'm—" I didn't know that, either. I burst into tears.

"Oh, well, we can't have that. Come with me." Standing up again, she offered her hand. I took it. Did she know where I was supposed to be?

Stepping over twigs and brush so that the skirts of her yukata made no noise, mindful of my much smaller legs, the lady led me down the wooded hill. We didn't walk very far to reach the open grass, long and waving in the afternoon breeze, and saw the village.

"Do you know where we are?" she asked gently. I shook my head—I didn't even know that. I didn't recognize the tiny thatch-roofed homes at all. Was one of them mine? Then I saw the mountains. Those I knew.

"Yes! Yes! I know—Tenkawa!" I laughed.

"Very good. And now, who am I?"

That was an odd thing to ask, but no odder than my not knowing who I was. "You're...Yoshi's new wife. You came last year."

"That's right. And I know who you are, too. You're Hope. And a very cute little Hope right now."

Chapter Twenty Eight

"Have you ever walked through a door and found yourself in yesterday? No? Have you ever [remainder of sentence redacted]? No? Then you've managed to live your life somewhere normal. Count. Your. Blessings. If I ever see those creepy [redacted] again, I'm making sushi."

Jacky Bouchard, aka Artemis *(An excerpt from heavily redacted files available in the Sentinels Historical Library.)*

I *was* six. Or somewhere around that tiny age. My feet were bare, my rough little yukata dusty from the dry earth, and I hadn't drawn Kitsune into my dream of a Chicago summer.

We sat on the grass, listening to the buzzing cicadas.

Kitsune laughed softly, like someone who had been thinking about a joke for a long time and who finally had someone to share it with. "Did you know that the story doesn't even give me a name? I'm just the fox-wife."

"Really?" Like I cared; I was six! I tried not to be too dismayed. Actually I tried not to have a screaming fit—six-year old emotions *were* intense.

"Really. You'd think they'd remember that, at least."

"Is this history?"

"Hardly." She ran fingers through my tangled hair, stopped. "In a way, I suppose. It's my story, and I can't say which one it is since it started with me already Yoshi's wife and with two beautiful little boys."

I blinked. "But, how can you not know?"

"Well, historians generally agree that the Kitsune of Tenkawa was a real woman. A lot of samurai and noble families lost everything in the wars of the period, so it is completely possible that she was the daughter of an impoverished family, married to a poor country samurai and brought home with him. She wouldn't have fit in with the uneducated townsfolk, her in-laws probably resented her, and she might not have liked them much, either."

"And that's you?"

"In this story. I just don't know how it ends. I disappear, remember." She did. In the legend, when Yoshi discovered his strange wife was a fox she vanished, never to be seen again.

"I'm still not sure if my mother-in-law is going to kill me and bury me in the woods now that I've given her two healthy grandsons, or if my father is going to recover his fortune and summon me back to Edo to marry somebody else with more connections." I gasped in horror and she stroked my hair again. "I think I'll likely be murdered—Yoshi's mother is nasty enough."

"Why are you here? Is the godfish trying to teach you a lesson?" I couldn't imagine being forced to wait around to see if you were murdered. What was the point?

"A lesson? Just where do you think we are?"

"Well—the underworld—" I stammered out an approximation of Kochi's guess about mythic underworlds and judges. Kitsune was laughing delightedly by the time I finished.

"I'm not going to let Kochi forget this!" She shook with mirth. "She's very, very good, and right most of the time."

"Then where *are* we?" I challenged crossly, and hiccupped in shock when I realized that I was almost hysterically upset because an adult was laughing at me.

"We're on a stage! Your 'godfish' isn't a judge—he's the spirit of Kabukicho. His gates can open in any entertainment district in Japan, but he's the embodiment of the Kabuki theater and all its drama and melodrama."

My mouth made a big 'O'. "It's keeping sleepers as players?"

"'All the world's a stage,'" Kitsune recited in accentless English, "'and all the men and women merely players; they have their exits and their entrances, and one man in his time plays many parts.'" She sighed. "That's also why I expect murder—much more dramatic."

"It's doing this to everybody? All of them? That's—that's—"

"Terrible? A kabuki needs drama—I suspect that Kabukicho has placed each sleeper into a period of drama in their lives. Hopefully good drama, or at least drama from which they emerged triumphant, but I doubt that most are that lucky. But you, dear Hope, why are you here?"

"Agent Inoue sent us here for you!"

"Oh?" A brow rose. "That's very resourceful of him, but all the way from America?"

"No—" I kept having to remind myself that I wanted to go home and home wasn't below us in the village. It was insidious—all my thoughts and emotions felt different, and just hearing Kitsune speak English was jarring. Her voice had been getting kinder and kinder, and now I wanted to cry and curl up beside her so she could stroke my hair until I felt better.

"I mean, just this time. We came to find you because of the tree."

"Do tell." Taking my suddenly quivering chin, she looked into my face. "But quickly. I'm a kami myself, with more control than Kabukicho's other guests possess. Any longer, and I think you're going to forget you're a player on this little stage."

"Shit!" Jacky jerked away when I jackknifed into a vertical curl by Kitsune's side.

I was too big. The world in my *head* was too big. My shoulder throbbed unbearably for the moment it took for my brain to remember how it felt to live with low-level pain.

"How long—how long have I been asleep?" My voice was too deep.

"Just a few minutes. What happened in there?" Kitsune still floated beside us, as much a sleeping beauty as ever.

"We're leaving *right now*."

"Right." Just to be safe, we rose to the surface first. When I gave her a boost out and we stood on the unbroken ice, I kept my hand on her shoulder.

"Ready?" She nodded and I closed my eyes. *There's no place like freaking home*. And we were there—as close to home as I could get, anyway. Spotlights lit the night again, making every puff of dust visible as Kaminari and Kochi slid-ran down into the crater to meet us.

I squinted to see beyond the lights. We'd been in there for hours. "I need to talk to Agent Inoue," I said as soon as the two Defensenet capes got to us. "Is he still on-site?"

"*He's here*," Shell let me know. "*Hasn't left all day*." I gave everyone an "excuse me" bow and lifted up, landed on the rim.

"Hikari-san," he greeted me when I landed. He stood in a circle of used cigarette butts and crushed coffee cups, but he said my name like he'd been waiting a couple of minutes to meet me on the street for a lunch date.

"We could not retrieve Kitsune, Inoue-san. But he did give me a message for you. Three names and an address."

"Thank you. Repeat them, please." When I did, he nodded. "You've kept your part of our agreement—sufficiently, at least, for none but lawyers to object to. I'm not a lawyer, nor are my superiors. Since you can reach Kitsune, may I ask you to stay with us for a few more days while we do what we can with what you've given us? I would also appreciate the opportunity to hear anything else you might be able to relate. However—" Now he bowed. "You have our gratitude. If you wish to leave Japan immediately, we will arrange your departure to any destination you wish and see you on your way. Your own business here is also done?"

"Ooh..." Shell whispered. "*That's the nicest 'Thanks for all your help, now don't let the door hit your butt on your way out' I've ever heard.*" I covered my mouth; I was wiped out and punchy, but Agent Inoue didn't deserve hysterical laughter.

I bowed back—just a few intense days and it was becoming second nature. "Thank you, Inoue-san. I would feel better for the opportunity to give a fuller debrief." He nodded acceptance; I couldn't tell if he was happy with me or not, and I really didn't much care—I wanted to sleep for a week. A natural sleep, without worrying about where I was going to wake up. And tonight I was going to get it.

A light rain had begun to fall when we left the mech units standing watch over the gate. Kaminari and Kochi disappeared. Jacky went off to collect kitty-Shell and all our stuff and meet us there while Ozma and I flew back to Defensenet Shinjuku with Agent Inoue; while all was forgiven, as long as we remained in Japan we were going to stay where they could see us. Looking down at the bright-lit crater that had been Golden Gai, I couldn't say they were being unreasonable.

Agent Inoue talked on his own earbug as we lifted off, and it sounded like a certain address was about to become a very exciting location. Then he turned his attention to me.

"Is there anything else that our asset was able to tell you?"

I nodded painfully. The ache in my shoulder had shot a spike up my neck into my head, and I was going to go see Dr. Arai as soon as we landed. "He told me that he'd gotten stuck by the yakuza boss's coercive power and was unable to leave or contact you once he found out that they were using the extrareality pocket to smuggle people and equipment. When their onmiyoji spotted O—Kimiko's magic in Shinjuku, our fox advised that she be taken." I laughed, winced.

"He set the whole thing up. He didn't share who we were, but he knew we'd come after her and that's what he told his boss—gave him the idea of "recruiting" us by sucking us into a fight in the pocket and turning us there. He knew you guys would be watching Kabukicho, and win or lose we'd lead you right to them. He didn't expect—" I waved a hand vaguely.

The agent nodded. "That is his style of play. And he remains trapped?"

"Not—not exactly. He has more freedom than the other sleepers there, and said that he expects to be able to slip away sooner or later." *After murder ends the play.* The thought made me cringe.

"That is good." A nice understatement. I looked out the windows.

On my first ride to Defensenet Shinjuku I hadn't exactly been able to appreciate the sights; this time I not only had a window to look out of, I had a great angle. Defensenet Shinjuku, also the Defensenet One Building, sat in the middle of Shinjuku's tall-towered business district. Not as tall as the buildings around it, it still managed to look intimidating; instead of the steel and glass style of its neighbors, it looked carved from white stone. The windows in its upper floors, long, narrow, and widely spaced, didn't compromise its solid strength one bit. Neither did the carved stone murals that ringed its first three or four floors.

Even so, to me keeping Defensenet's national nerve-center in the same location as its two premier teams felt like tempting fate. Too many eggs in one basket. On the other hand I was willing to bet that, as strong as it looked, it was really *much* stronger. And there was something to be said for not spreading out the targets you absolutely had to defend.

The heavy garage gates closed behind us, and now that I didn't have other things on my mind I could appreciate the layered security we passed through—perfectly sensible considering they kept holding cells in the same building.

Climbing out of our ride first, Agent Inoue signaled to a couple of base guards. "I will have someone take you back to the infirmary, Hikari-san, and show your companions to your rooms. You will find them very comfortable, and you will be able to come and go as you please except for specific areas."

I raise my hand, feeling like a school-kid on a field trip. "Um… Inoue-san?"

"Yes?"

"I would prefer the room I occupied last night."

He actually blinked. "Excuse me?"

"With the security seals active? If it's not too much trouble."

"May I ask why?"

Ozma smothered a laugh as my face heated up. *Please sir, can I spend the night in your maximum-security cell? That would be really, really nice.*

"It prevents a tree from kidnapping me when I sleep?" Although I felt much better about it after talking to Kitsune, I wasn't ready to go just yet. Of course I wouldn't be in the cell the next time somebody knocked me out, but I didn't see any fights looming for a while. Not with my shoulder the way it felt; in the old days of field-hockey injuries, if it had ached like this I would have been immobilizing it and packing it in ice.

"A tree."

"Yes, Inoue-san. I am haunted by a tree."

"And you sought our mutual friend because…"

"He knows the tree."

I was sure that Agent Inoue saw lots of weirder things than I did, so how weird could being stalked by a tree sound to him? He looked thoughtful for all of a few seconds, nodded like I'd just asked to switch to a room with a better view, and said he'd fix it. Showing us to the suite Ozma and Jacky would share, he assigned a staff assistant to see to Ozma's requests and an unthreatening uniformed aide to take care of me, and politely disappeared.

My sharply attentive aide, introduced as Leading Private Watabe, led me back to the infirmary where Dr. Arai waited. She was not happy to see me, and I wasn't happy to be there, but she looked me over and gave me a prescription for my shoulder: *Stop. Using. It.*

Then she gave me a what she called a neuro-block patch, informed me that it would dial down the pain receptors in my shoulder enough for me to sleep—and promised that if I did *anything* strenuous it would stop working real fast and she wouldn't give me another one.

Leading Private Watabe had obviously talked to someone while Dr. Arai was poking me. "Hikari-sama," he said respectfully once I'd gotten my coat back on and met him at the infirmary doors. "If you will follow me, we have your room prepared."

"Thank you. Nekokami?" *Kitty-Shell?*

"Neko, huh? *I should have gotten a codename,*" Shell laughed in my earbug. "Mamori *says to go to sleep, we're fine and settled in up here. But I want to know what the heck happened in there. We journey to the underworld...and come back with three names and an address? Did you at least get him to agree to a wedding date?*"

"Talk when I've showered?" Later, when Leading Private Watabe wasn't standing beside me. Not that I expected *privacy*, but I wouldn't really have any less than if I'd slept upstairs, either; Defensenet was being nice, but nice didn't mean stupid.

We didn't have privacy *now*—I was willing to bet that Defensenet was only letting me talk to Shell because they could hear what we were saying. Watabe looked at me funny when I chortled for no apparent reason. What would they think of Shell's last question? Maybe they'd think I was really pursuing Kitsune to press a paternity suit. *As if.* Watabe paid no attention to my sudden flush.

I vaguely remembered the way, and when the elevator doors opened on a bare cement hallway I led and he followed. Past a section of hall that featured large blast-doors and sections that obviously opened out into something bigger, we entered the cell block. Either I was the only guest tonight or all their guards were behind screens, or invisible. Watabe showed me to the only open cell door and handed me a remote.

"The red button activates the lock and will fully seal off the cell, Hikari-sama," he explained. "And the green button will open the cell. The orange button will sound an alarm and seal the detainment section." His smile made him look eighteen. "I don't suggest pushing it—the paperwork is a nightmare. Everything inside the cell is controlled by the monitor, so when you want to shower, for example, say 'monitor' to activate its listening function, followed by 'I wish to shower.' If your wishes are unclear, she will ask for clarification or connect you to someone."

He smiled again. "I have been instructed to tell you that, once you seal the cell, its monitoring instruments will switch to passive record; no video or audio feed will be viewed by a living person unless something happens, and once you have departed all recordings will be scrubbed."

"Oh? Then the monitor..."

"The monitor is an AI system, not a person. Goodnight, Hikari-sama."

He actually bowed and I blinked before hastily returning it.

"*Well that's interesting,*" Shell muttered as I stepped into the cell and found that someone had brought my suitcase downstairs.

"What is?"

"*Oh, nothing I want to talk about here.*"

"Then don't." Looking at my luggage, I decided that I didn't want Defensenet learning about my magical-girl ring. Propping Cutter in a corner and hitting the red button to seal off the cell, I got undressed and called for the shower—and almost melted under the warm water.

"*So, can you tell me anything?*" Shell asked. Obviously the base had provided a link so she could still bedevil me. I turned my face into the spray to give myself a moment to think.

"Just that Kitsune said I didn't have to worry about being trapped wherever the tree is." He'd been completely mute about where that *was*. "At worst he thinks I'll be 'home in time for tea.' And that's if the tree still even wants me." And that was all I could tell Shell with big listening ears around. The truth was that Kitsune had laughed and told me that the tree was as much a tree as he was a humble fox or the godfish was a school of golden koi. That hadn't surprised me, since trees didn't usually want company. But he'd hinted that it wasn't *just* some friendly tree kami either.

In fact he'd blamed my entire trip to Japan on it. He seemed to think that it had *known* he was in trouble and decided that it would be a fine thing to poke me because I'd come looking for him. Killing Heavenly Dragon, delivering the vaccines, laying the shinigami to rest, all that had been a happy bonus—it had been all about *his* mission.

Kitsune wasn't exactly humble, but the apparent stakes of his current game, he was probably right.

"*That's it?*" Shell whined when I didn't say anything else. "*What about, you know, wedding plans? On hold?*"

If her furry butt had been present I'd have flipped water at her. "Ha, ha. Funny cat. He didn't say, I didn't ask."

With the hours since the contest being so interesting, I'd barely given it a thought. Because really, a fox was a *wild* animal; there was no way he would ever swear service to my family. Right? We'd achieved a nice balance of promises that neither of us would have any interest in requiring payment on—not when the tradeoff was so very, very final. That had been the point of our choices in the contest; mutually assured *you don't want to go there*.

But Shell would tease me about my "engaged" status until the end of time. When we'd both still be in our teens.

Drying off, I put on my sleep-shirt and bottoms and asked the monitor for the sleep mode; this time the futon came with a pillow *and* blanket, which was thoughtful of someone. Firmly wishing Shell goodnight, I settled in for a night of purely natural dreams, if I had any at all.

I didn't. But I didn't sleep very long before the droning, grinding alarm woke me up.

Chapter Twenty Nine

Defensenet Alert: Retrieval of Asset 7-T has proven unsuccessful. However, the ronin enlisted in the attempt were able to speak with the asset and retrieve several items of intelligence. Defensenet is now aware of one location and three individuals germane to the suspected security threat.

Defensenet Recommendation: Mobilize all teams and support assets to secure the location and individuals; the potential for lost intelligence is minor against the objective of neutralizing the present threat.

DR107-TX [Classified]

A sadist had designed that alarm. It reached down into my bones, made my teeth rattle, drove nails into my ears. A corpse couldn't have slept through that alarm. *Jacky* wouldn't have slept through it when she'd been undead. Awake and with Cutter in my hands before the adrenaline-spike wore off enough for me to wonder where I was, I fumbled for the remote and hit the green button before thinking to yell for the monitor. When the cell door slid open, I could hear the evil alarm echoing down the halls.

"Monitor!"

"How may I assist you?"

"The alarm!"

"The alarm is a base-wide alarm. I do not have the authority to shut it off." The alarm chose that moment to shut itself off.

"Is there an attack on the base?"

"I am not able—"

"Shel—Nekokami!"

"*Hey sleepyhead! No idea what's going on, but it's not us and nobody's shooting yet. You might want to dress and come on up.*"

I'd already started to fly up the hall, and reversed with a four-letter word. "How did you know?"

"*Duh. Get your tiny ass up here before* Mamori *goes looking for something to shoot.*"

I did, setting a personal-best for speed dressing and slowed down only a little by the need to settle Cutter's harness right, and got to the elevator. The monitor proved perfectly able to pass me through the invisible layers of security and direct me to the appropriate floor and hall.

The suite of rooms Defensenet had given us was every bit as nice as Keio Plaza's, although I doubted it came with the same level of room service. I found Jacky and Ozma already dressed and looking out the single floor-to-ceiling window in the lounge. Kitty-Shell sat remotely working her epad.

Ozma turned away from the window. The day had just been one thing after another, taking care of business and no time to talk with even the illusion of privacy. Now looking me over, she smiled. "You weren't yourself, today."

"How did—" I closed my mouth. I hadn't even *thought* about it since coming back. Intentionally.

Ozma would never do anything as inelegant as shrug, but a hand waved delicately. "It shows, until you're comfortable in your own head and skin again. How are you?"

I shrugged, sighed. "I was six."

Her perfect lips quirked up. "A hat might have been easier. Being something so different...when you're you again, you have no frame of reference for it and the memory is rather like being drugged. But simply being younger, or a different person... Did you enjoy it?"

Behind her, Jacky listened while watching the wet night outside.

"Um." There had been that moment when I'd woken up, when *everything* had crushed me in a single unbearable heartbeat until my thoughts had deepened and filled out to push back at the renewed load. But before... *"Shinji ran this way. I think he's hiding in the cave."*

It would have been nice to get to find him. "Yes. I did."

"I'm glad."

"So, do we know anything yet?"

"There's lots of air-activity over Tokyo Bay," Jacky said without turning. "And you can see them lifting from the garage here—I'd guess that they're sending most of their mecha into whatever's going on."

"The civil-emergency channel is active." Shell's tail flipped and thumped the bed-covers. "It's a reported kaiju incursion outside the sea wall. They're not reporting a breach, but it's standard for the harbor districts to close up anyway. Everyone not going into shelter is evacuating. The rest of the city is on alert."

Evacuation or shelter; I knew what that meant. All of Japan's recent construction came with shelter requirements, and shelter-blocks were being built in all coastal metropolitan areas; the waterfront district's residents and night-workers would be underground or inside hard-points in minutes, and the streets and transit systems would be clicking over to Evacuation Mode, sucking visitors away into waiting areas in more distant districts. In Chicago we got superhuman fights downtown instead of kaiju attacks—the Chicago Godzilla had been our first and last—but even though we were big believers in defensive urban planning, Japan was ahead of us in civilian-protection policy.

"Are the Eight Excellent Protectors and Nine Accomplished Heroes involved?" If it was Chicago *we* would be, but then we didn't have Defensenet's mecha forces to deal with things.

Shell's tail kept twitching. "I don't know. The public channels are crap for intel. But the chances of a kaiju getting through the sea wall is almost zip."

The Tokyo Bay sea wall actually sat across the narrowest point of the Uraga Channel, between the bay and the open Pacific. Dug-in fortresses flanked the sea wall's ends and the fortresses were themselves Defense Force bases for launching airborn responses to attacks up and down the coast. Shell had every reason to be confident.

Still. I stepped up behind Jacky. "Mamori? What do you think?"

"I think I hate coincidences." Her face wasn't her stiff pre-fight mask, but her arms were crossed tight—the pulled-in tension that preceded explosive action. "Yesterday we shut down a criminal group that your government agent says was involved in a major national security threat, today we hand Defensenet names and a target, and *tonight* Tokyo gets attacked?"

I shook my head. "Agent Inoue didn't say anything about the threat including *kaiju*." Whatever their origin, the monsters were under nobody's control that we knew of. But...had the yakuza been smuggling in kaiju-lures? They did make a lot of their money in the construction industry—bigger profits through sudden urban renewal? *We are trying to keep somebody very dangerous and very angry from turning Tokyo into an ashtray.* Was that what the terrorist Verne-Type had? A way to control the kaiju?

How many kaiju were attacking the sea wall?

Shell *hissed*, caught herself and looked as embarrassed as a cat could. "Everyone? You're going to want to see this." She linked her epad to our reality-plus shades.

News channels with drones out over the bay were providing live images of at least *five* kaiju assaulting the wall, their gargantuan lizard-dinosaur bodies glowing in the spotlights that cut through the rain. As we watched, one of them flared with energy-discharge as attack helicopters fired missiles into it. I winced, but Japan's defense forces simply *had* to be fully EMP-hardened by now; the electromagnetic pulse wouldn't be knocking attack copters out of the sky or crashing communications. Tokyo's civilian power and communications infrastructure was probably just as hardened by now.

Still… "Monitor? May I speak to Agent Inoue?" For a moment I wondered if I'd stumped the AI, which couldn't be as smart as Shell.

"Hikari-san?" Agent Inoue's voice came over the speakers that carried the monitor's. "What can I do for you?" Even Blackstone wouldn't have sounded so polite.

"We would like to offer our assistance."

"Thank you. However, I hope you'll understand that you are not integrated into our defense plans or units." *Translation: you would get in the way, be a distraction, and likely get shot out of the sky.*

"I understand, Inoue-san. I only wished to know if we could be of service in the civilian evacuation. Back home—" Back home there would be jammed roads and deadlocked nodes of traffic, emergency vehicles that needed moving, pedestrians unable to move themselves. Prepared didn't mean *easy*.

"Follow the monitor."

And that was fast. "Shell? Wait here?"

"Yeah, sure, leave the cat behind." But her tail was settling; if we could get out in the field she'd be *learning* stuff. I hadn't really thought about how *small* she had to feel right now, limited to only local and public data sources and without her quantum-links. Cyber-Cat Shell didn't compare to Quantum-Ghost Shell.

Jacky left the window, scratching Shell's ears in passing. "It's wet out there."

"Hah, hah. Get going."
We got.

Monitor led us to the garage, where Leading Private Watabe waited to hand each of us an almost neon-white glowing armband.

"These are equipped with transponders which will inform all Defensenet units in the vicinity that you are active Defensenet reserves. The monitor is linking with your...cat to provide some communication and send you where your powers will be useful. Good luck, and return safely." That was all he had to say as the street doors opened to let the rain in, but he did send us off with a deep bow.

The rain soaked us immediately—me and Jacky anyway; Ozma was using some sort of minor charm to stay dry.

I *like* fighting in the rain. Energy-projection—flames, superheated plasma, electricity, whatever—are relatively common breakthrough types and energy projectors tend to start fires if they use their gifts with abandon; certainly the kaiju's "plasma breath" fit that category, and rain helps minimize collateral damage. Jacky hates the rain; she told me heavy rain pushes against her as mist, and all the water in the air limited the effective range of the elasers she normally used as Artemis (they worked by using a laser to "burn" a path of ionized air to guide the stunning high-voltage, low-current electrical discharge—not so useful in rain). Fortunately, tonight she had her Vulcans. Not that we expected her to have to use them.

I lifted off, Ozma on my back, and Jacky disappeared into mist to follow as fast as she could—saving Ozma's bottled wind so it wouldn't get tired. "Shell? Marching orders?"

"*They evacuate the closest districts first, and the residential towers have their shelters so Defensenet wants us to lend a hand in the clearing of Odaiba—it's a big waterfront amusement district. Upside, it's got a major expressway and a train line running directly out of it. Downside, it's a weekend evening and it's crowded. But we've got plenty of—"*

Lifting over Shinjuku's towers, we saw the eye-searing flash before we heard the boom. It lit the clouds above Tokyo Bay.

The bay. What was the worst possible thing that explosion could have been? "Shell, please please *please* tell me that wasn't the sea wall."

"I can if you want, but I'd be lying!" She put a drone-view image of the bay up on our shades; the sea wall lay shattered and mostly submerged, the kaiju flowing over it to disappear into the dark water of Tokyo Bay.

Of *course*. If you're an evil master-villain and you've got a kaiju lure, are you going to waste it letting your critters get held up outside of town? Nope. I reached back over my head to make sure Ozma had a good grip, and poured on the speed. Jacky dropped back out of mist to grab my foot and hang on. Shell started talking with the local Powers That Be.

"Defensenet wants us on the Rainbow Bridge, now! Odaiba's an artificial island with only two exits!"

"Got it! Point the way!" A red triangle popped up on my shades and I turned to center it.

The rain obscured a lot, but closing the distance it was easy to spot Odaiba; it had a huge and lit up Ferris wheel, a tinker-toy building supporting a big metal sphere, and what looked like four upside-down pyramids. Also, the Statue of Liberty and a sixty-foot Gundam-robot statue, right out of the old Pre-Event anime. Because sure, why not?

Rainbow Bridge didn't look very rainbowish—a double-span suspension bridge, it linked the island to central Tokyo—but it did look *packed*. And as we came down on it, it went black.

"Shell, the kaiju aren't close yet are they?"

"They're still south of us in the bay! That EMP hit came from something else and its pulse-strength is too high!"

Whatever had made it, our job had just gotten impossible; nearly a third of the cars on the bridge went dark, their sensitive controller chips shorted out by the pulse. And the effect wasn't limited to the bridge—if anything it was on the periphery, and anyone in the city behind us not able to get into a shelter was a walking target. Where were the Eight and the Nine?

"New instructions!" Shell called out. *"Clear an exit on the bridge for the cars that can still move and then rendezvous at the Gundam! They're going to keep it, the Ferris wheel, and Lady Liberty lit up as bait—try and suck the kaiju onto the island where the mecha can deal with them!"*

Good plan if it worked—keep the big monsters concentrated instead of trying to hold them back wherever they decided to come ashore—but hard on any civilians who didn't make it off Odaiba. I dropped Jacky and Ozma at the mainland end and we moved up the bridge.

Ozma and Jacky settled the mob as we went—Ozma with her words, Jacky by "pushing" with her vampy mind-power—while I tossed abandoned vehicles into the bay to make room. The two of them had to jog to keep up. Behind us, the lights of Tokyo died as Defensenet shut down the ones not taken down by the pulse to provide focus on the target. We were helped by a half-dozen pedestrians who turned out to be unpowered Defensenet reservists; they'd brought their own white armbands, and just seeing all of us moving calmly down the road and directing people past us settled the crowd tremendously.

Lucky for us, traffic had already been at a standstill when the EMP hit—there were no injuries from rear-end collisions into dead cars. Getting to the end of the bridge, I looked out over the rain shrouded bay.

"Shell, what's the biggest kaiju attack they've dealt with before?"

"A couple of Second-Gen kaiju off of the Port of Nagoya. Why?"

Nagoya—Japan's biggest port, and totally open to the Pacific. "Just checking my master-villain hypothesis."

"Oh, d'you think? Defensenet's already called the play for that and is activating every reservist they've got. But forget about government capes—with the mecha tonnage they're dropping, none of those lizards are going to make it to shore."

"Yeah, but—" It still didn't make sense; the EMP hit hadn't stopped Tokyo's mecha-deployment—mech units were all EMP-hardened to handle the kaiju. All the hit had done was slow civilian evacuation. "Let's get to the rendezvous."

The second EMP hit caught us halfway there and this time I *felt* the sticky static discharge wash over us, like standing too close to one of Lei Zi's local pulses. The lights lighting up the Gundam statue and Lady Liberty died and then came back.

And *virtual* Shell appeared in the rain beside me, looking thrilled and *shocked*.

"The quantum interdiction-field is down! The pulse knocked it down! But EMPs don't do that—they're not that kind of event!"

"Tell Defensenet! Assuming they don't already know."

"Working it." She did a twirl, morphing into a Remarkable Ronin version of herself, and vanished. I could imagine the insanity breaking out back at Defensenet Shinjuku, but we had our own monkeys to deal with—assuming they got through the mecha-launched missile storm getting ready to greet them when they poked their heads up out of the bay.

Why was I beginning to think it was likely?

Arriving at the rendezvous told us at least one thing—six of the Eight Excellent Protectors were already there, their crisply pleated skirts and tailored jackets practically shining under the media's camera-lights as they stood watching the bay. Considering they were surrounded by mecha—including an even dozen BFRs (Big Freaking Robots, Shell's term for the fifteen-foot tall street-mecha)—loaded with rocket batteries and pointing at the water, their vigilance would have looked over-the-top if not for the cameras.

I nodded; it wasn't exactly how we did things in Chicago, but half of winning tonight would be keeping the city calm; probably every news channel was running this—certainly millions of Tokyoites were watching on their cellphones and epads. They needed to see that Defensenet was ready to defend them.

"Look dangerous, people," Jacky whispered before I spotted the camera pointed our direction and the field-reporter in front of it talking into his mic.

Lights, cameras, action! I kept us walking forward, stopped us maybe twenty feet from the Eight and copied their casually observant pose to watch the bay. Checking out the Eight's visible preparedness (one of them was a cyborg loaded with more bristling fight-mods than Shell wore as a battle-ready Galatea), I casually unsheathed Cutter and stuck him in the sand with a one-handed flourish. Jacky snickered beside me, but I could hear the rising hums as she drew, readied, and re-holstered her scary looking Vulcans.

"Five-second delayed broadcasts." Virtual-Shell popped in beside me, again a dark-haired fourth Remarkable Ronin. Smart—Kochi stood with her team by the water, and magic-types had the habit of being able to see my BF. "Defensenet can cut all media transmissions in a second if the situation goes bad or they need to keep someone special from seeing it. You ready for this?"

I smiled whimsically, making sure my face was angled so the camera would catch it. "I would really, really like a spa-day. With aggressive shopping. You know, the Bees would love Tokyo. Especially Isetan Shinjuku—those ladies were really, really nice."

"That's a lot of reallys."

"I'm really tired and my shoulder really really hurts." I rotated it carefully; I'd managed to clear the bridge mostly one-handed, but just the strenuous movement had stripped away the numbing protection Dr. Arai had given me, just like she'd promised.

Jacky touched my elbow. "Camera's gone, now look clever." With the news crews pointed elsewhere, Kaminari headed straight for us, her glowing naginata held over her shoulder so its butt didn't brush the sand. She very carefully *wasn't* limping but I could read it in her stance. Controlled rage practically poured off her in waves.

I folded my arms and almost stepped back before I stopped myself. Beside me Jacky loomed taller.

"Thank you for coming. Truly." She said it with the briefest bow, which I automatically mirrored. Were the cameras back without my seeing them?

Again I nodded automatically. "What happened to you?"

"Agent Inoue sent us to collect one of the persons you named tonight. It did not go well."

"They found the Verne-Type guy—" Virtual-Shell whispered beside me "—but he blew himself and his workshop up before they could get through his booby-traps and stop him. Two of the Eight are in the hospital."

I winced. "I'm sor—"

Kaminari cut my instinctive apology short with an impatient slash of her hand; her anger wasn't pointed at me. "We needed what you brought us. The Nine Accomplished Heroes are now in Kyoto protecting the Asian delegates from a One-Lander attack, and there has been hard fighting. The conspiracy was widespread and they began executing their plan yesterday when your actions removed the Kabukicho yakuza from play."

"Do you know what the conspiracy was about yet?"

"A powerful attack." She scowled. "The yakuza family involved was getting paid very well to use the gates to smuggle men and contraband—the furthest gate we're now sure of is in Okinawa. And they stood to make even more money skimming construction contracts in the rebuilding. They believed that they were working for an ultra-nationalist group that wants to remilitarize and reestablish our prewar hegemony." Turning around she looked out at the bay. The Tokyo Bay Aqua-Line had gone dark as the rest of Tokyo; hopefully the kaiju would ignore the bay-spanning bridge.

It had certainly been emptied—probably what the Eight had been doing while we'd cleared the much shorter Rainbow Bridge. If there'd still been traffic on it we wouldn't be standing here.

"And they were—the nationalist group exists—but its strings were being pulled by One Land. And One Land prepared for more than just an attack; they were preparing for a blow that would cripple Japan. Your interference made them kick off their plans early."

The chill had been settling into my gut as Kaminari spoke. So maybe we'd done some good—but our enemy had gained a whole day to begin, once we'd gotten the Kabukicho yakuza trapped and before I'd talked to Kitsune. If I had gone straight to Defensenet when Ozma had been taken, told them who we were and why we were here, they'd have known we could find Kitsune for them and tonight would all be playing out very, very differently.

But if they hadn't used Kitsune to spy on us, then we could have asked for their help instead of sneaking in.

It *sucked*; if we'd trusted them enough to ask, they would have learned we could find him for them. If we'd used Ozma's magic fish to track him down and then gone in with the full might of Defensenet behind us... I felt sick. "So then, we just hope that this was the big plan? Destroying the sea wall and sending a bunch of kaiju into Tokyo?"

Kaminari actually snorted. "No, Hikari-san. Every Defensenet team across Japan is on alert, with every Defense Force base." A new EMP hit washed over us, the static charge raising my neck-hairs and inducing tiny arcs of snapping current on the station-keeping mecha around us. She sighed and pushed wet strands of hair out of her face. "Thank you for being here, Hikari-san."

I stared at her retreating back as she rejoined her remaining teammates.

"The kaiju just passed the Aqua-Line," Shell reported.

Get your mind back in the game. "Why aren't they using torpedoes on them?"

"They moved the torpedo batteries out into the Uraga Channel when they built the sea wall, and air-dropped torpedoes are too risky in the bay. Here they come!"

Back in full quantum-neural link with me, Shell was using all her processing power to analyze what I was seeing with my super-duper vision. Now she painted virtual markers on the faintest of water-trails, barely visible in the night and rain. Fast-moving markers, closing on Odaiba's artificial beach. I didn't have to ask to know that she was passing the images through her cat-Shell links to Jacky and Ozma's shades.

I drew Cutter from his sheath of sand. Beside me, Jacky held a Vulcan in one fist, her free hand resting on her sash where she kept her bottled wind. Ozma stood easy, looking mildly interested but with her wand-baton held ready.

And the night exploded into furious fire as the BFRs flushed their rocket batteries at the rising hills of water. So did The Eight's cyborg—Shell tagged her as Arashi. The screaming roars that shook the air almost drowned the sound of auto-cannon fire as the five monster lizards rose through the rain of hypervelocity and explosive rounds to tower over the beach, the two in front already dying.

"They've got them!" virtual-Shell yelled by my ear. "They've—what is *that*?"

That was the bay water around the embattled kaiju, and it looked like it was *boiling*, rising around the monsters' legs.

The heaving mass exploded.

"Shell! Analysis now!" The explosion resolved into thousands of *things* that looked like flying stingrays, if stingrays were made of seaweed and covered in tiny bubbling membranes. Jacky swore and fumbled to reset her Vulcan as the rest of the Eight leaped into action and the cloud of flying nightmares swept over us.

Chapter Thirty

When your time comes to die, be not like those whose hearts are filled with fear of death. Sing your death song! And die like a hero going home.

Tecumseh

When your time comes to die, kick someone's ass first.

Artemis

Jacky stopped trying to reset her Vulcan and disappeared into wind and mist, a whirlwind battering at the flying creatures. Ozma spun in a circle to trace a line in the sand with her wand-baton and before she'd finished the circle the sand flowed up into human shapes around her, literal sand-*men* that flailed at the flapping shapes descending on us. The creatures the sandmen touched dropped to the beach outside her circle.

Because sandmen brought sleep, of course.

I swung Cutter in broad one-handed arcs, cutting the creatures down in bunches as Cutter moved in my grip to carve his path through the swarm. The cloud of flapping seaweed made it hard to see more than a few feet.

"Shell! What's going on?"

Virtual-Shell just stood there, turning in circles, as the things flew through her. "The Eight are okay—they've got an energy projector pushing back with her fields and they're moving to cover the news crews—" A rolling, concussive explosion to our right almost blinded and deafened me. "—but hitting them with anything hot or electric lights them off!"

"What *are* they?"

"Really frisky seaweed! They break down water into gas—the bubbles in their skin are full of hydrogen to make them floaty so it doesn't take much flapping to keep them airborne! And they've got some kind of toxin coating them—contact with skin is raising blisters and welts!"

"What's their zone?"

"They're staying on the beach, acting like mobile chaff for the kaiju—a living smokescreen!"

Even with Cutter's help all my swinging couldn't kill every flapper that came within our reach—I had to keep pulling them off me. Fortunately whatever secretions they were slimed with didn't bother me; I just *really* needed to shower. But I wasn't worried about them—they were *nuisances* and I needed to know where the—

The beach shook and the roaring came from damn near overhead; another rippling shockwave signaled the fiery mass-death of a cloud of flappers.

"I've hacked a drone-feed!" Shell shouted. "The kaiju are on the beach, plasma-jetting the fat flapper clusters around the street mecha! Good thing they're piloted remotely—the big guys are going down!"

Great—we were losing our heavy artillery.

Another EMP hit washed over us and this time the arcing sparks ignited whole clumps of flappers.

And what was *that* about?

And— "Shell! Where's Ozma?" She'd vanished into the dark green airborne mass.

"Our magical princess is headed for the Gundam statue! Kaminari says we need to hit the kaiju!"

That I could do. "Point me!"

The one upside to the flapper-clouds was that the kaiju couldn't see us through the flying things any better than we could see them; these monsters were Second Gen kaiju—bigger and tougher than the Chicago Godzilla—but they still had the signature plasma-breath and Shell confirmed that three of them were still standing.

I could have launched myself low and chopped at the first legs I found, but an instant vision of an injured kaiju blasting away at whatever was below it—a beach crowded with powered-armor mecha, news crews, and assorted capes—killed all possibility of a low shot. Instead I told Shell to pass the word that I'd be providing a platform, and went straight up.

The flapper swarm was thickest close to the ground, and as I cleared its densest layers I stayed low to eyeball my targets. Jacky dropped out of mist to stand on my shoulders as she drew her humming Vulcans and leaped into mist again. Kaminari used me as a stepping stone—a nice trick since she couldn't fly and I was at least thirty feet up. Landing soft-footed on my head she jumped higher into the sky, multiplying as she sailed upward to become a swarm of naginata-wielding Kaminaris that descended on the closest kaiju.

"Okay, that's impressive," Shell allowed.

I closed on the one Jacky and Kaminari hadn't targeted, circling around in the rain to come up behind it. Diving to bury Cutter to his hilt, I felt the shock through my body as he drove down through hide and bone into the back of the monster's skull. The kaiju roared and twisted violently, almost throwing me off despite my two-handed grip on Cutter's hilt and I clung tight as my shoulder screamed. I had no idea if I could kill it—the thing was so huge it made Heavenly Dragon look like a Chihuahua. Then we saw the Gundam.

Shell started *laughing*. "And that's just crazy."

All I could do was hang on and nod—I literally had no words.

With all the flappers flying around its legs, the brilliantly white, blue, and red Gundam robot statue waded towards us through a dark green tide. The "energy sword" it lifted glowed almost too bright to look at and our kaiju saw it coming, all sixty feet of impossible steel.

Common sense would tell you that one jet of a kaiju's superheated plasma breath would reduce the walking statue to melted wreckage, but common sense checks out the instant magic is involved. Ozma hadn't just animated the giant Gundam statue—she had transformed it into something close to the real deal and the first plasma-jet to hit the Gundam splashed off it without doing more than scorching the paint. The mighty symbol of all Giant Robot Anime struck back with a swing of its energy sword that half-decapitated the most aggressive kaiju.

"Kaminari says to pull back!" Shell yelled. Turning my attention I saw that all of the Eight-leader's duplicates had disappeared as she leaped away from her own now one-eyed opponent. Jacky stopped dancing in and out of mist and pouring Vulcan-shots into her target's face to vanish a final time. Cutter came free with my pull and I shot up and away.

Our moves had bought time and the surviving BFRs opened fire again, rockets and auto-cannons ripping the air as I narrowly missed a Defensenet drone in my climb.

The gut-churning reek of ruptured and burned lizard filled the air.

"And that's how they do it in Japan," Shell said, floating beside me. Below us, the Eight were doing something to thin the flappers; for whatever reason, the things seemed to want to remain close to the definitively dead kaiju—the only break we'd gotten tonight. "You okay?"

"I'm tired." I'd never felt so utterly done; Cutter weighed nothing but I felt every breath give more weight to my bones. I'd be able to sleep even without another pain-patch. For *days*.

Landing, I found Ozma by the de-animated Gundam. It had frozen in a stable posture but not its original at-ease pose, and I wondered if Tokyo would just rebuild its base down here on the beach and leave it like this to commemorate the attack.

"I thought you said your belt was almost tapped out?"

Ozma smiled. "The Magic Belt absorbs and stores magic. Think of it as a solar battery."

"Okay…"

"Taking it to the godfish's realm was like wearing it to sunbathe on Mercury."

"So—*oh*. Then…" She'd told me once that the Magic Belt wasn't as powerful, outside of Oz, and I really had no idea what that meant for her now.

She shook her head. "I used up a great deal of it, just now. But I think our metal defender was effective, don't you?" She patted the Gundam's foot affectionately.

I nodded dazedly. "Yeah, you could—"

Beside me Shell *jerked*. "What the actual *fu*—"

"Shell?"

She was grabbing fistfuls of her currently dark hair, almond eyes wide. "The EMP hits are coming from a *generator*. It's cycling up, which is why the hits have been getting stronger."

"And this means…"

"Defensenet just found the source, and I'm trying to tell them what they're looking at."

"*You* know— Shell, what's going on?" Jacky dropped out of mist down the beach and I waved her over.

"The crazy-powerful Verne that suicided built a zero-point energy generator. The pulses are phase-discharges as the thing cycles up. It sucks up energy from the decaying virtual particles in the quantum foam—knocking down the quantum-interdiction field is just a side-effect of that. It's something that becomes more than just theoretically possible a hundred years from now—the Chinese Verne must have used his weirdass superscience to skip steps."

"Okay." So we were looking at an exotic power source; maybe I was too tired, but that didn't seem like enough to be making Shell pull her virtual hair out.

"So freaking *not* okay. The pulse strength tells me it's passed its critical threshold." Her eyes were wide. "It *was* a generator. *Now* it's a bomb."

I wasn't tired anymore. "Where is it?"

The zero-point generator had been buried at the address the Eight Excellent Protectors raided earlier tonight. Buried *literally*—the conspirators had assembled it in the empty foundation of a soon-to-be built Shinjuku skyscraper (construction had been halted when the financing company went bankrupt) and buried it in cement. I grabbed Jacky and Ozma and flew as fast as I could safely carry them, landing us in the open pit with the Eight Excellent Protectors still far behind us.

The open pit looked like what it was: the site of a serious superhuman fight. A couple of street-mecha left to guard the scene had done more to rip up the site, using their ordnance to crack open the cement over the buried generator. In their spotlights the generator shone too dim, the exposed mirror-smooth shell of the huge dark sphere looking almost black and seeming to suck in the light—Shell said it was absorbing more photons than it was reflecting, another clue it was now a bomb.

"The pulses aren't centered on the generator!" Shell explained. "They're quantum-eruptions popping up anywhere in the generator's disbursed subtraction field! Defensenet didn't find the source until the generator passed the threshold and flared detectable tachyons in time with a pulse—that's when I realized what it was."

Standing beside me, she stared down at the sphere. Her face was a study in despair. "Defensenet's sending a superhuman lifter but he won't make it on time." A new pulse washed over us.

"Can we destroy it?"

"No. It will just release the energy it's stored and it's already got enough."

"Enough for what?"

"Enough to incinerate Tokyo and break Japan. Japan is a volcanic island chain. This thing will blow it a new one."

"So we move it! How fragile is it?"

"Its outer wall is two-meter thick carbon alloy—you're not going to crack it!"

"I don't want to crack it!" Dropping into the newly smashed hole, I landed on top of it and drew Cutter. "Don't let go," I told him.

"Do your part—I know what to do, girl."

I screamed and buried Cutter in the sphere like Excalibur in the stone, screamed again as I *pulled*.

The street-mecha helped by blasting away at the engine's cement bed with their autocannons, fracturing the concrete and surrounding me with a blizzard of cement chips and fragmented rounds as I pulled with everything I had.

"How! Much! Time?"

"Minutes! We've got to drop it over the ocean! Past the coastal shelf!"

Every breath was a grinding scream and my vision started to gray out before the engine moved and came free of its cement anchor. "Shell! I can barely lift this! I can't— I can't—" We weren't going to make it.

If I broke it now, before it built up *more* power, would it help at all?

"We will succeed," Ozma said, opening her magic box and taking out...her little ivory netsuke? She whispered "Fly," and the tiny white dragon uncurled to dart around her head. She smiled at it, touched the Magic Belt where it hid beneath her sash. "Grow."

It grew. The street-mecha stumbled back as the happy little guy ballooned outward, snakelike body wrapping around the sphere. Ozma calmly stepped up and across his expanding back to join me as she told it what to do.

"Mamori." she called to Jacky. "Hold me here?" Jacky misted over to wrap an arm around Ozma and another around me. "When you're ready," Ozma let me know.

I lifted again, sucking air between my teeth. My shoulder was on fire, but we rose. "Shell! Point me! Tell the Eight to stand off!"

A red marker gave me my direction as we lifted out of the construction pit, picking up speed. Little Dragon tightened his scaly grip to take the strain, horned and whiskered head pointed towards the bay.

Shell reoriented. "We need to get out of the Uraga Channel and head southwest, away from Oshima Island!"

"Got it." Every breath made my vision swim, but I could follow Shell's virtual target and Little Dragon was happy to be guided.

"Agent Inoue says that he's alerting the coast. He says 'Good luck.'"

"Good to know." I tried to blink away visions of blast-generated tsunamis—what could happen if we were *lucky*. I couldn't see down past the engine, but from the sides I could see as we passed over Tokyo Bay and the Aqua Line.

"Jacky, when we hit deep water take Ozma and go—I'm going to get this as far under as I can." I could *push* the thing easily enough if I was going the way gravity wanted me to.

"No! You've danced with a bomb once already! That should be *your* career limit!"

"We're past the sea wall..." Shell sang out and I angled to follow the new direction and accelerate while trying not to black out.

"Everyone will be safe!" I didn't have *time* for this.

"Almost there...we're past the shelf—drop!"

I stopped trying to hold the engine up and dove for the rain-swept sea: Jacky would take Ozma to safety.

Instead she *bit* me. With no warm-up I felt the bite like stinging ice before the warmth flared down my neck and over me, washing away the agony of my shoulder. I didn't have time to draw breath or even think before she grabbed my head and put her mouth next to my ear.

"*SLEEP!*"

Chapter Thirty One

The last of the Three Deeds of Hikari and the Three Remarkable Ronin was saving all of Tokyo during the Yi Guo Attack. The Shrine of The Deeds built near the Kannonzaki Lighthouse and within sight of Hikari Island commemorates all of the deeds of Japan's greatest ronin, and their festival day culminates the week when The Sword makes its four-stop return from the Chinese sister shrine in Anhui.

A History of the Brief Career of Hikari and the Three Remarkable Ronin.

I didn't hurt anywhere, but the brush of warm blossoms on my forehead made me open my eyes. There were no blossoms; the lady whose lap I lay in gently traced her fingers across my brow.

"Good." She smiled. "I do not think your friend meant for you to sleep forever."

I blinked. Even looking at her from upside-down, she was the most beautiful woman I had ever seen. She wore brilliant court robes, but although the fashion was ancient Chinese her rich dark hair hung loose and flowing, shifting in the breeze. The rising sun lay behind clouds, but she glowed brighter and warmer than even my by-now familiar dream country.

Except there was no cherry tree above us.

And I knew her; even if she wasn't holding a baby and there was no parrot. Little Dragon lay draped contentedly across her shoulder, and I had prayed in front of her statue in the Dome's chapel more times than I could count.

"Quan Yin!" I jerked into a sitting position, only her hand on my arm keeping me for springing to my feet. And still nothing hurt.

"Kannon, dear, in Japan. God let me borrow you for a while. Do you mind?"

The world is full of weeping. How can I go? I should have realized: Kannon, the Goddess of Mercy, "who hears the cries of the world."

"Yes." She rose with infinite grace and helped me up, her smile turning merry. "I met young Kitsune here one fine morning, and tricked him into my occasional service before he realized I was more than simply a lively tree. And *you*. You were praying to your Mary of The Pagans but I heard you anyway, once Kitsune introduced us."

She let go of my hand and, as good as I felt, I suddenly remembered my friends. I didn't see them anywhere on the hill.

"You have slept the hours away," Kannon said before I could ask. "And you were safe with me so they wandered. Shall we find them?"

"Is everyone..."

"You saved them. All of you saved them." She led me down the hill.

At the base of the hill I had to stop and dip a hand in the bubbling spring. Everything was crystal clear and vibrant as it had been in my dreams, without the dreamy lassitude—my thoughts ran as clear as the water. We followed the stream down through the lower tree-covered hills to the island's shore.

"There they are." There was laughter in her voice as she pointed to the small building near the beach. The building looked a lot like a traditional raised wooden shrine, except that instead of walls hiding the chamber where the *shintai*, the sacred object that housed the kami, was kept, the platform sat open to the air with four posts supporting the peaked roof. It made the whole thing a kind of Japanese gazebo beside the stream where it flowed into the sea.

And it was crowded. Jacky, Ozma, Shell, and a man I didn't recognize sat talking. Well, Jacky and Ozma were talking—Shell was teasing the gray-haired man holding the fishing pole. All of them wore breezy summer yukatas, but the older man also wore a flat-brimmed cowboy hat and smoked a stubby rolled cigarette...

"Cutter?"

Shell looked up. "Hope!" Using Jacky's shoulder as leverage, she bounced to her feet and jumped off the platform. Sand flew under her feet, and I barely had time to reach up before she threw herself onto me. "You're awake!" She squealed. "Isn't this amazing?"

"Yes, I—" Turning my head I realized we were alone; Kannon was gone.

"Come *on*! We've got to tell you what's been happening!" She grabbed the hand Kannon had held, tugging me towards everyone.

"Girl." Cutter nodded when I joined everyone else. For a man in what looked like a fancy bathrobe he still managed to look totally cowboy.

Jacky looked almost as improbable in her yukata as Cutter did, but Ozma wore hers perfectly and looked like of course they had been invented just for her. Looking down, I finally realized that I was wearing a blue yukata of my own. With a white star-pattern, naturally.

Shell pushed me down to sit where she had been, folded her legs to squeeze between me and Cutter. "You slept for*ever*. You know it's been days back home?" She waved a hand to vaguely indicate the Real World.

I poked her. She was *real*.

"Yeah, since I was in your head at the time I got sucked in here too. Heck, when Jacky sent you to sleep she expected just *you* to vanish. Or not, in which case she expected Ozma to turn you and herself into fashion accessories so she could get you all out of there. Instead we *all* came. Well—" She stopped smiling. "Except for Cutter. You left him stuck in the engine. And Little Dragon. He stayed with Cutter."

"But—" I looked past Shell's red head to make sure Cutter was still there. He took his cigar out of his mouth and chuckled.

"I'm dead, girl. Searchers found my hilt and part of my blade—Vulcan made me tough—but that's it."

"Searchers? What's happened?" So Shell explained, Jacky adding details to her enthusiasm and Ozma gently correcting now and again.

It had been *three days* since our wild flight.

The zero-point engine had sunk into the Pacific and nearly buried itself in the deeps beyond the shelf before exploding and turning billions of cubic meters of seawater into superheated steam. Fortunately the wind had been blowing *east*; the instant and lethal cloud simply drifted out into the Pacific to cool, just missing Oshima Island. That was the good news.

The blast had kicked off a seven-point-eight earthquake along the east coast of Japan, caused a miniature tsunami to flood much of Sagami Bay with the seawater that had rushed to fill the void, and cracked the actual seabed. Smaller quakes continued to unsettle the Japanese islands, and it looked like there was going to be a new volcanic island appearing soon in the middle of the Sagami Sea.

The amazing thing was that, because of the kaiju alert, everyone had been sheltered or evacuating; between that and all of Defensenet's capes, the death toll was miraculously low. But there were still deaths. There always were.

"So, does anyone know we're alive—*mostly* alive?" I'd think about what Cutter and Little Dragon meant later. Much, much later...

"Nope. And yeah." Shell shrugged. Her being here *and real* was just as strange. "Since the zero-point engine's gone the interdiction field is back, but I'm still linked with quantum-me from here. Ozma's transformation ended and cat-me has reverted back into a drone, and I used the drone's link to Defensenet to let Agent Inoue know we'd made it. But I don't think he's told anyone else. Weird but true, it looks like he's using your 'heroic deaths' to quietly erase all evidence he can find that might tell anyone who you really are."

"Why?"

Ozma giggled, looking a lot younger than her triple-digits. "For the *story*. An epic to conjure by—Hikari, Mamori, and Kimiko, the Three Remarkable Ronin. Shell tells us there is already public talk of building a shrine for us on the Muira Peninsula, next to the Kannonzaki Lighthouse. You'll be able to see the new volcano from there. They'll probably name it after you."

The look on my face had her bursting into more un-Ozmalike giggles. "Kannon told all of us the story of Tenkawa's kitsune. Interesting people become kami all the time in Japan."

"*Historically*, but—"

She laughed harder and I gave up.

We decided that since I was awake it was time to go *home*— and as divinely beautiful as the High Plane of Heaven was, the thought of waking up for breakfast with the parentals was positively blissful. Shell decided to stay with Cutter and explore, since her virtual-self would be waiting for me back home, too. But before we left (which according to Ozma was now as easy as leaving the godfish's weird pocket of extrareality), I went back up the hill to see the tree. Or the goddess.

Kannon waited for me there, and I wondered if the cherry tree would be here if I returned. If I *could* return. Now that she'd shown herself, would I ever see her again?

"You'll still be able to dream your way here," she answered the biggest of my unasked questions. "I promise."

"Thank you." We sat. The sun had risen high over the string of green islands. I could see a larger mainland behind them, and wondered if my island sat in a spirit-realm analogue of the Inland Sea. I didn't wonder very hard; watching Little Dragon chase startled seabirds was much more fun.

And I just had to know.

"How— How did Cutter and Little Dragon..."

Kannon laughed, and it was a sound I could listen to forever. "Even simple objects have their own kami. And the kami of objects animating by magic are certainly aware. Dying, Cutter followed you here. He was *your* sword, after all. Little Dragon followed the rest of you. I believe I will keep them."

She gave me the smile that had brightened her face when I opened my eyes. "And your real question, Hope?"

I blinked, realized my face was wet and didn't know why. "You hear the cries of the world. How can you be *happy*?"

"Oh, my dear." Her gentle smile didn't waver, but her eyes grew solemn and she reached up to stroke my chin. "I am happy because I also know how it ends."

"How what ends?"

"Everything. 'And they all lived happily ever after.'"

The warmth of her kiss on my forehead didn't fade until I'd been home for days.

Epilogue

There were a lot of awkward conversations. First there was the one with Blackstone, who we had to tell that we'd lost a multi-million dollar piece of NASA equipment east of Japan. Then there was the one I *didn't* have with Veritas, where I *didn't* explain what we *hadn't* done and what his boss *didn't* need to know about, and the one I had with Father Nolan about Kannon. The worst was the one with the parentals—there were going to be a *lot* of home waffle-breakfasts over the coming weeks.

And then there was the news coming out of Japan. The worst of *that* was my Catholic horror and guilt over being turned into a Shinto kami—and Chinese *shen*! But there were leaders in Japan and the Chinese states who were milking the nation-hopping adventures of the beatified Three Remarkable Ronin for all they were worth, and I supposed I couldn't blame them. It was one more step to burying China's memories of Japan's early 20th Century crimes against it, one more tie that could bring them together in the League of Democratic States.

And one more reason for the Three Remarkable Ronin to forever remain *Japanese* heroes. Nobody would ever, *ever* find out that I, Hope Corrigan, had been made a kind of *saint*—before I was even dead.

One possible downside to not disappearing down the rabbit-hole, one that occurred to me with my mother's reminder a week after my return, was I wasn't going to miss the Silver and Green Ball. I couldn't even plead injury, since all the post-operation damage I'd done to myself seemed to have gone away and Dr. Beth had been able to put me on a workout regimen to help me compensate for the lost muscle.

    The ballroom had been decorated with silver lights and green potted topiary—textured bushes, shrubs, and mosses in the shapes of real and fanciful creatures. I even found a Chinese dragon. Julie had picked my dress since we'd all come together with Dane as our escort; I wore a jade green strapless floor-length gown with a patterned silver ribbon that ran over and beneath my minimal bust before crossing to hug my waist, doing my shape some justice. I'd known I was in for a lot of handshakes and conversation since Hope Corrigan had long been outed as Astra—but despite that everybody *looked* at Annabeth and Dane, and Julie and Megan too, when they took the floor to dance together. Which was how it should be.
    "Are you having a good time, Hope?"
    Mrs. Lori's question shook me out of my mellow reverie. *Grande dame* of Chicago and Mom's charity-rival she might be, but she had introduced me to five "nice young men" since I'd arrived. Blood of the bluest blue, of course, even if one had the misfortune of being the scion of a *Boston* family. I was feeling too good to care.
    "I am! Thank you Mrs. Lori. Next year I'll be able to drink the champagne, and then it will be even *more* fun."
    "Scamp." But she smiled approvingly. "You've done your duty and can run along with your friends if you desire; the young always have more interesting places to be. But before you go, I wanted to bring you one more gentleman who seeks an introduction." She stepped aside and I finally saw the man standing beside her.
    "Hope, may I make known to you Mr. Yoshi Miyamoto. His is an old Japanese family. He has come to Chicago to acquire some art, and even to buy some property in town."
    "It is a pleasure to meet you." Kitsune bowed formally, and I bowed back without thinking. Same narrow face, high cheekbones,

night-black eyes; his dark hair was longer, feathered to lie almost like fur on his head, and he sported facial hair again—the shadow of a mustache and fringe of a beard along the edge of a strong jaw I'd seen on a different face.

And he looked really, *really* good in a tux; I knew without looking that a flush had started to creep up my chest, and his smile grew as I desperately scrambled for a thought, something to say, anything at all.

"Have—have you found anything you like?" *What did I just say?* I turned beet red as he opened his mouth, closed it without taking dastardly advantage of my idiocy, and smiled again.

He held out his hand. "May I have this dance?"

The End

Waiting for Wearing the Cape, Book 6?

Sign up for the Wearing the Cape Newsletter at wearingthecape.com for a quarterly newsletter, updates, and the 2016 pre-release read of the first five chapters of Mr. Harmon's next Astra adventure!

Also, watch for the *Wearing the Cape: the Roleplaying Game* Kickstarter campaign in 2016.

ABOUT THE AUTHOR

Marion G. Harmon (Marion for his great-grandfather, George for his father), is a former financial advisor and sometime bagpipe player living in Las Vegas. *Wearing the Cape* was his first novel, quickly followed by *Villains Inc.* and *Bite Me: Big Easy Nights*, and *Young Sentinels*, and *Small Town Heroes*. *Ronin Games* is his sixth book, fifth in the Wearing the Cape series, and he guarantees that there will be more stories to come set in the Post-Event world. He also promises that he will get to his comic space opera science fiction story, *Worst Contact*. Really.